I0606571

Flood

Elaine Cantrell

Flood

Caleb's eyes twinkled as a smile spread across his face. "I don't see you at a loss for words too often."

"What do you mean by that?"

He wound a lock of her hair around his finger. "You're a take-charge kind of gal. You're decisive, confident, and very capable, but right now you can't put two words together without stuttering. I think that's a good sign."

Aria felt hot blood rush to her face. "I think you should go, Caleb. It's been a long day."

His eyes, filled with heat and desire, met hers. "Are you sure you want me to go?"

She was sure she *didn't* want him to go, but she had told him the truth. Things were moving too fast for her. "Not tonight, Caleb. Tonight you have to go."

He let go of her hair and picked up his tee shirt. "Okay. I'll go." He grinned at her. "Do I have to walk back to the motel?"

She sighed and rolled her eyes. "Of course not."

Grabbing her purse, she drove him back to his rental house. For a moment neither of them spoke, then Caleb reached for her hand. "You can come in if you like."

Aria bit her lip against the desire to take him up on his offer. Her body still burned in the places where his hands had rested, and if they could be alone together for five minutes, she'd burn all over. Had she ever wanted a man so badly? No. No, she hadn't. The urge to give in was almost overwhelming.

Flood

Elaine Cantrell

A Wings ePress, Inc.

A Contemporary Romance Novel

Wings ePress, Inc.

Edited by: Jeanne Smith
Copy Edited by: Joan C. Powell
Executive Editor: Jeanne Smith
Cover Artist: Trisha FitzGerald

All rights reserved

Names, characters and incidents depicted in this book are products of the author's imagination or are used fictitiously. Any resemblance to actual events, locales, organizations, or persons, living or dead, is entirely coincidental and beyond the intent of the author or the publisher.

No part of this book may be reproduced or transmitted in any form or by any means, electronic or mechanical, including photocopying, recording, or by any information storage and retrieval system, without permission in writing from the publisher.

Wings ePress Books
www.books-by-wings-epress.com

Copyright © 2017 by Elaine Cantrell
ISBN 978-1-61309-702-1

Published In the United States Of America

Wings ePress Inc.
3000 N. Rock Road
Newton, KS 67114

Dedication

For the real Rascal, my inspiration for the book.

Prologue

Dr. Aria De Luca threw a newspaper onto her cluttered desk and reached for a tissue to dry her eyes. How could anyone let such a terrible thing happen?

Her lead vet tech Lila Monroe breezed into her office and held out a clipboard. "Sign this. They just delivered our order of dog food."

Aria scribbled her name for Lila who vanished as abruptly as she had arrived. The cute assistant came back a couple of minutes later without a hint of her usual perky smile. "Why are you crying, Aria? Did the collie's surgery not go well?"

"No, she's fine. I'm almost sure the tumor was benign." Blowing her nose, Aria reached for the morning paper. "Look at this."

Lila perched on the edge of Aria's desk and made herself comfortable. "I'm not wearing my contacts. Forgot them. Just tell me what it says."

"Okay, have you heard of the Second Chance program?"

"No, can't say that I have."

Aria's chair squeaked as she leaned back. She made a mental note to get some oil for it the next time she went to the store. "Well, the Second Chance program is a new initiative for convicts. It's sponsored by the Department of Corrections."

Lila laughed in the way that made all of her friends want to laugh too. "Convicts, huh? I didn't know you knew any convicts, especially not convicts that would make you cry. You've been holding out on me."

"This is serious," Aria insisted even though she did smile at Lila's teasing. She tossed her tissue into the trashcan. "The Department of Corrections partners with community organizations to place model convicts in out-of-prison job settings. It's supposed to let the convicts learn a skill they can use when they're released."

"That's no reason to cry." Lila blinked. "Uh, we aren't getting one, are we? Not that I dislike convicts, but still... Come to think of it, I don't know anyone who's been in prison. Besides, I bet your dad wouldn't like it at all if you started staffing the clinic with criminals."

Aria snickered. "No, we aren't getting a convict, but one of the big animal shelters in Pine City has several. Listen to this. They took in an abuse case, an adult dog that nobody but one of their convicts could reach." She sniffed. "Since the dog isn't especially friendly or pretty, nobody wants to adopt it. It's scheduled to be put down on Friday unless someone steps up for it, and guess who'd have to walk the dog to the killing room?"

"The convict?"

"Yep."

Lila studied her fingernails for a moment. This week she had painted them neon green which clashed with the blue scrubs she was wearing. It didn't look all that good with her red hair and freckles either, but Lila had her own style and always had.

"What are you going to do about the dog, Aria? I know you're going to do something. I've seen that look on your face a hundred times before."

Aria laughed and started to tidy the papers and medication samples on her desk, a huge, mahogany antique that she had bought at a junk store and refinished just because she loved it. "What look?"

"The one that says you're determined to save the world."

"Not the whole world," Aria teased. "Just my little corner of it." She took a sip of cola from the can on her desk. No matter how hard she tried, she couldn't give up colas. Probably she'd get fat when she got older. "What do you think, Lila? Do we have room here for an unwanted, difficult dog?"

Lila rolled her eyes. "Sure. When do we pick her up?"

~ * ~

The next day Aria parked her SUV near the front door of the Pine City Animal Shelter. She and Lila got out of the vehicle and stared at the grounds of the place they'd driven two hours on a beautiful spring day to reach.

"The shelter looks nice," Lila said.

Aria nodded. "Yeah, that's what I was thinking."

The red brick building was only one story high. From the parking lot, Aria saw fenced dog runs and a small enclosure occupied by two goats. The grass had been freshly cut. All in all, it looked neat and well cared for.

She and Lila made their way to the front door, which was made of institutional-looking gray metal and went inside where a pretty receptionist greeted them with a smile. "Hi, can I help you? We have a special on kittens this week. The adoption fee is fifty percent off, and if you take two, we'll knock another twenty five percent off. We have some little beauties in the back."

Aria smiled. "Thanks, but we didn't come for the kittens. I'm Aria De Luca, and ..."

"Oh, Dr. De Luca, I can't tell you how glad I am to see you! We've all been so upset over Peaches and Caleb." The woman ran around her desk and hugged both Aria and Lila. "Thank you so much for taking her." She yelled to a man who'd just entered the lobby from the back of the room. "Ed, go get Peaches. This is Dr. De Luca."

Ed rushed forward and shook her hand instead. "We're so grateful to you, Dr. De Luca. It would have killed Caleb if Peaches hadn't been saved. I'll go get her for you."

"Have a seat," the receptionist urged as Ed left to get the dog. She gestured toward a collection of folding chairs to the right of the reception desk. "It'll be a minute."

When Aria and Lila sat down, she brought them a soft drink and took the chair beside Aria. "How did you hear about Peaches? We've all wondered about that ever since you called us."

"I saw it in our local newspaper," Aria replied as she popped the top from the soft drink can. "It just sounded like something that shouldn't happen."

The woman nodded and sent dark curls bouncing. "You're right. Caleb and Peaches needed each other. Once they connected, both of them just bloomed. It would have been a shame to put her to sleep."

Lila pursed her lips. "What did Caleb do to get himself a prison sentence?"

"Stole a car."

"That's grand theft auto," Lila said.

Aria giggled. "Stop borrowing terms from your favorite crime show. Seriously, though, how long will Caleb be in prison?"

The receptionist sighed. "Another eighteen months. Caleb's a nice guy. He made a mistake, but we all think he's paid his debt to society. The director already told him if he wanted a job at the shelter once he was free, it wouldn't be any problem."

She laid her hand on Aria's arm, her eyes wide and intense. "You know what Caleb did?"

Aria shook her head.

"The director told him he didn't have to come to work on Friday if he didn't want to. That's the day Peaches was scheduled to be put down, but he said he had to be here. He said he couldn't leave her to die alone. He wanted to hold her and comfort her until her soul went free."

Aria's lip quivered. Blinking away the mist in her eyes, she pulled a card out of her pocket and handed it to the receptionist. "Please give my card to Caleb. If he wants to email me, I'll be glad to keep him updated about how Peaches is doing." Beside her, Lila sniffed.

The receptionist, who was obviously a hugger, leaned over and hugged Aria again. "You're a wonderful woman, Dr. De Luca. Only a person with a heart of gold would do what you're doing for Peaches. Maybe you can help her learn to trust again."

"What happened to her?" Lila asked.

Anger spread across the woman's face. "Some monster poured gas on her back and lit her up. By the time a good Samaritan brought her in, she was at death's door. She lived but only by a miracle. Dr. Ballard, our staff doctor, knows his stuff, but it was all he could do to save her."

Aria shivered. "Monster is the right word. Did they ever find out who did it?"

The receptionist shook her head. "No."

"Anyone who'd do a thing like that doesn't deserve to live," Aria cried. "Don't such people have a conscience? How could anyone take pleasure in causing pain for another living creature?"

Nobody responded because no one knew the answer and because Ed and Peaches arrived. Well, the paper hadn't exaggerated when it said Peaches wasn't pretty. She was a medium-sized animal, maybe fifty pounds with over-long legs, a dull, yellowish coat, a head that was a bit too big for her body, and a scarred back. Her ears were down; her eyes looked scared.

Aria slowly approached the pair. "Hello, Peaches." She squatted down until she was on eye level with the dog.

Holding out her hand, she stared at Peaches' feet. Eye to eye contact might make the dog feel threatened.

Peaches tensed, but when Aria made no other move, she took a tentative stop forward, then another. Her nose bumped Aria's hand.

Aria gave the dog time to inspect her before she stood. "Let's go home, girl. You're gonna like Saint Francis."

Ed passed the dog's lease to Aria. "What's this about Saint Francis?" He pulled a small St. Francis medallion on a chain from under his tee shirt and showed it to Aria.

"That's the name of my practice. Saint Francis Animal Hospital."

Ed smiled. "Since Saint Francis is the patron saint of animals, that's a good name."

Ed and the receptionist both patted Peaches. "Good luck, girl," Ed said. "We'll tell Caleb you're fine."

"Didn't he want to say goodbye to her?" Lila asked.

The receptionist gave Peaches one final pat. "He already did. Caleb doesn't come on Thursday so he said goodbye yesterday. I wish you could have seen his face when we told him Peaches had found a home with a vet. It looked like Christmas and his birthday all rolled into one." She beamed at Aria and Lila. "I'll give him your card."

Aria took a firm grip on Peaches' leash. "Thanks. Tell him I'll take good care of her. Let's go, Peaches."

As Aria left the shelter parking lot and turned onto the highway, she saw Ed and the receptionist standing in the door with two other men, all of whom were waving goodbye and undoubtedly wishing good luck to Peaches.

One

Caleb Hawkins fingered the dog-eared card in his pocket as the bus ate up the miles between Pine City and Fairfield. He should have bought a ticket to Greenville, the little town about twenty miles outside of Pine City where his grandmother lived. She might or might not have been glad to see him, but it was the logical place to go.

Instead, he had spent his prison traveling money going to Fairfield, the place where Peaches lived with a lady vet. It had somehow seemed important to know that things had gone well for the dog who had been as broken and injured as he had. He also wanted to thank the woman who had saved his good friend.

Beyond that, he didn't have any specific plans other than finding a job. Maybe he'd go back to Pine City and work at the animal shelter there. He'd rather not unless he had to, though. In that place, he would still feel like a prisoner instead of a free man. It would be better to start over in a new place with no ties to his past.

In the distance he saw a group of buildings. "Approaching Fairfield," the driver called.

The bus came to a halt outside the terminal. Caleb hefted his bag and waited his turn to get off. Then he went inside to an information desk near the front counter. "Hey, I'm looking for the Saint Francis Animal Hospital. Could you tell me how to get there?"

The woman, a young blonde who smiled prettily at him, pulled a map from a drawer and showed him where the hospital was. "That's Dr. De Luca's place. It's about five miles away, so you'll need a ride."

"Thanks for the help."

The woman gestured to an old man dozing in a plastic chair positioned to catch the sunshine. "That's Bob Roach. He has a taxi if you'd like to wake him."

Caleb smiled at the sight of the relaxed old man. In prison you learned not to sleep too deeply. "Thank you."

He touched the man's shoulder, hoping not to startle him. "Mr. Roach?"

"Huh?"

"Mr. Roach, I'm looking for a ride to the animal hospital. Are you interested?"

The old man blinked and wiped his face. "Yeah, give me a minute."

Actually, Mr. Roach took ten minutes to wake up, but he took Caleb right to the animal hospital. It was a pretty drive.

The hospital was located in a relatively rural area with freshly plowed fields just waiting for the weather to warm up enough to plant. Pale green fuzz decorated most of the trees and gave the promise of shade once the leaves grew a little more.

"Want me to wait?" Roach asked as he stopped in front of the animal hospital.

"No, thanks." He had seen a motel not a mile from St. Francis. He'd stay there for the night.

He paused for a moment to look the place over. The hospital was set in a grove of oak trees that would provide shade in the summertime and let the sun in during the winter months. The building was made of concrete blocks that had been painted dark green. It had white shutters and a white door. Someone had added window boxes and filled them with spring flowers in shades of pink, red, and yellow. A curvy walkway made of small gravel led from the parking lot to the front door. All in all it looked like a nice place, a place where the doctor and her staff cared about the animals entrusted to them.

He drew a deep breath of the fresh air and noted that for the past three years he'd mostly missed out on the beauty of the springtime. From his cell he hadn't been able to see even a sliver of the sky. The Department of Corrections initiative that had let him work at the animal clinic had been a lifesaver for him. If not for that escape from his cell, he had no idea what would have become of him, but he suspected it wouldn't have been anything good. He loathed being cooped up and always had.

He saw movement out of the corner of his eye. A big, yellow dog with floppy ears was following a slender, dark-haired woman from behind the building. Eagerness filled him. Peaches. The dog was Peaches.

He called out and waved to the woman who turned and walked his way. All at once Peaches bayed and took off at a dead run in his direction. He held out his arms, and she launched herself at him, bowling him over, licking his face and whining while her tail wagged a mile a minute. "Good dog," he crooned as he stroked her head and fondled her ears. "Good Peaches. I missed you." Swiping his eyes, he hoped nobody was watching him make a fool of himself over a dog.

She looked great. Although she had some scars on her back, her coat shone. Her eyes were bright and clear, and she must have gained ten much-needed pounds. Her attitude was better too. He saw no trace of fear or aggression in her eyes.

He struggled to a sitting position when the woman reached them. The sun shone directly into his eyes so he couldn't see her face. "Hi, I'm Caleb Hawkins. Can you tell me where to find Dr. De Luca?"

"I'm Dr. De Luca." She reached for Peaches' collar, but the dog evaded her and resumed licking him. "Sorry about the dog jumping you. She didn't hurt you, did she?"

He escaped Peaches' embrace and scrambled to his feet. Good grief! Now that the sun was out of his eyes he saw that the doctor was the best looking woman he'd ever seen. The dark hair that he'd previously observed gleamed blue-black in the sun and curled gently on the ends. Her eyes were dark velvety brown, her skin on the olive side. He gulped. She was slender, but she had curves in all the right places.

He forced himself to stop staring at her. "Do you know who I am?"

"What did you say your name was?"

"Caleb Hawkins."

She glanced at Peaches, who was still busy licking his hand. "You're Peaches' friend from the shelter, right?"

He nodded. "I hope it was okay for me to come. It was important to me to see for myself that she was okay." Smiling, he caressed the dog's face. "She's better than okay. Thank you, Doctor."

The doctor beamed at him as though he were an honored guest instead of an ex-con come to see a dog. "Of course it was okay. I hoped you would come to see her. Won't you come in and have something cold? It's warm today."

"Yeah, I'd like that. Thanks."

Caleb followed her into the clinic, noting with approval that it seemed clean and well kept. A big yellow cat lay in the sun on a deep windowsill. The staff smiled at him with friendliness too. Warmth spread throughout his veins. After a dreadful start in life, Peaches had gotten lucky.

The doctor took him into her office and removed two soft drinks from the small refrigerator behind her desk. "What do you think of Peaches?"

At the sound of her name, Peaches gave the doctor one of those soulful looks that she used to give him, but her head still rested on his knee. "I think she looks wonderful. You've done everything that needed doing for her."

The doctor smiled as if his compliment really did please her. "Thank you. We tried. It took a while for her to heal, but with the groundwork you laid we thought we could help her, and we did." She took a sip of her drink. "Have you decided what you want to do now that you have your freedom?"

Caleb shrugged. "I don't know yet. I just got out of prison yesterday."

The doctor's eyes widened just a touch. "You must have come straight here."

"I did. Like I said, it was important to me to see that she was okay."

Dr. De Luca took a big pull on her soft drink. "The receptionist at the Pine City shelter told me that the director had offered you a job when your sentence was over."

He nodded. "That's right. She did, but..." How could he make her see? What words could describe his despair over the loss of every single freedom he had? Someone else had told him when to go to bed and when to get up. Meals consisted of something someone else said you should eat. His gaze fell to the blue denim shirt he wore. It was the first thing he'd had to wear in over three years that wasn't regulation prison issue. Unless you'd been in the same situation, you'd never understand why he didn't want to work there.

The doctor's next words blew him out of the water. "You still feel like a prisoner there, don't you?"

He laughed at himself. "And here I was thinking nobody could understand that."

"It's the way I'd feel," she assured him. She assessed him for a moment. "We have a girl out on maternity leave.

Would you be interested in filling in here until she comes back? We're looking at a six week time frame."

Were vets and animal shelter directors all nice people, or had he gotten lucky to meet two women willing to give him a second chance? He should probably head on over to Greenville, but the prospect held little appeal. Peaches sighed and licked his hand again. "That sounds real good. When do you want me to start?"

"Tomorrow?"

"Yes, ma'am. I'll be here."

~ * ~

Aria watched as Caleb Hawkins shouldered his pack and walked down the driveway. She had offered to drive him to the motel, but he had turned her down, saying that after spending three years sitting in prison, he enjoyed walking.

She didn't know what she had expected, but whatever it was it didn't fit Caleb Hawkins. The man could have been a male model, selling everything from designer clothes and jewelry to outdoor sports equipment. He stood about six one and didn't have an ounce of fat on him. The way his muscles bulged when he picked up his pack had sent a thrill racing through her. His hair was dark, his eyes a deep blue shade that reminded her of the sky just as the sun set in the evening.

Would she regret offering him a temporary position? Maybe, but probably not. Melissa's maternity leave would be up in six weeks so he wouldn't be around forever. He could use the time to acclimate to being out of prison before he set about finding a permanent job. His room and board would eat up some of his pay, but he'd still have a few dollars left over. He could save it or maybe buy a few clothes and other things he needed.

She went back into her office, but before she could tell Lila she was ready to see patients again, the phone rang. The number belonged to her mother.

"Hey, Mama, what's up?"

Clariee De Luca laughed, which made Aria laugh too. Her happy mama laughed at anything and everything. "Lila called me and said Peaches' friend had come to see her."

Aria nodded, even though her mother couldn't see her. "He did. His name is Caleb Hawkins. You should have seen Peaches. When she saw him, she ran across the yard and knocked him over."

"Did he look like a dangerous man?"

"No, Mama, he didn't. In fact, I hired him to fill in for Melissa."

"Then I want to meet him. Invite him to come to dinner tomorrow night."

Aria giggled. "Do you want me to come too, or do you just want Caleb?"

"Hmm. Let me think. If he's cute maybe he should come alone." She laughed. "Of course I meant you too."

"That's good. Daddy probably wouldn't like it if you took up with another man."

They made their arrangements, and Aria went back to work. Her patients wouldn't wait all day. Even then, she could hear Mr. Simms' Siamese cat howling like a soul in torment.

Two

Caleb cut off the hose and used his stiff-bristled broom to sweep the water from the concrete floor. He had spent the morning cleaning kennels and dog runs. The doctor had some kind of little cot things on legs that the dogs slept on, so he hadn't had any blankets to wash except where a couple of dogs who'd had surgery had been covered to keep them warm.

This was the kind of thing he'd done at the shelter in Pine City. It was enjoyable work because it made the animals more comfortable. He smiled to himself. If not for his years in prison, he never would have known how much he liked animals. It would be great to be a vet himself, but with his means, that was an impossible dream. Even if he could somehow raise the money for tuition and books, he'd still have to have money to live on, money he didn't have.

Lila Monroe, the doctor's lead vet tech, entered the boarding area carrying a smoky gray kitten with blue eyes. Lila was pretty with her red hair and curvy body, but she couldn't compare to the doc. He liked the efficiency, calmness, and strength that he sensed in Aria De Luca. She was all business at work, but the way her eyes twinkled and the corners of her mouth often turned up, he'd bet she was a lot of fun once she left the office.

Lila passed him the kitten. "We're boarding this little guy while his mama and daddy are out of town. Can you put him in cage five and fill the water dish for me?"

Caleb nodded and stroked the kitten's tiny head with one finger. "He's a beauty."

"Yep, sure is. Say, Aria wants to see you as soon as you finish here."

"Okay."

Caleb settled the kitten and headed for the office. He hoped she wasn't going to fire him. Not that he could remember doing anything wrong, but when you were an ex-con, the rules were different. This was a good place to get back on his feet so he crossed his fingers for good luck as he made his way to Dr. De Luca's office. The door stood open so the doc saw him before he could knock. "Hi, Caleb, come in."

"You wanted to see me?"

"Yes, if you aren't busy, my mother wants you to have dinner with us tonight."

When she laughed, he guessed the astonishment he felt was written on his face. Why on earth had the doc's mother invited him to dinner? He'd never even met the woman, but it would be silly to turn down the chance of a home cooked meal. In his world, they were few and far between. "That's nice of her. Can I bring anything?"

Now it was the doc's turn to look surprised. She hadn't expected him to offer, probably thought he didn't know that people sometimes offered to help out the hostess. "No, just bring yourself," she said. "Mama loves to cook so she never lets anyone help her. You're staying in John's Home Away From Home aren't you? How about if I pick you up at six thirty? Mama lives too far away for you to walk."

"Yes, the motel isn't far from the clinic so it works for me. I'll be ready by six thirty." He smiled. "I'm looking forward to it." He rubbed his hands, which were still damp on his pants. "I'm finished with the kennels."

She grinned. "Melissa takes a bit longer to get them done. Go ahead and take your lunch break now. We have a horse coming in at one, and we might need you to help with him."

As it happened, they did need help. The horse, a big chestnut stallion, was buck wild. He rolled his eyes, laid back his ears, and tried to bite anyone in his vicinity. A dangling tumor that looked huge to Caleb hung from the horse's stomach. "We have to get him into the stocks," the doc said. "I don't want to treat him with hooves flying around my head."

"I don't suppose he'd let us get a twitch on him," Caleb muttered.

The doc laughed. "Not likely."

Caleb remembered the first time he'd heard a vet talk about putting an animal in the stocks. He'd pictured a cow with her head and front legs in a frame the way they used to do to people in the old days, but it wasn't like that at all. Stocks were basically a metal enclosure that restrained the animal but allowed the vet access to treat it.

It took a while to get the horse in the stocks, but once they did, he settled down and let the doc remove the tumor without much fuss. The doc had handled the horse exactly right. She'd been firm but kind to him and never raised her voice or hit him. This lady knew her business.

"Is this anything to worry about?" he asked.

Aria shook her head. "No, I don't think so. I'll send it off for testing just to be sure, but I'm almost certain it's nothing. You see things like this sometimes."

At the end of the day, he hurried to the motel to clean up. He didn't want to meet the doc's family smelling like a horse or dog. *Sorry, Peaches. It's nothing personal.*

~ * ~

Caleb stared at the De Luca home as they turned into a long, paved driveway bordered by a white fence. Several nice looking horses and a few donkeys grazed inside the fence. At the end of the driveway stood a large, three-story brick house with a small front porch supported by white columns. Aria parked her truck in an area to the right of the house. As he got out of the truck, he saw that all of the grounds were manicured to perfection. "You've got quite a place here."

Aria pushed that lovely dark hair away from her face and gave a cursory glance at the house. "Yeah, it's nice. My great-grandfather built it. It's been in the family ever since."

She smiled as if the idea of family pleased her. "I'm an only child," she said, "so eventually, it'll come to me."

This came as no surprise. The house obviously wasn't new. "If you don't mind me asking, what did your great-grandfather do for a living?"

"Oh, he was a doctor."

A doctor. That explained the air of wealth and privilege that clung to the place.

He followed Aria into the house where they entered a wide, central hallway. An oriental runner ran the entire length of the hallway. Small, highly polished tables and a few chairs lined both sides of the hall. On one table he saw a huge bouquet of pink roses. A silver tray filled with mail sat beside the bouquet.

"Aria?" A lilting voice sounded from the back of the house.

"Coming, Mama."

She led Caleb down the hall and turned right into a huge, bright kitchen filled with white cabinets and stainless steel appliances. A gray tabby cat perched on a padded bar stool and supervised all the kitchen activity. The cat blinked when it saw him and turned its back on him. It only had three legs.

"Caleb, this is my mother, Clariee De Luca. Mama, this is Caleb Hawkins."

Clariee De Luca looked very much like her daughter. She had the same slender frame and coloring, and like the doc her eyes were filled with laughter. "Welcome, Caleb. I hope you're in the mood for some good Italian food. I've been cooking all afternoon."

She didn't have to tell him. A fragrant aroma filled the room and made his stomach growl noisily.

"Oh, that won't do," Clariee cried. She pushed a plate toward him. "Try this shrimp bruschetta. I think you'll like it."

Aria popped one into her mouth. "I like it, that's for sure."

Caleb willingly tried the bruschetta. In prison you didn't get food like this. Come to think of it, he'd never had food like this. Before he went to prison, most of his meals consisted of institutional food served at school or things like meat loaf and mashed potatoes that his grandmother favored. He took a bite and his eyes closed in appreciation. "Delicious."

Clariee beamed. She liked getting compliments on her cooking. Well, who didn't like compliments? It had done him a world of good to be appreciated when he went to work for the Pine City shelter.

"Where's Daddy?" Aria asked as she tried another piece of bruschetta.

"He had a late appointment in town, but he'll be here for dinner. I made his favorite since he had to work late."

Aria drew a deep breath. "Mine too." To Caleb she explained. "She made braciole."

Caleb laughed. "And that is?"

"Stuffed flank steak. Mama's is the best ever."

"Don't tell him that," Clariee exclaimed, brandishing a fork in Aria's direction. "I can't live up to those standards."

"Oh, yes, she can," Aria cried. "Just you wait and see, Caleb."

Caleb glanced out the kitchen window and saw a black BMW entering a garage. Probably Aria's father. Some moments later a door opened on the far side of the kitchen, and a man with dark, graying hair and strong features entered the kitchen. He looked surprised when he saw Caleb.

"I didn't know we were having company," he said. He set his briefcase on a shelf just inside the door and joined them around the kitchen island. He held out his hand. "David De Luca."

"Caleb Hawkins." De Luca took his hand, but the man's face changed. He'd heard of his visitor. Grim amusement filled Caleb. Ex-cons probably didn't eat here very often.

"Daddy's a lawyer," Aria explained as she gave her father a hug.

Well, that explained a lot.

Clariee indicated the plate of bruschetta. "Have one, David. We're almost ready."

De Luca's face softened as he reached for the bruschetta, but his eyes never left his wife's face. Clariee looked a few years younger than her husband, but maybe not. He'd never been any good at determining a person's age. At any rate, that look on De Luca's face told him the man was deeply in love with his wife.

They had dinner in a formal dining room filled with more highly polished furniture that looked as if it had been in the family for generations. It probably had been. The accessories had a more contemporary flavor, though, which gave the room an updated look. The careless arrangement of fresh flowers that sat on the table lent a cheery air to the dining room.

Clariee smiled at him as De Luca carved the meat. "Do you enjoy working at Saint Francis, Caleb?"

"Yes, ma'am. I like animals, and Dr. De Luca is good to work for."

"He's doing a nice job," Aria joined in. "The animals like him too."

Clariee beamed as if she had personally chosen him for the job. "Do you know about St. Francis, Caleb? Aria named her clinic after him."

Caleb shook his head. "No, I've heard of St. Francis, but that's it. I don't know anything about him."

Clariee picked up a bottle of red wine. "Let me refill your glass for you. Aria, tell him about St. Francis."

Aria didn't hesitate, which made him think she liked this story and had probably told it before. "Okay, here's the story of St. Francis and the wolf. I like this one. A long time ago, there was a small village that was having trouble with a hungry wolf. The villagers tried to kill the wolf, but they couldn't get it done. The creature kept right on killing the villagers.

"St. Francis heard about it and went out into the woods to talk to the wolf, even though the villagers begged him not to go."

Caleb laughed. "I probably wouldn't have gone. I saw a wolf once in a zoo. They're huge."

Aria smiled and nodded at him. "Neither would I. Anyway, when the wolf saw him, it rushed toward him with its jaws open wide. St. Francis rebuked it, and it lay down in front of him without trying to hurt him."

"Oh, I love this story," Clariee broke in. Caleb smiled at her, amused by her childlike enthusiasm. It was easy to see why David De Luca loved her.

"Go ahead and finish the story, Mama," Aria urged.

Clariee laughed. "Only if you insist. St. Francis made a deal with the wolf. He made it promise not to eat anyone else, and in return the villagers promised to feed the wolf. It actually laid its paw in his hand to seal the deal. The wolf lived in the village for two years and never hurt anyone."

"What happened to it?" Caleb asked, hoping for a good ending.

"Oh, it died of old age."

Aria passed him a basket filled with bread. "There are a lot of other stories about St. Francis and his relationship with animals, so when I opened my practice that seemed like a good name."

"When does Melissa come back to work?"

David's change of subject and abrupt entrance into the conversation brought stories about St. Francis to a close. Since finding out his visitor's identity, he hadn't had two words to say.

"Six weeks," Aria answered.

De Luca passed him a plate that looked and smelled delicious. "What will you do when Melissa comes back?"

That was a good question, but he didn't know the answer. He had called his grandmother one night from the motel to tell her he was out of jail, but she hadn't seemed too interested in seeing him. "Keep your nose clean and find a job," she'd said, but she hadn't invited him to come and live with her until he got on his feet. Not that he'd expected her to. His grandmother had made her opinion of him very clear. In all the years he'd been in prison, she hadn't visited him once, not even at Christmas.

"I might go back to the Pine City shelter," he said. "They like my work."

De Luca nodded. "That's a good plan. Don't wait too long to go and see them. If they hire you, they might send you through a vet tech program at a technical school. You'd make more money that way."

Both Aria and Clariee nodded and smiled as if De Luca were trying to help him and had said something profound. They didn't get the same message he was getting. De Luca was telling him to get out of town and leave Aria alone.

His jaw tightened as anger nipped him, but he'd be worried too if an ex-con went to work for his good-looking daughter. Since he was a lawyer, De Luca had probably seen a lot of tough troublemakers. No wonder he was worried for Aria.

Clariee buttered a piece of homemade bread and took a bite. "Where are you from, Caleb?"

"Pine City, ma'am."

The doc joined the conversation. "There's a bus that runs from Fairfield to Pine City almost every day. You could visit people and still get back for dinner."

"I might do that," he said, knowing that he wouldn't. It was easier not to explain about his lack of family so he didn't try.

"Getting a vet tech certificate is a good idea," Aria said. "I could let you do a whole lot more if you were certified."

Wow, that sounded intriguing. "Like what?"

"Well, you could give medications, draw blood, put in IVs, give anesthesia, assist me in surgery, do lab work. Lots of things."

This sounded like the next best thing to actually being a vet. "How long would it take to get a certificate?"

Aria thought for a minute. "About two years if you go full time. A little more if you don't."

Caleb nodded. "I'll give it some thought." He would too, but first he had to find out how much money they were looking at. Paying the rent and buying some grub wasn't cheap. Any job he took on a permanent basis had to pay the bills.

As dinner concluded, Clariee smiled at him and said, "If you have a refrigerator in your room, I'll fix you a plate to take with you for tomorrow night."

"Thank you. I'd appreciate it." After buying a few things to wear to work, he was having a ramen noodle and peanut butter and jelly week so the food would be a godsend.

De Luca rose from the table. "Think about the vet tech degree, Caleb. I think it would be in your best interest."

He turned to Clariee. "I'll be in the study if you need me."

Caleb gave a mental shrug. He hadn't really expected De Luca to shake his hand or tell him to come back. Still, the man hadn't been very hospitable.

Clariee came from the kitchen with two plates wrapped in foil. "One is real food; the other is dessert."

Caleb laughed at the expression on her face when she looked at one of the plates. He'd bet the farm Clariee liked dessert better.

Aria kissed her mother, and smiled at him. "Ready?"

He nodded. After thanking Clariee, he followed Aria outside. "Do you live with your parents?" he asked as they got into the doc's truck and fastened their seatbelts.

She shook her head. "No, I bought a house not too far from the clinic. It's right on the river. I can sit on my front porch and watch the water flowing downstream."

"Sounds nice." Or he guessed it would be nice. He'd never lived outside of town in his life. Cars and sirens had sung lullabies for him, not rivers.

"Oh, it is nice." She beamed at him. "There's nothing better to relax me after a hard day at the clinic."

After the doc dropped him off at the motel, Caleb stood and watched as her truck drove down the road. Even though Aria came from money, she acted like a regular person and did useful work. She could probably have been a debutante and spent her time going to parties and shopping for expensive clothes and shoes. Instead, she had chosen-to his way of thinking-a better life.

He unlocked his door and went inside. Although he didn't know the De Lucas well enough to say for certain, it seemed to him that Aria was more like her father than her mother. She projected the same competent certainty that her father did.

Still, the doc had inherited her mother's kindness. If she'd hadn't, Peaches would be dead today, not running around in the sunshine and having the time of her life. He himself had been the recipient of her kindness too, hadn't he? She didn't have to let him work at St. Francis for six weeks, but she did. The money was coming in handy too.

Yep, no doubt about it. Aria De Luca was an admirable woman.

Three

"Caleb! Aria needs you ASAP in exam one."

The scared look on Lila's face sent Caleb bolting from the waiting room where he'd been setting up a display of collars and leashes. He peeped through the door and saw Aria backed into a corner. A huge, black, mixed-breed dog stood in front of her. The animal's hair stood up all along its back, and he could hear it growling from the hallway.

He darted to the equipment room and grabbed a catchpole. As he eased the exam room door open, the dog lunged at him. It was no match for a man who'd spent several years working in a dog shelter, though. Within seconds, he subdued the animal.

As soon as he had the dog in hand, Aria gave it a sedative. "I owe you one," she said. They watched as the dog's head nodded. It yawned and lay down on the floor.

Caleb removed the noose from the animal's neck. "Where did it come from?"

"It's a stray. The local animal shelter brought it in this morning. They said it was feral, but I didn't expect it to freak out that way."

Caleb sighed. "That's a bad lookout then."

"Maybe. Let's get him up on the table."

After they heaved the animal onto the stainless steel exam table, Aria took a blood sample from the dog. "Tell Lila to do a heartworm check."

By the time the exam ended, they had wormed the dog and started heartworm treatment. Caleb scooped him up and put him in one of the doc's nice kennels. When the dog woke up, he could rest in the kennel or go outside into a dog run.

Aria checked to make sure the kennel had water. "I was thinking. You did so well with Peaches, maybe you'd like to see what you can do for this boy."

"Peaches was never this bad, and I only have a short time to reach the dog, but I'm willing to try."

Her smile just about blinded him with its intensity. His heart jumped around in his chest and almost left him breathless. All she'd done was smile at him!

The doc removed her white lab coat and tossed it onto a coat rack with several others. "Let's go to lunch. My treat. If you hadn't been here, I might be getting treatment for a dog bite."

"All part of the job," he assured her, "but lunch sounds nice." Yes, it certainly did. His heart had settled down, but he wouldn't mind receiving another killer smile.

They walked toward Aria's truck, which was parked not far from the dog runs. The new dog was curled into a ball sleeping in the sunshine.

"I guess you get to name him. Do you have anything in mind?" Aria asked. She clicked her electronic door opener for him.

"I think Rascal would be perfect."

Aria nodded as she backed out of her reserved parking space. "I like that. Rascal it is, then."

"I was just wondering," Caleb began as he fastened his seat belt.

"Wondering what?"

"Why'd they sent a dog like Rascal to the vet? We got a couple of feral dogs in Pine City, and they got put to sleep."

Aria laughed. "The director of the animal shelter is a friend of mine. She sent him here because she knew I'd do everything I could to help him. This isn't a rescue, but ..."

"I get it," Caleb teased. "Everyone knows you're a softie."

She rolled her eyes, not a good thing since she was driving. "Don't tell anybody else."

Like he had to.

They parked in front of a neat, brick building whose parking lot was filled with cars. A tasteful, old-fashioned looking sign in the window invited people to enter Ned's Place. "The restaurant is new," Aria said as they made their way across the parking lot. "Everyone says Ned Simmons spent a lot of money on the decor. He spent a lot of time too. It took forever for him to open."

Caleb held the door for the doc, and they went inside. Wow, look at that big rock fireplace on the far wall. It sure was pretty. The tables were round and had real tablecloths and small vases of fresh flowers. One wall was filled with booths that also had fresh flowers. Big windows let in lots of light. No wonder people in Fairfield liked coming here.

Aria spoke or waved to a good many people as the hostess escorted them to their table. "You know a lot of these folks," he observed.

She nodded. "I do. Most of the people I spoke to are pet owners that bring their animals to St. Francis."

As they sat down, a man unfolded from one of the booths across the room. He had to be six four at least and was slim built. His hair was blond, his skin fair. Nothing about his face stood out in any way. He looked...generic. Yeah, that was the word. Generic. He waved to Aria and strolled over.

"Aria, how are you?"

"I'm fine. And you?"

"Fitter than a fiddle."

Aria laughed when the man glanced at him. "I'm forgetting my manners. Jason Lee, this is Caleb Hawkins. He's taking Melissa's place while she's out on maternity leave."

Lee gave him the once over before offering to shake hands. "Good to meet you."

"You too." He usually didn't lie, but he had lied this time. Something about Lee set his teeth on edge. He couldn't put a finger on it, but he didn't like the man. As irrational as it seemed, he didn't think Lee liked him either. Well, maybe Lee didn't like seeing Aria with another man. The doc's love life was a mystery to him. For all he knew, this might be one of her boyfriends.

"Jason's a contractor," Aria said. "His latest project is a housing development about ten miles past Mama and Daddy's house."

"What kind of houses?" Caleb asked. "Single family, apartments?"

Lee snorted. "Only one kind if you want to make money. Luxury homes with huge rooms and fancy finishings."

That sounded odd. A major recession had the country by the throat, and this guy was selling luxury houses? Last he heard the housing market was still depressed. Still, Lee must know his business.

"I do have a few low cost homes in a development out River Road if you'd be interested in looking," Lee said. "I can cut you quite a deal to get the inventory off my hands."

Caleb smiled. "Not right now. I'm not sure about my plans yet."

"Call me if you decide." He nodded at the doc. "Aria, I'll see you later."

"Bye, Jason."

Caleb watched as Lee crossed the parking lot and drove away in a very nice SUV. "How's he doing it? Selling expensive houses, I mean."

Aria shrugged. "I don't know. He talks about his luxury development, but I bet he sells more on River Road. Those houses don't stay on the market long, but the ones in the luxury development take forever to sell. Jason just likes building big houses."

The talk moved away from Jason Lee, but Caleb thought of him off and on that afternoon. It wasn't common for him to take an instant dislike to someone. If only he could figure out what he disliked about the man. The guy had shaken his hand and been friendly on the surface, and he'd even tried to sell him a cheap house. It really must have something to do with the doc, but he barely knew her. He had no right to feel territorial about her, a fact he'd do well to remember.

~ * ~

The next morning, Aria and Lila stood at the window and stared at Caleb and Rascal. After a rodeo of gigantic proportions, they had finally got a leash on Rascal and tied him inside a portable, wire enclosure. Caleb had then brought a chair into the pen. Turning sideways to Rascal, he had seated himself in the chair to read a book he had taken with him.

"Is that all he's going to do?" Lila asked. "I expected something a little fancier."

"He's trying to win the dog's trust. Rascal has never been around people, so Caleb is showing him that he doesn't have to fear humans."

Lila sniffed. "I'd just give him a piece of chicken. That ought to do the trick."

"He has the chicken in his pocket. Chicken strips from Epic Chicken."

Lila giggled. "For real?"

Aria nodded.

Lila strolled away to get started with her day, but Aria stayed at the window. Watching the way Caleb Hawkins moved took her breath away. He was graceful with an economy of movement that made everything he did look effortless. Those shoulders of his were something to see. If there was one thing she liked, it was a nice pair of shoulders. The gray tee shirt he had worn this morning strained across his chest and hinted of rock-hard, six pack abs. He had probably worked out in prison when he wasn't at the shelter. Of course, that was a cliché. Prisoners on TV and in the movies did it, but that didn't mean everyone did.

Reaching into his pocket, Caleb brought out the food he had taken with him. His arm hung limply toward the ground. Rascal's nose twitched when he smelled the chicken in Caleb's hand, but he refused to come any closer.

Caleb sat there for a couple more minutes before tossing the meat to the dog. After Rascal gobbled it up, Caleb untied him and quickly stepped out of the pen.

He saw her at the window, smiled, and waved. "Pretty good for the first day," he said as he entered the clinic.

"If you say so," Aria answered. "You're the one with experience here."

Her heart gave a little bounce when he smiled at her. When Caleb smiled he looked like...like a movie star. Good grief! What was the matter with her? She had work to do. Standing around ogling her employee was a super waste of time even if he did look like movie star.

"Now that you've finished with Rascal, why not take Peaches for a walk?" she asked, thinking how Peaches would love a walk on this fine spring morning.

His face lit up. "I'd be glad to. I need a walk myself." He laughed. "I was the favorite dog walker in Pine City. I was big enough to control the larger, stronger dogs."

Yes, he certainly was. As Caleb hurried to find a harness and leash for Peaches, Aria forced herself to go and see her patients, but she spared a moment to watch as he and the dog left the clinic and walked down the driveway. Too bad she couldn't go with them.

~ * ~

That evening Caleb borrowed a car from the woman who was living in the motel room beside him and drove over to see Jason Lee's luxury housing development. If there had been anything to watch on TV he wouldn't have done it, but then again, maybe he would. He felt restless tonight, and Lee had rubbed him the wrong way.

As he approached the place, he saw that eventually the upscale development would be a gated community. Probably the construction vehicles coming and going were the only reason they didn't already have the gate installed. When they got around to it, the gate would probably be something impressive, something that would match the huge, river-rock wall that surrounded the property.

He turned inside the development and drove down the first street he came to. Nice cul-de-sac. Safer for kids. Oh, look at that. There was an open house sign in the yard of the house at the very end of the street. Why not go inside and take a look?

He parked in the driveway and went inside. Where was the real estate agent? Well, no matter. He'd give himself a tour.

Actually, the house looked nice. The rooms were spacious, and the hardwood floors and real stone baths would be a lot easier to care for than carpet. Oh, good. The bonus room wasn't finished yet. Uh oh. This room confirmed what he'd suspected from the beginning. Lee was cutting corners.

The framing was 19.0 plus an inch instead of 16. Lee had used finger studs instead of solid wood. And look at the lone window on the far wall. It was cheaply made of metal and probably wouldn't hold up to the elements.

Exiting the bonus room, he wandered into the kitchen, a beautiful room that had granite countertops, stainless appliances, and stone floors. Nice, but look at the floor. Lee's men had used as much grout as they had stone.

He left the house and drove over a couple of streets. Here was a home they were in the process of building. He got out of his car, and after a short examination, he exclaimed, "What a mess!"

It was obvious from the grading job that the house would have water problems. The lumber was cheap; the copper piping for the plumbing was undoubtedly type M instead of the more expensive type L. Everywhere he looked he saw something wrong. Lee had given people what he termed 'fancy finishings,' but he had scrimped on the things that really mattered most. If this was how Lee built what was supposed to be a nice house, he couldn't imagine what the cheap homes were like.

Of course, most buyers probably wouldn't know what they were looking at. The only reason he did was because in high school he hung out with a guy whose father was a contractor, and the guy had shown him a few things.

Should he say anything to the doc? Of course not. It wasn't any of her business. His either, for that matter. And nothing he'd seen here was illegal, just shoddy workmanship. *Forget you ever saw it, Caleb. You'll stay out of trouble that way, and haven't you had enough trouble in your life?*

~ * ~

Lila was humming a catchy tune when Caleb got to St. Francis the next day. "Good morning," she warbled. "Isn't it a lovely day?"

"I guess. It's kinda hot, though."

The doc breezed in just in time to hear his comment. "It's too hot for me this morning too, Caleb. Lila's just happy because she's going to the dance with Seth."

"That's right!" Lila enthused. She grabbed Aria's arm and spun her around. "I'm going to dance all night with the man of my dreams."

Caleb grinned at her. He liked the spunky redhead. "Seth's a lucky man."

"Thank you, sir," Lila gushed as she curtsied to him.

She sashayed out of the room and turned toward the office, still humming her cheerful song. "You should think about going to the dance," Aria said. "The town's celebrating its bicentennial with street dances every Friday."

Caleb shrugged. "I probably won't go. I don't know anyone, and it isn't fun to go by yourself."

Aria giggled. "I know a hint when I hear it. Okay, why don't we go together?"

Caleb rapidly backtracked. "Hey, I wasn't hinting or anything."

Aria arched one eyebrow. "So you don't want to go with me?"

entered his mind. He was just a man with a desirable, beautiful woman in his arms, and he wanted her with a ferocity that amazed him.

They had just bought a snow cone of all things when Jason Lee saw them and sauntered over. "Hi, Aria, Caleb. Are you having a good time?"

Aria laughed. "We sure are. I just taught Caleb to square dance. Well, not really. He picked it up just by watching."

Something flickered in Lee's eyes and was gone. "Isn't that nice."

Aria licked her snow cone that was slowly turning her tongue blue. "He's a fast learner."

"Probably because you're such a good dance partner," Jason said.

"Oh, I doubt it. Caleb has natural rhythm."

A muscle jumped in the man's cheek. "I'll see you later. Have a good time."

"Okay, bye."

She stared at Jason as he merged into the crowd. "Wonder what's wrong with him? He left so abruptly."

Caleb shrugged. "Do you really want to know?"

"Yes, of course I do."

"He didn't like seeing you with me."

"Oh." She thought for a moment. "That isn't really any of his business, is it? We've gone out a few times, but he doesn't have any claim on me. We're friends, but that's it."

The relief brought by her words dimmed. "Maybe he thinks you shouldn't be hanging out with an ex-con."

She thought that over too, just as deliberately as he'd seen her mulling over a difficult case. "Jason Lee does not pick my friends or my dance partners." The little line between her eyes smoothed out. "Let's dance, Caleb. Forget about Jason."

Grabbing his hand, she pulled him toward the dance floor, or in this case the center of the street.

~ * ~

Caleb groaned and flipped over on his hard, motel mattress. Seconds later he flipped the other way. He had known he wouldn't sleep before he ever even lay down. Sighing, he turned on the bedside lamp and sat up.

Melissa, the woman who was on maternity leave, would come back to the clinic in four weeks. That's when his temporary job with Aria would end, and he didn't want it to end. As ridiculous as it sounded, he had fallen hard for Aria De Luca. Having her in his arms tonight had been the sweetest form of torture he could imagine, but he liked more than just Aria's looks. He liked her kind heart and the way she treated the animals just as much.

Scrambling to his feet, he left his room and went to the vending machines outside his door to buy a pack of crackers. Just because the doc was a kind woman didn't mean he was anything more to her than an employee. All he'd seen in her eyes tonight was pleasure over a nice evening dancing and talking to friends.

It was better that way. Even if she did feel the same way he did, what could he offer her? He didn't have a penny to his name or any prospects for the future. Besides that, her daddy didn't like him.

Be careful. Don't let yourself get hurt again.

Four

"Caleb, would you mind helping me out during your lunch break?"

Caleb tightened his hold on Rascal's leash. The dog was doing better, but Aria knew Caleb would never take the chance of Rascal biting anyone.

"Sure, Doc. What can I do for you?"

Aria giggled. As far as she knew, Caleb was the only person who'd ever called her Doc, and she had to admit she liked it. It tickled her every time he said it. "My mama called this morning. She said a stray cat holed up under the barn and had a litter of kittens. The mama looks bad, so she wants me to see if I can do anything. I don't know how hard it'll be to catch her, which is where you come in. Mama said she'd give us lunch so you don't have to worry about missing a meal."

"I'd never pass up your mama's cooking. I'm your man."

"Good. We'll leave after I see my eleven-thirty appointment."

~ * ~

As the car stopped in front of the De Luca house, Clariee De Luca stepped onto the porch to meet them. "Welcome, Caleb! How're you doing at the clinic?"

Caleb laughed. "You'd have to ask Aria."

"He's doing fine," Aria assured her. "I think we'll try to catch the cat before we eat if that's okay, Mama."

Clariee nodded. "I'll show you where it is."

They passed by the door of an immaculate, white barn and went around back. "We need to get someone in to work on this hole," Clariee said.

Aria stooped over and stared into the hole at the back of the barn. A yellow cat glared at her and hissed as it prepared to defend the three babies at its side. Aria handed Caleb a pair of heavy, leather work gloves and pulled on a pair herself. She reached inside. "Catch it if it comes your way, Caleb."

The cat shot out of the hole and darted away. Caleb grabbed for it, missed, and gave chase, but the cat vanished into the woods behind the barn. "Sorry," he yelled.

Aria removed her gloves and stuck them in her pocket. "Let's see if we can track her."

She and Caleb entered the woods and followed a small path made smooth by the passing of generations of wild animals. They hadn't gone far when Caleb froze. "Listen."

Aria heard it too. A wet, sobbing, snuffling sound came from a thicket of ferns just in front of them.

"What is that?" Caleb breathed. He grabbed her arm when she took a step forward. "No, let me."

Aria held her breath as he slowly moved forward. "Be careful," she whispered.

"Aria! Look."

Aria rushed forward. A skeletal, brown and white pit bull lay on its side in the ferns. Almost every inch of its body was covered in fresh wounds, but the most horrible thing of all was the animal's nose. Part of it had been ripped off, exposing the poor thing's gums, teeth, and nasal passages.

Aria's curses rent the air. Remembering that she wasn't alone she contented herself with kicking a tree and pounding it with her palm. "Can you carry him, Caleb? We need to get him to the clinic right away."

"Yeah, but how should I pick him up? I'm afraid I'll hurt him."

"It can't be helped. Just pick him up as if he were a healthy dog."

She ran ahead to make a bed for the dog in the back of her truck with her mama darting along behind her. "Hurry, Aria," Clariee urged. "Help him."

"Dog fighting?" Caleb asked as the truck turned onto the highway.

Aria nodded. "I know there's a dog fighting ring around here, and I've tried to find out who's behind it, but nobody's talking. I hope whoever did this rots in ..."

She broke off and concentrated on driving. How could anyone be so cruel? She'd never understand it. No, not even if she lived to be a hundred. The minute she stopped the truck in the clinic parking lot she jumped out and ran to unlock the clinic door that had been locked during lunchtime. "Bring him in here," she cried as Caleb eased the dog out of the truck.

The dog groaned and breathed wetly as Caleb gently placed him on the exam table. "We need to shave the fur off his leg so we can get an IV in." She pointed to an electric razor on the shelf, and Caleb took it from its box and handed it to her. A few minutes later she had the IV in the dog's vein.

"I put some pain medication and an antibiotic in the IV," she said. "He's dehydrated so I had a hard time getting the needle in, but he'll be comfortable enough for us to examine him now."

Caleb pointed to one of the deepest cuts on the dog's shoulder. "He has ticks in his wounds."

Aria groaned. "They're all over him. Let's get rid of them first." It wasn't legal for her to let Caleb help her, but she wasn't tending a client's dog. This dog belonged to her now, and she needed his help.

It took what seemed like forever to get the ticks off the dog. Afterward, she gently ran her hands over him, searching for broken bones. "I don't think he has anything broken, but we'll do an X-ray just to make sure. Then I'll stitch these wounds and we'll do some blood work on him. He probably has Babesia and no telling what else."

"What's Babesia?"

Aria took off her gloves and reached for a clean pair. "Babesia is a tick borne illness. It's a protozoa that causes malaria-like symptoms. In many cases, it's fatal. Fighting dogs especially are susceptible to it because when one dog bites another, it can be spread."

"What can you do about his nose?"

She frowned. "Nothing. He'll have to go to a specialist for that."

"Aria? Is that you? The door was unlocked." Lila who had just returned from lunch cautiously poked her head around the door. "Oh, sweet goodness!" she exclaimed, horror registering on her face. "From the dog fighting ring?"

Aria nodded. "It's bad, Lila. We need to get a blood panel right now."

Two hours later, they had done everything they could for the dog who had turned out to have no broken bones. "Will he survive?" Caleb asked.

Aria shrugged. "I wish I knew. His wounds, while extensive, will heal, and I think we can treat the Babesia, but the nose and starvation... I don't know, Caleb. I don't know. Carry him to the kennel for me, please."

Caleb did and Aria gently covered the dog with a warm blanket. "You poor thing," she whispered. "I'll do what I can for you, and if I ever find out who did this, he'll pay. You have my word on that."

Lila breezed into the room that she called the intensive care room. "I rescheduled all your afternoon patients so you can have a break."

Aria nodded. "Thanks, Lila. I feel like I've been run over by a car."

"Will we do all night care?"

"Yes. We'll each do a shift. I don't want him alone for even a moment."

"Count me in," Caleb said.

"I was." Aria glanced at her watch. "Lila, call Dr. Pickford and alert him to the situation. Provided everything goes okay I want him to work on the nose."

"Will do."

As Lila went to make her call, the phone in the intensive care room rang. With a sigh, Aria picked it up. "St. Francis Animal Clinic. How may I help you?"

"Hi, Aria, it's Jason Lee."

"Hello, Jason. What's up?"

He laughed lightly. "Nothing to do with any animals, if that's what you meant. I just wondered if you'd let me take you to dinner tonight."

If they hadn't found the dog she would probably have gone. She and Jason had grown up together, and she liked him, but her patient came first. "Any other time, Jason, but not tonight. I have a really urgent patient that I don't want to leave."

He sighed in her ear. "Do you want some company? I could bring some Chinese to the clinic."

Tempting, but... But somehow she'd rather have dinner with Caleb. He had carried the dog with such care. She had seen his heart in his eyes and knew how much the pitiful sight had moved him. What was wrong with people? How could anyone be a part of such cruelty?

"I'm sorry, Jason, but no. Another time."

"Okay. I'll call you."

She hung up the phone and turned around to find Caleb watching her.

"No dinner date?"

She shook her head and told the truth. "I'd rather have dinner with you tonight. Why don't you come over to my house? Mama stocked my freezer with plenty of soups and casseroles, so all we'd have to do is heat one."

Something, she didn't know what, leaped in his eyes. "Sure, that sounds nice." He laughed. "I smell a little like a dog, though."

Aria laughed too, which dissipated some of the tension that had hung over the room for hours now. "So do I. Get out of here and get cleaned up. I'll pick you up in an hour."

~ * ~

After giving Lila instructions about the dog's care, Aria drove to the motel to pick up Caleb. Peaches rode shotgun, a place of honor she often claimed for herself. Caleb saw her coming and went outside to meet her. What would it be like to see life from Caleb's point of view? As a child of wealthy parents, she took a lot for granted. Caleb had no transportation and was living in a motel for six weeks. She wondered where he got his meals. He usually had lunch at the clinic and ate a sandwich he brought from the motel. Her cheeks burned. She'd never seen him eat anything other than peanut butter.

There had to be another side to him. After all, he spent five years in prison for auto theft. In spite of his time there, he'd never let her see anything except his basic goodness. Basic goodness? From a car thief? A criminal she'd given work to just because he was nice to animals? As strange as it seemed, the answer was *yes.*

Working as a vet, she saw a lot of people each week, and the way they cared for their animals told her a great deal about their character. Mr. Williams, for instance, didn't like animals. He only brought his wife's cat in for the animal's yearly shots because she was an invalid, but he always looked irritated and in a hurry. People said he was always irritated with his wife too.

Another client, Margaret Martin, had four rescued terriers that lived in the lap of luxury. If she even suspected one of the dogs wasn't feeling up to par, she called and made an appointment for the animal to be checked out. The little creatures were devoted to her.

Caleb was a lot like Margaret Martin. Compassion and love for the animals in his care filled his heart to the brim. Without a doubt, that compassion and care spilled over into every aspect of his life.

She stared at Caleb as he neared her truck. The evening was warm, but he was wearing jeans, and he didn't need them in this heat. Probably he didn't have any shorts. The money she paid him wouldn't go far, and he did have his rent to pay. Not that he didn't look good in the jeans. They had molded themselves to his lean hips just as his blue tee shirt molded itself to his chest. *My oh my! Bring me a fan!*

He slid into the truck along with the clean scent of the soap he'd used. Who knew soap could smell so sexy? "Well, you clean up okay," she teased as Peaches rubbed her head on his chest and howled a bit.

He laughed. "So do you. That peachy color suits you."

Warmth chased through her veins. She felt the heat in her cheeks. "Thank you."

"I've been trying to imagine your place," Caleb admitted as they left the motel parking lot behind them.

"We aren't too far from my house. One of the reasons I bought it is because it was only nine or ten miles from the clinic. I think you'll like it. I've been living on the river for three years now."

Aria gestured at a gravel road a few yards ahead of them. "That's my driveway. The previous owners wanted to live right on the water so the driveway is pretty long."

She turned onto the driveway and almost immediately they crossed a wooden bridge that spanned a small creek. "That's Pigeon Creek. It runs parallel to the river for a few miles." She laughed. "Unless we have a lot of rain, there isn't much to it."

Caleb looked out the window. "You don't have many neighbors. Aren't you scared being off in the woods by yourself?"

Aria laughed. "No, I'm not. I have an alarm system, and I also have a nine millimeter pistol loaded and ready to use."

"You know how to shoot a pistol?"

Aria grinned. "Surprised? Sure, I know how to use it. Daddy insisted that both Mama and I learn to shoot. He deals with some bad people, so it colors his attitude about things."

"You have Peaches too."

Aria rolled her eyes. "I'm not sure how much help she'd be, but she's great company. Anyway, once it gets dark you'll be able to see a few lights from other houses, and in the winter when the leaves have fallen off the trees, you can actually see a couple of my neighbors."

"Do a lot of people live on the river?"

"Oh yeah." She slowed down to take a little curve. "People love it and pay top dollar for a home on the water. My house is one of the last before the river enters Fairfield. I guess there's maybe a twenty to twenty-five mile stretch of river with no houses after you pass my place." She sighed. "It's only a matter of time until some developer buys it up and starts building McMansions on it."

Aria gestured as the house came into view. "There it is."

Caleb studied the house. "I like that grayish-green siding. It looks rustic."

"Thank you." She smiled. "That's exactly why I picked it. The previous owner painted the whole property an orangey color that I couldn't stand to look at. The house is small, but one person doesn't need a whole bunch of space."

Caleb's eyes had lit up. He really did like her place. "You have a big porch overlooking the water," he said. "Man, I love that river."

"Me too. It's a treat to sit out here at night and listen to the river rush by."

Caleb got out of the truck and walked to the edge of the yard. "This is wonderful. You didn't even plant any grass. Everything looks natural. Do you ever have a problem with flooding?"

Aria shook her head. "Nope, not ever. We're on higher ground here even if we are near the water. Notice how the yard slopes downward? If we did have a flood, it would go toward the other side of the river."

He drew a deep breath. "It smells great. Really fresh and clean."

She nodded, pleased that he too felt the charm of the river as it climbed across rocks and rushed on its way to the sea. "Let's go in, and I'll give you a house tour."

Caleb followed and waited as she unlocked her front door. "This is the living room/dining room/kitchen area," Aria said as she pushed the door open. "Originally there were walls, but I took them down. Since the place is on the small side, I wanted an open concept."

Caleb surveyed the big room. "It doesn't look like your mother's house, but I see things that might go in her home." He gestured toward a lamp sitting beside the sofa. "Like that lamp and the sofa, for instance."

Aria laughed. "You have a good eye. Do you think a crystal lamp and a blue Chesterfield sofa are a bit much for a cabin on the river?"

"No, I don't. Overall, I guess most everything is rustic, but it all looks nice together." His eyes twinkled. "Even that orange wall behind the cabinets."

"I did keep that much of the original color scheme."

Caleb tapped the floor with his foot. "Are the floors real stone?"

"They are. Stone is a little chilly in the winter, which is why I have so many rugs in here."

"They shouldn't match, but they do," Caleb observed. "That's an oriental in front of your sofa, but the orange and blue stripe under the table looks modern to me."

Aria laughed. "I just put together what I like. It works for me." She ran her hand across the dining table. "I made the table myself."

"You did?"

The look of surprise on his face made Aria laugh again. "I bought some legs from a catalogue and had a local woodworker make the table top."

Caleb walked over to inspect the table. "What wood is it made from?"

"That's cedar. It came from a tree that Daddy had to cut down. I used the same wood to make a headboard for my bedroom."

"How many bedrooms do you have?"

"Two. The other one is set up as an office."

Aria beckoned to him and led him to her bedroom. "Don't be shocked," she warned.

Caleb burst into laughter. "Wow, a zebra print rug and stripes on one wall. You've got a wild streak, Doc."

"Is it too much? I painted the furniture black except for the bed and bought a white comforter, so I thought the zebra would go well."

"It does."

After they finished their tour, Aria put a casserole in the oven to cook. She grabbed a beer for Caleb and a glass of ice water for herself. "Let's sit on the porch while we wait for the food to cook."

On the porch, they both stretched out in some very comfortable lounge chairs. "Tell me about yourself, Caleb."

Caleb hesitated. Had she embarrassed him?

"There's nothing much to tell," he said.

"Oh?" She heard the skepticism in her own voice. Gah, he'd think this was an inquisition if she didn't knock it off.

He took a sip of his beer and shrugged his shoulder in a way she could only describe as defensive. "My mother died when I was born, a fact my dad never let me forget even though he didn't care for her at all."

Aria scowled. "That's rotten! It wasn't your fault."

"I know. He probably felt guilty because he hadn't insisted that she take better care of herself when she was pregnant. My dad isn't what you'd call a nice guy. Nothing like your father."

"So, he's still alive."

"Oh, yeah."

The look of suppressed anger and the cold tone of his voice told Aria exactly how he felt about his father. "Don't you have other relatives?"

"Nobody except my grandma, my mother's mother."

Aria set her glass down on a red, lacy, metal table between the two chairs. "Is that a good thing?"

He shrugged. "I guess. She did more for me than my dad ever did, but after that car thing she pretty much washed her hands of me. I called her a few days ago. She told me to get a job and keep my nose clean, but she didn't invite me to visit." He paused. "Not that I expected her to."

The contrast between their lives was so great it was hard for her to imagine it. Maybe she really was her mama and daddy's spoiled princess. That's what her cousin had called her when they were children. "You should go to see her anyway. Let her see how well you're doing. Maybe she'd forget that you made a mistake."

Caleb stared at the river as though it could wash away all of his pain. It took a moment before he spoke. "How well am I doing? I have a temporary job, but when Melissa comes back, I'm out of work."

Aria flinched. How did you answer that one? He was right about his job situation. Oh, thank goodness; the timer was going off in the kitchen. "Let me get that," she said and ran inside. Something should be done for Caleb, but she'd have to think what. Just like the people at the Pine City Shelter, she thought he had paid his debt to society.

~ * ~

Caleb watched as she deftly removed the white baking dish from the oven. The way she moved reminded him of the river in front of her home as it gracefully and joyfully made its way to the sea. She was very beautiful. The flickering candles on the table made her eyes look like molten, brown fire. Her skin was so satiny smooth he guessed his fingers might catch on it if he were stupid enough to touch her. And her lips. He repressed a groan. Lush was the only way to describe them. Lush, pouty, and so kissable. He picked up his wine glass and held his fork at the same time just to keep his hands from reaching out to her.

What would she say if he did? She had wanted to have dinner with him instead of that jerk Jason Lee. Aw, she'd probably slug him one. He'd deserve it too. A man like him had no right to a woman like her, a woman who came from a good family and owned her own business.

A fission of anger bubbled to the surface. Her father would probably approve of Jason Lee, that sorry, good for nothing, low-life cheater. He took a deep breath and tasted his wine again. Right now he was in a good place. Lusting after his boss lady would ruin everything for him. Whether he liked it or not, he had to forget his attraction to Aria De Luca. If he didn't, he might end up on his grandmother's porch begging for a handout, and that was something he'd almost rather die than do.

Five

Caleb had just reported to relieve Aria at the clinic that night when he and Aria heard a knock on the front door. "Are you expecting someone?" Caleb asked, concerned about a knock in the middle of night when the clinic was closed.

Aria shook her head. She didn't look scared to him, but she did look cautious. "No, but let's see who it is."

"I'm right behind you."

When they reached the front door, Aria started to smile. "It's only Jason."

She unlocked the door and pushed it open. "What in the world are you doing here in the middle of the night? Aren't you afraid you'll lose some much-needed beauty sleep?"

Jason laughed and placed a hand over his heart. "Did you hear that, Caleb? This is the way she's treated me from the time we were kids." He smiled and held out a bag and a cup to Aria. "Coffee and chocolate doughnuts."

"Guess you know my weaknesses," Aria replied with a laugh. "Come on back and keep us company."

Caleb trailed behind them back to the intensive care room. The dog moaned, which sent Aria hurrying to its side. She checked his IV and patted his head, and he went back to sleep.

Jason strolled over to the kennel. "Who's the patient?"

As he looked into the cage, a look of something between horror and terror briefly flooded his face, but in the time it took Caleb to blink, Jason had control of himself. "Do you know who he belongs to?"

Aria shook her head. "No, but I'd like to find out. I have a little something I'd like to say to him."

"I just bet you do."

Caleb's blood burned in his veins. How dare that slime ball look so patronizingly at Aria? She was too smart to be fooled by this jerk. Why couldn't she see that he wasn't one of the good guys? Maybe it was because they had grown up together.

Jason sat down on the counter below the cabinet where they kept their medicines. What was he trying to do... spread contamination everywhere? Of course all the medicine was supposed to be in the cabinet, but looking behind Jason, he saw a vial of painkiller, which he knew Aria had put into the dog's IV. It should have been locked up in the secure cabinet, but someone had dropped the ball big time and left it out. That stuff would fetch a pretty penny on the street. At least it would have in the neighborhood where he'd grown up.

Another knock on the front door startled everybody. "We're sure popular tonight," Aria said with a laugh as she mopped up some coffee she had spilled when she heard the knock. "Caleb, would you see who it is?"

It turned out to be a police officer that had come in response to a call saying that there was a lot of unusual activity at the clinic. "Come on in," Caleb offered. "Dr. De Luca is in the back room."

Aria greeted him with a big laugh. "Hey, Stan, what brings you by so late? Or early, as the case may be." She giggled. "I have doughnuts."

"I ought to arrest you for that," Stan quipped. After he explained why he'd come, Aria motioned him forward to look at the dog. "I'm glad you're here. I was going to call you this morning anyway. I want to make a report on this dog."

Jason slid off the counter. "I'll see you guys later. I think I'll go home and try to get a couple of hours sleep before I have to get up."

Aria threw him a sweet smile that Caleb would have almost died to receive. "Thanks for the coffee and doughnuts. Caleb, could you walk him out and lock the door behind him?"

Caleb nodded and let Jason out. He returned in time to hear Stan say, "Come down to the station tomorrow and file a formal report. We'll do what we can, but you know we aren't likely to find anything." The look of frustration on the officer's face told Caleb that he'd just met another animal lover.

"I know. Lila took and printed some pictures when the dog came in. I'll get them off my desk and walk out with you."

She turned to Caleb. "I'll see you tomorrow morning. Call me if you need me."

"I will."

Aria left with Stan, and Caleb sat in a rocking chair beside the dog's kennel. 'Call me if you need me,' she'd said. What would she say if she knew just how bad he did need her? He'd dreamed of her too, and in his dreams she was always warm and willing, in his arms, and in his bed.

~ * ~

Aria was hanging up the phone when Lila breezed into her office the next morning. "I brought you some coffee, fearless leader," she said. "From Starbucks."

Aria laughed as she took the cup from Lila. "Thanks. I'm still sleepy this morning."

"I figured you would be. How's the dog?"

A smile creased Aria's face. "Much improved. We have a long way to go, but we've made a good beginning." She leaned back in her chair. "Guess who just called me."

Lila shrugged. "I don't know. Your mama?"

"Good guess, but no, it was Melissa. She said she doesn't plan on coming back to work."

Lila removed the lid on her cup and took a sip of her own coffee, filling Aria's office with the smell of vanilla. "I thought she might not. She mentioned to me that it would be awful for your children to be raised by strangers."

Aria scowled at her. "You might have clued me in."

Her scowl rolled off Lila's back as usual. She wasn't worried about a scolding from her boss and never had been. It was part of her charm. "Why bother you for nothing? She might have come back."

Aria stared out the window and saw Caleb rolling a wheelbarrow filled with small gravel across the yard. He saw her in the window and waved at her. "Lila, I thought I might offer Melissa's job to Caleb. What do you think about that?"

"Everybody likes him, and he's a hard worker, so why not? He's done a much better job than Melissa ever did."

"I think so too." She took another sip of her coffee and stood up. "I'll go and talk to him."

She found Caleb dumping the gravel into a small drainage ditch. He greeted her with a smile that made her heart flutter. And oh those shoulders! In that sweat-darkened tee shirt he looked like a romance novel cover model, only better.

"Hey, Doc."

"Good morning." She took a deep breath and willed herself to forget about shoulders and hot guys. "I wanted to talk to you about something."

Apprehension filled his face. "I guess Melissa's maternity leave is almost over."

"No, quite the contrary. She called this morning and said she isn't coming back."

Relief leaped into his eyes. Did he want her to offer him Melissa's job? He had certainly seemed content at St. Francis. "I was wondering if you'd like to stay on permanently."

He didn't hesitate. "I'd like to. I want to see if I can turn Rascal around, and I'd like to see what happens to the bait dog."

Aria laughed, relieved that he had taken the job. She hadn't liked the idea of him leaving at all. "Consider yourself a permanent employee. We've got to get you out of that motel, though. It isn't cheap to live there. Are you busy after work?"

He shook his head.

"Good. I know of a little house not far from here that would just suit you, and as luck would have it, the place is vacant."

"Is it within walking distance? I still don't have any transportation."

"I remembered." She smiled. "It's within walking distance."

"I don't have a lot of money saved," he warned. "How expensive is this house?"

A brilliant idea came to mind, but it wasn't something she wanted to mention to Caleb. Not ever. "I think you can afford it. You'll probably be paying less than you do at the motel."

Having made their plans, Aria left him to his work and went back to her office where she saw Lila sitting in the chair in front of her desk.

"Well? Did he take the job?"

"He did." She looked at the doughnut on Lila's plate. "What kind is that?"

"Lemon filled. Want one?"

Aria giggled. "Is the pope Catholic? Of course I do."

"I'll get you one." She returned a moment later with two doughnuts. "You can have one for a mid-morning snack and one now. It's amazing to me how you stay so slender. You eat doughnuts all the time."

"So do you."

"I'm fatter than you are, too." Lila took a big bite of her doughnut. "Yummy as usual. What's your dad going to say about you offering Melissa's job to Caleb? You told me he didn't want Caleb hanging around."

Aria scowled. "Daddy can't tell me how to run my business, Lila. Caleb's a good worker. He's a nice addition to our operation."

"Uh-huh." Doughnut crumbs flew everywhere, and Lila wiped them up with her hand. "Is that why you looked so misty eyed after you talked to him?"

"What?"

Lila giggled. "You're so funny. Caleb is a good worker, but I don't think that's why you want him to stay. I think you want him here because you're falling for him. Am I right?"

Aria gasped. Her ears burned. "No, no, it's nothing like that. I just want him here because he's one of the best workers I've ever hired."

"Uh-huh." Lila threw her paper plate into Aria's trashcan. "Think about what I just said. Caleb's a nice man, and he does good work, but I'm not sure he's the kind of guy you'd want to get involved with. I hope I didn't make a mistake when I encouraged you to hire him. It was just easier to keep him than to train someone else." She paused on her way out the door. "I was filing some invoices a minute ago and found something odd."

"Odd?"

Lila nodded. "According to the invoice, AKA Pharmaceuticals billed us for ten vials of pain reliever. Everything checked out when I opened the box, but this morning there's only nine vials there. Did you use one for the dog last night?"

"I used part of one, but it had plenty of medication left in it."

"I'll see if I can find it."

Aria absently tapped a pen against her desk, a habit Lila hated. Losing pain medication was serious. Naturally, such losses were a financial drain on the business, but worse yet, the medicine was a controlled substance. The practice might get into trouble if someone found that medication, took it, and got sick afterward.

An ear-splitting howl brought her out of her chair. Mrs. Watson's dog had arrived for his shots, and as usual he wasn't happy about it.

~ * ~

Aria picked Caleb up around seven. When he opened the truck door, the clean scent of male skin and freshly washed hair filled the air. "You're prompt," he observed as he fastened his seat belt. "Most of the women I know would be late to their own funerals."

"And do you know a lot of women?"

Caleb laughed. "I refuse to answer that one, Doc."

She laughed too. It was easy to talk to Caleb. For one thing, they had the animals in common, but for another, well, he was just ...just... just easy to talk to. The occasional silences that had fallen between them didn't seem awkward either. Bottom line, spending time with Caleb was a treat. Looking at him was no problem either. The man just oozed sex appeal.

The little house she had in mind for Caleb wasn't any farther from the clinic than the motel where he was currently staying. "I have a key," she said. "I stopped by at lunch and picked it up. The rental agent is a client of mine."

They got out of the car, and Caleb paused for a look at the house. "I like it, Doc. It looks homey."

Aria stared at the house, trying to see it from his point of view, but no, she couldn't do it. All she saw was a small, white, shotgun house with little charm to recommend it. The yard didn't have much grass, and nobody had planted any shrubbery or flowers around it. That would make it easier on Caleb maybe. He didn't have a lawn mower to cut grass with.

"Let's go in," he said.

They unlocked the door and entered the living room. The red and blue plaid sofa screamed 1980 but looked in good repair. She also saw a blue recliner and a television on a table sitting in the corner.

Caleb pointed toward a lamp sitting on an end table. "Look at that blue lamp, Doc. I've never seen a blue lamp before."

He left the living room and entered the kitchen. "White stove and refrigerator. That's clean looking."

"Classic."

From the kitchen they entered the bedroom. "The bed's bigger than I thought it would be," he said.

"I think it's a queen size. Do you like the bedspread?" She didn't. Mustard yellow had never been one of her colors.

"It's okay." He laughed. "I bet a girl with zebra rugs doesn't like this yellow color. It reminds me of mustard. Let's look at the bathroom."

The bathroom was basic and beige, but was clean and in good repair.

Caleb made his way back to the living room and tried out the sofa. "It's comfortable. How much is the rent?"

"Five fifty a month. No lease to sign either." If she had anything to say about it, Caleb would never find out she was giving free vet service to the home's owner as long as he was living there. If not for that, the rental price was six fifty a month, which was really too much for him to afford. She knew because she'd spent a part of this afternoon calculating expenses for him. After all, she knew what she paid him.

She sat down beside him. "I've been thinking about your salary. Melissa worked mainly for something to do because her husband has a good job, but in your case you'll be paying the bills. I can offer you a ten percent raise. I know it isn't much."

He laughed. "It's better than zero percent. Thanks, Doc. I'll make out fine."

Maybe. At the moment, his life looked pretty marginal. He didn't even have basic transportation for himself, but there was nothing she could do about that. "Well, then, are you ready to go?"

"Yep."

Aria looked at her watch. "It's dinner time. Want a hot dog to celebrate your new job? If you haven't been to the Dog House, you're missing the best hot dogs in the state, maybe even the world."

Eyes twinkling, he answered, "If they're the best in the world, I'm in."

~ * ~

This couldn't be the place the doc wanted to go, could it? That white cinderblock wouldn't be real pretty even if it had been freshly painted, which it hadn't. The Dog House hadn't seen fresh paint in a long time. And look at those booths against the far wall. Someone had mended some pretty serious rips with duct tape. He stepped on something soft. Super. Squashed French fries littered the floor around several of the tables.

Aria caught him staring at the French fries. "Oh, I know the place isn't fancy, but the hot dogs can't be beat."

The waitress took their order and returned with their hot dogs on a piece of waxed paper. Classy. Real classy. He took a big bite, and all of his reservations evaporated. "You were right, Doc. They're great."

"Told you so. Oh, look, there's Daddy."

De Luca smiled and hurried over to their table. "Hi, honey. Give your old dad a kiss."

Caleb had to look away. That little peck on the cheek made Aria seem like a spoiled little princess whose daddy doted on her. A part of it at least was probably true. Love and trust shone from her eyes when she looked at her dad. That was good, right? Aria was anything but a spoiled princess, so what was his problem?

It bothered him because it gave David De Luca power over her. She would respect his opinions, and David didn't like seeing a car thief, an ex-con, with his little princess. His hands clenched under the table. This wasn't the first time he'd questioned the decision he'd made about the car. At the time it had seemed like the noble, the right thing to do, but if he had it to do over, things would be different.

De Luca was clever. The man spoke pleasantly to him and didn't reveal his dislike to Aria. "Hi, Caleb, are you still enjoying your work at the clinic?"

Caleb nodded. "Yes, very much." Probably he should have said sir, but knowing how DeLuca felt about him, he couldn't do it.

At any rate, De Luca was finished with him. "Your mama and I would love to have you come over for dinner tomorrow. Think you can make it?"

Aria laughed. "Of course I can. Tell Mama I'll bring dessert."

"She won't like that. You know how she loves to cook."

"Okay, tell her I'll just bring me."

De Luca nodded. "See you tomorrow then. Caleb, it was nice to see you."

Beaming at Aria, he went to pick up his hot dogs and left.

"Maybe Mama will do cassata for dessert. If she does, I'll bring you a piece. It's made of Italian ricotta cheese, sponge cake, candied peel, and filling of chocolate or vanilla. I like chocolate better."

"Sounds good."

The waiter wandered over to their table carrying a huge paper carton of steaming fries. "Ben said to give you these. Said to tell you thanks for saving his cat."

"It was my pleasure," Aria answered. "Tell him I said thank you."

"Will do."

As the waiter left, both he and Aria reached for a fry at the same time. Their fingers brushed together. An arc of fire shot through his entire body and set him to burning. He had to remind himself to breathe. Frozen by the fire, he couldn't move his hand. Aria didn't try to move her hand either. Had the fire burned her too? Her face had flushed, and her eyes glittered like two brown stars.

With a sharp intake of breath, she pulled away and shoved the fries toward him. "You take them."

He forced himself to move. Taking a couple of fries, he dropped them on his waxed paper and fumbled for some ketchup. Chancing a peek at Aria who was doing everything she could not to look at him, he lost his breath again. His heart hammered in his throat. "Uh, I'll...I'll take them home if you don't wa...want them."

She nodded but said nothing. Her hand fluttered to her throat where a pulse pounded so strongly he could see it. "Restroom," she croaked and ran for what was probably the nastiest bathroom in town.

She came back five minutes later, looking as poised, efficient, and pleasant as she always did. "That restroom is a mess. Ben needs to clean it up a little. I wouldn't let one of the dogs use it."

She reached for the check. "Are you ready to go?"

He nodded. "Give me the check."

"Oh, but I invited you. I'll get it."

Caleb laughed. "You just gave me a raise. I'll get it."

She looked unhappy about it, but she handed over the check so he could pay. "How do you think Rascal is coming along?" she asked as they crossed the parking lot to her truck.

"He's a good dog. Eventually he'll be fine."

And so it went for the entire drive back to the motel. Something had happened between them, something that Aria refused to own up to. If things had been different—like no prison record and a decent job—he'd have pushed her, but as it was, he'd have to leave it alone.

~ * ~

Aria patted Peaches' head and sat down on the porch swing. The sounds of a summer evening filled the air while in the background the river gurgled and sang. Fireflies blinked as they flitted to and fro. In the distance a dog barked.

Her fingers clenched when she thought of touching Caleb's hand. Unable to sit still, she jumped up. "Let's walk, Peaches."

Together they strolled down to the riverbank where Peaches lapped up a big drink of fresh water. Nothing had happened between her and Caleb, so why was she so unsettled? She *ran* from him at the Dog House. Touching him had upset her so much that she ran away to gain her composure. And wasn't that ridiculous? Running away from things was cowardly, and at the risk of bragging on herself, she wasn't a coward. Hmm... what was going on here?

Nothing, yet everything. Denying her attraction to Caleb would be stupid. She had liked his looks from the first time she saw him, and the longer they worked together, the better she liked him. Hot blood rushed to her face. Was she falling for him?

She picked up a rock and slung it into the river. Falling for Caleb wasn't an option. No matter how much she liked him, it wouldn't work between them. They came from different worlds, and while she could accept his world, she doubted he'd ever be welcome in hers. That alone put a significant barrier between them, but there was more.

He had no education to speak of, which meant that he was unlikely ever to hold a high paying job. Not that that was the most important thing in the world, but men were so proud that she doubted he'd want a relationship with a woman who brought home the bacon.

And there was his prison record. She had tried to tell herself it didn't matter, and in most ways it didn't, but if he had stolen once, would he do it again?

Sexual attraction. Relief flooded her. It was nothing more than a sexual attraction. Caleb was hot. No wonder she'd noticed him. She laughed and Peaches nuzzled her hand, expecting a pat. "Oh, Peaches, haven't I been silly? Here I was thinking about relationships and serious commitments, and all along this thing is nothing more than sexual attraction."

Peaches licked her. "Let's go back to the house, pretty puppy. I've been attracted to guys before. I know how to handle it."

Relief made Aria slightly light-headed. She liked her life just the way it was, thank you very much. There was no room in it for a romance with a sexy ex-con.

Six

Jason Lee dropped by the office the next morning. He had a scrawny, ugly kitten with him. The kitten wreaked havoc in the clinic by hissing and spitting nonstop at all the other animals in the waiting room. The air was filled with hisses, yowls, barks and growls. "Let's take him on back," Lila shouted to Jason, whose face looked like a thundercloud.

Once they got the kitten into a room, he retreated into the back of his carrier and settled down. Aria breezed in a moment later with a smile on her face. "So this is the cause of so much angst at my clinic."

Jason and Lila laughed as Aria peered into the carrier. "Why, Jason, I didn't know you had a kitten."

"I don't." He looked slightly horrified at the idea of a cat in his life. "It belongs to my mother. She has a cold and asked me to bring it in."

"Oh, that's too bad," Aria said. "Tell her I hope she feels better soon. Lila, you'd better find me some gloves. Kitty isn't happy to be here."

Lila ran for some gloves that allowed Aria to pull the kitten out. She did her examination and gave Jason her diagnosis. "We'll test for parasites and give it its shots, but I think you have a healthy kitten here."

"That's good news for Mom. What are you doing tonight?"

Aria laughed. "That's an abrupt change of subject. I'm not doing anything. What are you doing?"

"Taking you to Pine City for dinner?"

"I'm your girl. What time will you pick me up?"

"Seven."

Their arrangements made, Jason took his kitten and left.

"What's next, Lila?"

The rest of the morning passed quickly. At noon Lila produced a plate of chicken that she heated in the office microwave. "Leftovers from yesterday. Help me eat it. I have potato salad and cake to go with it."

After working all morning both of them were hungry and dug in. Lila reached for her second piece of chicken. "Did you find that bottle of painkiller?"

"Oh, gosh, I forgot about it. Maybe we can look for it when we finish eating."

They made an extensive search but finally concluded that the bottle wasn't in the clinic. "It's the strangest thing," Aria fretted as they returned to her office. "I guess I threw it into the trash by mistake. After seeing that poor dog, I was so mad I might have done it without thinking."

Lila pursed her lips. "That doesn't sound like you. You're one of the most conscientious people I know. Losing a bottle of painkiller isn't something you'd do."

Aria sighed. "I really was mad, Lila. I guess that's what happened."

Lila frowned. "Maybe... No never mind."

"Tell me. What were you going to say?"

Lila looked into her eyes. "You weren't the only one here that night."

Aria gasped. "Are you saying that Caleb, Jason, or Stan might have picked it up?"

"Yes. It makes more sense than to think you did it."

Aria opened another cola for herself. "Oh, Lila, I don't think so."

"Why? Because you don't want it to be true? I don't either, but I think it is."

"Lila..." What could she say? If Lila were right, smart money would be on Caleb as the thief, and that couldn't be true. It couldn't!

She got up and put her lab coat back on. "Forget it. I was distracted that night and half out of my mind with rage. There was a lot of dirty gauze and empty boxes around. I picked it up and threw it away by mistake. None of the guys did it."

Lila tossed the remains of her lunch into the trashcan. "Be careful, Aria. Do you think I'm blind? I see the look on your face when you're around Caleb. You're falling for him.

Have you admitted it to yourself yet? You're taking the blame for the painkiller because you don't want it to be Caleb. If it were only Jason or Stan, you'd be chomping at the bit to check it out."

Aria answered by walking out of the room and leaving the clinic. Heart pounding, she got into her car and turned toward her mom's house. Clariee could help her make sense of all this.

She found her mother weeding a petunia bed. Clariee's yard always looked like something from a gardening magazine, which was no surprise considering how many hours she spent working there. Her mother had come into the world loving plants and with the instinctive knowledge of how to make them thrive.

She stood and wiped her hands when Aria's car turned into the driveway. When Aria got out, her mother ran to hug her. "Honey, what a nice surprise! Did you come for lunch?"

"No. I...just something to drink."

Clariee shot her a keen look. "Okay, come on inside."

They went into the kitchen where her mother poured her a glass of iced tea. "Are you sure you don't want a roast beef sandwich?"

"I'm sure."

Clariee poured more tea for herself and sat beside Aria at the table. "Why don't you tell me what's wrong, baby."

Thank God for her mother. "I ...something happened today. No, a couple of days ago."

"I'm listening."

Aria nodded and told her mother about the missing medicine. "Lila said that one of the guys could have taken it."

Clariee sighed. "And which one did she pick for the thief?"

"Caleb."

Clariee reached for her hand. "You don't want it to be Caleb, do you?"

Tears filled Aria's eyes. Since she couldn't speak yet, she nodded instead.

"He's very handsome." Clariee tapped the table with her fingernail. "Have you fallen in love with him, honey?"

Aria took a deep breath. "I don't know."

Clariee sat back and thought for a minute. "Aria, I like Caleb very much. I sensed great good in him, but you have to be careful. He *has* been in prison. Wait until you know him better to lose your heart."

Aria ran both hands through her hair, tugging as if she could tug all thoughts of this man from her soul. "I don't want to lose my heart to anyone. My life is great just as it is."

Clariee laughed. "Sometimes we don't have a choice about it. It was that way for me when I met your father. I took one look at him and knew he was the one."

"But how did you know?" Aria beseeched. "I like Caleb's looks, but there's nothing between us. We've never even kissed. For that matter, we've never even held hands."

Clariee laughed. "You don't really have to ask me that, do you?"

Aria thought of the last lunch she and Caleb had shared and how she was so moved she had to run to the restroom. "No, I guess not."

"Then do what I say. Wait and see where this thing is going. Then you'll know if Caleb is the one for you or not."

"I have a date with Jason Lee tonight."

Clariee's lips tightened. "Why? You've never shown any interest in Jason before. Is this a knee-jerk reaction to the way you're starting to feel about Caleb?"

Aria rolled her eyes. "Mama, it isn't that way between me and Jason. We've been friends like forever. Don't you remember how we climbed trees, played in the creek, and went trick-or-treating together?"

"Oh, I remember, but don't kid yourself." Clariee refilled her tea glass. "Jason wouldn't mind if you had romantic feelings for him. I've noticed a certain look in his eye lately."

Aria sighed. "I wish you hadn't said anything. Now I have something else to worry about."

Clariee shrugged. "Your father and I are friends with Jason's parents and have been for a long time, but there's something about Jason that sets my teeth on edge. He's always polite, pleasant, and entertaining, but every now and again you get a flash of something underneath his genial manner. I wish I could be more specific, but I can't. Your father and I have talked about it more than once, but like me, he can't put his finger on the problem."

Aria thought for a minute. "He's never done anything out of the way around me."

"Well, you think about it. I'm not pushing Caleb at you, far from it, but I'm not happy that you'd go out with Jason." She gave Aria's hand a squeeze. "Frankly, my darling, he isn't good enough for you."

~ * ~

A soft murmur of voices and smooth, gentle background music filled Le Monde, the Pine City restaurant where Jason had chosen to dine that evening. A fresh bouquet of roses sat in the center of a table covered with expensive-looking, beige linen. White bone china accented in turquoise and gold gleamed in the softly lit dining room. From her chair near the window on the twelfth floor, Aria could see the city laid out below her. Sparkling, twinkling lights made a breathtaking picture that enchanted her.

"You should have told me we were going to Le Monde, Jason. I would have worn something a little dressier."

Jason smiled warmly at her. "You're perfect just the way you are. Your outfit is classic."

Uh oh. She was preening, but she appreciated a compliment just as much as the next girl. She was wearing white slacks and a white camisole with a black blazer. The lovely gold statement necklace her father had given her for Christmas last year dressed up the outfit considerably.

A waiter approached their table to take their order. "Would you like for me to order?" Jason asked.

"No, thank you. I know what I want."

Jason pursed his lips and looked almost insulted, but so what? She didn't need him to choose her dinner, not after having dined here regularly for years. "I'll have the pork belly with caramelized onions and spiced apples to start with. For my entrée, I'll have the red snapper with fennel, and for dessert, the dark chocolate gelato." Smiling inwardly, she threw a bone to Jason. "You pick the wine, please."

After the waiter left, Jason smiled and nodded his head toward the view out the window. "Beautiful, isn't it? This is my favorite restaurant."

"Yes, it's nice. My mother and father love it."

"A lot of influential people come here." He nodded at Aria as if to impress his words on her. "Important business gets conducted at these tables."

"What kind of business?"

Jason's smile was positively condescending. "Big business, darlin'. Billion dollar deals."

"And have you been a party to these deals?"

He laughed, but his eyes didn't look happy. "I've made a few deals, but nothing to brag about yet. I'm working hard, though. I'll have my day."

"I'm sure you will." Money. With Jason it had always been about money. If he had grown up in a poor family she could have understood it better, but he hadn't. He'd had the same privileged, upper class upbringing that she did. Maybe he felt like he was in some kind of competition with his father. Mr. Lee had always been super nice to her, but the relationship between a grown son and his father could probably be challenging to say the least.

Jason took a sip of wine. "Nice. The wine steward here knows his business. Say, how's that dog doing? The one you were working on the night I stopped by the clinic."

Oh, that poor miserable creature! "He's better. Since I got him, he's gained a pound and a half, which is great since he was skin and bones. We're treating him for mange and trying to clear that up. He clawed at himself so much he has a lot of secondary infections on top of the mange. There are bite marks all over him. Some are new and some are old, but he has one on his back leg that's so bad I may have to amputate." She ground her teeth in frustration. "I'm pretty sure we can't save it."

Jason toyed with his dinner of lobster that had just been delivered. "Maybe you shouldn't let the dog suffer any more. Think about it. If he does recover, he'll only have three legs. What kind of life is that? And he's a fighter. No one will want to adopt him. Everyone knows pit bulls are dangerous."

Clenching her hands under the tablecloth, Aria hissed, "Be quiet, Jason! You don't know what you're talking about. You don't even have a dog. I only give up on a dog when he gives up first, and this dog is fighting hard to get well. I'll never desert him. And as far as the fighting is concerned, a good trainer and the proper home eliminate that problem. He may be a special needs dog, but I'll find him a home. Caleb has a way with animals so he can probably help Logan."

"Who's Logan?"

"The dog, Jason."

Jason's lips were compressed into a thin, straight line. "Caleb will get his butt chewed off too. I don't know why you're letting that convict hang around the clinic. Why, just the other day Mother told me that Mrs. Jenkins said she was taking her animals to see Dr. White now. She's afraid of being around a criminal."

"Good!" Aria scowled at him. "I can't stand that old bat. Ever since I was a child she's been nothing but a mean old gossip. Good riddance to her."

"You're missing the point, Aria. If she feels that way, so will other people."

Aria took a deep, cleansing breath and blew it out. "If such a thing should happen, I'll deal with it as I see fit. Let's drop the subject."

Jason obeyed, even though he'd already taken a breath to say something else.

It was close to eleven before they got back home. After Jason opened her door for her, he stood at the bottom of her steps and drew a deep breath. "The river smells nice."

The tension in her shoulders relaxed a bit. After their disastrous conversation at dinner, Jason had seemed like a stranger to her. The guy who enjoyed the earthy, clean smell of the river seemed more like the young man she had grown up with. "You should get a permanent house on the river for yourself. I know you have that little fishing camp, but it's old. By now I bet it's falling down. No matter how bad a day I've had, the river is so soothing. Sometimes I think it's taking all my cares and problems with it as it moves toward the sea."

"How poetic," Jason teased. "Not only is she a vet, she's a poet as well."

Aria laughed quietly. "I have too much of my father in me for poetry."

"I don't know so much about that." Jason took a step closer. "To me, you're poetry in motion each and every time I see you."

Without another word he kissed her, a gentle brushing of lips that was over almost before it had begun. He tensed and stepped away when they heard the sound of a dog howling in the distance. "I'd better go. I'll call you."

"Okay."

He paused when he reached his car. "I don't know why you would, but don't ever go to my fishing camp. It's in such an isolated spot I worry that tramps might use it. I check the place periodically to make sure that doesn't happen, but there's no use in taking chances."

Aria's eyebrows shot up. "I have no plans to invade the fish camp, your male bastion."

He laughed as if her answer amused him, but the way his face had relaxed she thought her answer had relieved him. "I'd better go. Let's do this again real soon." He gave her a mock punch on the arm. "Next time you can order my dinner if you want to."

Aria laughed. "If you like."

"I'll call you soon."

Aria watched as he got into his car and drove away. Why was he in such a hurry? He had seemed relaxed and happy until the dog howled, but from that time on he'd been in a dither to leave. Oh well, it didn't matter one way or the other. She still liked Jason, but it could never be anything more. Their values and attitudes were poles apart.

She whistled to Peaches, who was curled up on the porch, and walked down to the river to look at the stars.

Seven

"Aria De Luca?"

Aria fumbled for her bedroom lamp and switched it on. Four thirty in the morning. "Who is this?"

"Fairfield Police Department. We need you at your clinic. There's been a break in."

"On my way."

Aria sprang from her bed and fumbled for her jeans and tee shirt. She tripped and fell, slamming her knee into a sharp corner on her dresser. "Oww, that hurt!"

She arrived at the clinic fifteen minutes later and was almost blinded by lights flashing from four patrol cars. The clinic was as brightly lit as if they'd chosen to have an early morning party. Aria bolted from her car and dashed inside. Were the animals okay?

In her hurry, she ran right into Caleb's arms. "Whoa," he cautioned, holding her shoulders to steady her. "Slow down."

"Are the animals okay?" She gripped his arm. "Tell me!"

"Yes, they're fine. I checked them first thing."

"Dr. De Luca?"

Aria spun around to see a policeman standing there. "I'm Tom Wheeler," he said. "After your security alarm went off around four, the alarm people notified us. We got here by four-fifteen. Come inside and I'll show you what we found."

Both Aria and Caleb followed Wheeler into the clinic. The reception area looked okay, but Aria's office was a mess. Papers lay on the floor and were scattered everywhere. Someone had tried to open the locked drawers in the desk. Judging from the look of it, they had used a screwdriver or a knife to try to open the drawer, but the desk was old and well made. They hadn't been able to get into it.

Wheeler gave her a moment to process the chaos. "Do you keep money in this room?"

Aria shook her head. "Never."

"We think that's what happened in here." Wheeler turned down his radio as it squawked and made Aria jump. "The intruders thought you might have cash locked in the desk. As soon as possible, I'll need you to do an inventory in here and tell me if you find anything missing."

"I'll do it this morning." She peered closely at one of the locked drawers. "What's that powdery stuff on the drawers?

"Oh, we dusted for fingerprints in here. I don't think we'll find anything, but you never know until you try. Don't forget about that inventory. Now, step this way, please."

At St. Francis the lab, medical equipment, and medicine were housed in a long, back room that ran parallel to the exam rooms. The area looked as if a small tornado had swept through, leaving widespread destruction in its wake. Microscopes and other equipment lay broken on the floor. Cabinets stood ajar, their contents swept onto the floor or counter.

The medicine cabinet was the worst. The lock on the door had been destroyed, and the door itself hung by one hinge. Boxes and jars of medication were scattered everywhere.

Aria shivered. Man, she felt cold. She wrapped her arms around her middle for comfort. Why would someone do this? What sick, twisted mind could conceive such an idea?

The police officer cleared his throat. "Dr. DeLuca, I know the room's a mess, but do you see anything obvious missing?"

Aria picked up several of the medication containers on the counter and then searched the floor. "Narcotics. I don't see a single painkiller left." Remembering the first missing bottle, her stomach clenched.

Her eyes found Caleb's. "How did you know to come to the clinic? You got here before me."

"I couldn't sleep." He shrugged. "I had a bad dream. When so many police cars came by heading toward the clinic, I decided I'd better check it out."

The officer stuck a small notebook into his shirt pocket. "Do an inventory, Doctor, and as quickly as possible let me know what's missing."

"Yes, I will."

He touched his hat to her. "Thank you. We'll expect your report. Everything is wrapped up here. Would you like us to stay until you lock up? When something like this happens, it's scary."

"I'll stay with her," Caleb said. "I'm one of her employees."

Officer Wheeler nodded and left them alone amid the chaos.

Before her legs refused to hold her up any longer, Aria righted a chair lying on its back and sank into it. "Oh, Caleb, how could such a thing have happened?"

Caleb dropped to one knee and reached for her hand. "It's okay, Doc. Everything can be replaced, and the most important thing is that all of the animals are safe."

"I know," she choked and burst into tears.

With a sound low in his throat, Caleb reached for her and pulled her into his arms. He felt so warm and solid! Aria leaned into him and buried her face against his shoulder as he stroked her hair and murmured in her ear. When his arms tightened around her, Aria pulled away and wiped her eyes.

"I ...I'm sorry, Caleb. I didn't ...didn't mean to fall apart on you. It's just that nothing like this has ever happened to me. I ...I'm not sure how to handle it." She laughed, but even to her it sounded shaky. "I don't like being so emotional."

He stood. "You're entitled. This would shake anyone up. Shall we start cleanup now, or do you want to go home?"

Determination flooded Aria and chased away the shaky feeling. "Now. With any luck, by later this morning we'll be back in business."

"Let's get started."

His warm smile of approbation made her heart flip flop. She had felt so safe, so ...so at home in his arms. It had seemed only right for him to comfort her during this awful crisis. She marveled at how much better he had made her feel. Honesty compelled her to admit that no one else could have helped her as much as he did.

She pushed up her sleeves. "I'll go get some garbage bags for the trash."

By the time Lila got to work, things looked almost back to normal, if a vet's clinic could be called normal with very little medication and lots of broken equipment. "I meant to open this morning," Aria lamented, "but I don't think we can. We're missing too many things."

Lila patted her shoulder. "I'll call the insurance company after I cancel your appointments. They may replace some of the equipment you lost."

"Good idea," Aria agreed. She sighed and took a pull on the soft drink Caleb had given her. "It's going to be expensive to replace everything. I'm just glad they left the x-ray machine alone. The microscopes and defibrillator are expensive enough."

"The anesthesia machine is what worries me." Lila's lips pouched. "I bet your daddy'll help out if you need it."

Aria smiled at the thought of her father. "He would, but I hate to even ask him. I guess I should call Mama and tell her about it. I don't want her to hear it from someone else. She's going to freak out anyway."

Ten minutes later, Clariee arrived at St. Francis. She blew into the room like a small whirlwind and hugged Aria so fiercely that Aria couldn't breathe.

"Tell me what happened!"

After Aria explained about the break in, Clariee dropped into the chair in front of Aria's desk and buried her face in her hands. "Oh, my darling. What if you had been here because of an emergency?"

Aria put her arms around her mother. "Please don't worry, Mama. I don't think anything would have happened if I had been here. The doors are always locked after hours."

"Not good enough." Clariee's face turned fierce. "We have to ask your father. He'll think of some way to make sure you're safe."

By the time he reached the clinic an hour later, David De Luca had arranged for someone to come and start beefing up security. Of course, the security system already in place had proven its worth, but David wanted the doors and windows changed to security steel with a decorative iron pattern. "It's pretty," he said. "It won't look bad at all."

He also wanted a better parking situation for Aria. "I'm building a garage for you to park in with an enclosed, secure entrance to the clinic."

"Daddy, aren't you going a little overboard?"

He looked at her with all of a father's love in his eyes. "No. I'd do anything to keep you safe. Unless you want me to have a heart attack worrying about you, let me put in the garage."

"Daddy, that's blackmail!"

Clariee patted her hand. "Let him do this. It'll make both of us feel much better."

"Okay." Aria gave in with a loud, gusty sigh. "I don't like it, but okay."

"There's something else, Aria," her father said.

Aria looked into her father's face. Uh oh. He had that stern look he got whenever he thought she'd done something she shouldn't have. "What is it?"

"Didn't it occur to you that it might not be the police who called you? You just jumped out of bed and raced over there. What if someone had been waiting outside for you, someone you wouldn't like very much? I want your promise that you'll never leave home that way again, not until you verify the information you're given."

Aria's hand flew to her throat. "I never thought of that!"

"I'm not trying to scare you, honey. I want you take care of yourself, that's all."

Aria nodded. It did make sense. "Don't worry, Daddy. It won't happen again."

He leaned over and kissed her. "That's my girl."

The parents eventually left, and Caleb went outside to work with Rascal, leaving Aria and Lila alone. Lila cleared her throat the way she did when she had something to say she thought was important. "Aria, why was Caleb already at the clinic when you got here this morning? The police didn't call him; they called you. What was he doing here?"

Aria tucked a lock of dark hair behind her ear and picked up a stray medicine bottle that had somehow rolled under her desk. "He heard the sirens heading toward the clinic and went to see what was wrong."

"Are you sure about that?"

She threw the empty bottle into the trash. "What are you saying, Lila?"

"I'm saying that twice now someone has taken medication from the clinic, and both times Caleb was present. Don't you think that looks suspicious?"

Oh, why did Lila have to say anything? As long as no one said anything, she could ignore the suspicions in the back of her mind, the ones that had been trying to break free for hours now. *Everything Lila said is true. There.* She'd admitted it. It did look suspicious. *Okay, time to analyze this thing.*

The first bottle was no big deal. She *could* have thrown it away during the terrible night when she had been working on the bait dog, but the fact that Caleb was there last night bothered her. Of course, he could be taking his job seriously enough that he would have run the mile or so from the motel to the clinic. He still had a week to go before he could move into his house. On the other hand, she didn't know much about him other than the fact that he liked dogs and was good looking. And made her heart race and her pulse pound.

The only way she'd ever be at ease with this thing was to find out more about Caleb's past. She didn't want to do it, but if she didn't, it would gnaw at her until she couldn't stand it. She took a deep breath and blew out hard. Why did everything have to be so complicated? It would be a lot easier to be like her trusting mother instead of her logical, rational father.

~ * ~

Caleb dropped into the chair that sat in the window of his motel room. What a long, crappy day! Feeling the effects of the non-stop tension at the clinic, even Rascal had misbehaved. He sucked in a deep breath and blew out hard. At least Aria was going to open tomorrow. Some of her equipment was still missing, but she thought she could do what she needed to.

He got up and ambled to the drink machine to get a soft drink. It had irritated her when her father came in and forced more security on her, but personally, he was glad of it. No use taking chances; although, if his suspicions were correct, she wouldn't have been in any danger even if she had been at the clinic last night.

The first bottle of narcotics had gone missing when Jason Lee was in the room. It wasn't too far of a stretch to think Lee was behind this break in as well, but what was his motive? He didn't need money, so why would he rob a clinic belonging to a woman he hoped to get cozy with?

His fists clenched. There was one explanation. Maybe Lee hoped that Aria would blame the ex-con in her employ for the theft. If she did, he'd lose his job, and the way would be clear for good old Jason to have a shot at the doc's heart.

Arriving back at his room, he slammed the door behind him, wincing at the noise. Who would believe such a story about a prominent member of the community? Not Aria, for sure. Lee only showed his best side to her, but after you spent time in prison, you learned to read a man. Whether she believed it or not, her good friend Jason wasn't the nice guy he pretended to be.

There was nothing he could do about it. Aria would have to see for herself what kind of bad guy Lee really was. In the meantime, he'd be there to watch over her. As long as he had breath in his body, he'd take care of her.

~ * ~

A week later, Lila dumped Aria's mail on her desk. "Here you go. Looks like mostly bills." She grinned. "If I didn't just spoil your appetite, go to lunch with me."

Aria shook her head. "I can't. I'm up to my neck in paperwork for the insurance company. They've caused me more grief than the break-in. I hope there's a special corner in hell for animal abusers, child abusers, and insurance companies."

Lila snickered. "Very funny. I'll bring you a ham sandwich and tea from Ned's Place."

"Yummy. Er... bring Caleb one too. Peaches found his lunch and ate it." Aria laughed. "You should have seen her trying to get the peanut butter off the roof of her mouth."

Lila rolled her eyes and left the clinic. She had taken to rolling her eyes every time Caleb's name was mentioned in anything unrelated to business. Lila was like a dog with a bone once she got an idea into her head, and she had decided that Caleb had taken the missing medication. She had even asked if he had an alibi for the time when the robbery took place.

Aria quickly ran through her mail. Most of it was either bills or advertisements for new veterinary products, but the big manila envelope at the bottom of the pile caught her eye. The return address said Brittany Silver.

Oh crap, here it was, and it was making her feel like a criminal herself. Before anyone else could walk in, she locked her office door. She didn't want anyone bothering her until she finished the file she hoped to find inside. Ms. Silver was a well-recommended private investigator. People said she got results, but could anyone have found information so quickly? She pulled a small folder out of the envelope and started to read.

Caleb Hawkins had been born in Pine City. His parents were Charles Hawkins and Ellen Jefferson Hawkins. Charles had spent most of his life in and out of jail, mostly petty stuff like drunk and disorderly, vandalism, etc. Ellen came from a working class family with steady jobs. She was a member of a local church. Unfortunately, she had died when Caleb was born.

Charles had raised his son haphazardly, to say the least. He hadn't bothered with doctors and childhood immunizations. Until the courts got hold of him, he hadn't even bothered about school for his son.

The school provided free breakfast and lunch for Caleb, which was probably all he had to eat. Charles never held a job for long, and when he had one, he spent his wages at the local pool hall, drinking and associating with women who were no better than he was.

In spite of these disadvantages, Caleb was a good student. He was always on the A/B honor roll, and his teachers had only nice things to say about him. When he made it to high school, he had tried out for football. He excelled as the team's quarterback. In fact, several scouts had been interested in him, but somehow nothing ever panned out, so after he graduated from high school, he took a series of dead end jobs, and several years later he ended up at a local big box store.

Things finally went well for him. After a few months, he was promoted to department manager with a nice increase in pay. He became friendly with Molly Daniels, a woman who worked in the customer service department.

Aria grabbed the photo attached to the sheet and eagerly studied the woman Caleb once cared for. Molly had blonde hair that looked natural and porcelain pink skin, blue eyes, and a curvy figure. Her clothes didn't look like designer stuff, but she was well dressed and seemed to have a sense of style. All in all, she looked like a nice woman.

Daniels had nothing good to say about Caleb. She accused him of promising marriage and then breaking up with her. The woman created an extremely ugly scene at work that resulted in her losing her job.

About a month later, Caleb was arrested for auto theft. Nobody could understand it. Most of his co-workers refused to believe it until they talked to Caleb themselves. There was no trial because Caleb pleaded guilty. The judge sentenced him to seven years.

At the prison he was a model inmate, never causing trouble for anyone. That was why he was chosen for the program at the animal shelter. He was released on parole after three years and six months.

His only living relations were his father and his maternal grandmother, Delia Jefferson. As far as could be determined, he hadn't contacted either of them, going instead to St. Francis the minute he got out of jail.

With a frown, Aria laid the folder down. This didn't make sense. Why would a man who'd walked the straight and narrow his entire life suddenly steal a car, especially a man who'd just gotten a raise? Could he have been framed? No, he pled guilty. Did Molly Daniels find a way to hurt Caleb?

Did she steal the car, and he went to jail for her? No, probably not. because he had broken up with her before the car incident occurred. Could it be connected in some way to his grandmother? True, most grandmothers didn't go around stealing cars, but something weird was going on. Perhaps it was time she met Caleb's grandmother.

A knock on the office door brought Aria's head up. She put the folder in her desk and locked the drawer before she got up to see who wanted her. Caleb stood outside her office looking so much like a male fashion model that it almost stopped her breath. His blue tee shirt was molded to his body and showcased some six pack abs and thrilling pecs. It was a wonder her tongue wasn't lying on the floor. "Do you have a minute, Doc?"

She smiled. "For you, yes."

Caleb came in the room and sat in the turquoise chair in front of her desk. She had found the chair at a local junk store and bought it because she liked the color. It had been a surprise to find it was an original Ames chair made in 1955. He ran his hand through his hair. "I've been thinking," he said. "What are you going to do with Rascal?"

"Find him a good home, I guess. Why? Do you want him?"

Caleb laughed. "I can't afford a dog that big. He'd eat me out of house and home in a week flat."

"Vet care would be free, and I bet you could get his food wholesale. Come on, Caleb. You know you want him."

"I think Rascal would enjoy living on the river with you and Peaches."

Aria laughed. "Okay, but if you change your mind, he's yours." She grinned at him. "He'd be nice company for you at night."

Eagerness replaced the laughter on his face. "I bet there are a lot of animals like Rascal around here. I don't necessarily mean fighting dogs or feral dogs. I mean animals that have been abused and need a second chance. I'd like to start a rescue and find good homes for them."

"That sounds great, but I think it would be expensive." She spread her hands. "You'd need a building and money for that."

Caleb smiled, leaned back and crossed his ankles. *Hmm. Nice legs.* Aria cleared her throat and focused on the matter at hand.

"I don't want to do the traditional model," he said. "The rescue would be run entirely by volunteers who'd keep the dogs in their homes. We'd ask for private donations to pay for any vet care and training they needed. Once we re-homed the animals in our care, we'd start over with new ones."

"I see a lot of potential here," Aria agreed with a smile, as she realized what he had in mind. "I'd be glad to offer vet care at a reduced cost, and that would help. You'd need a website and maybe a Facebook page so people would know about the rescue. Probably a PayPal account so it would be easy to donate. If it wasn't easy, I think you'd lose a lot of spur-of-the-moment money."

Caleb laughed as if her enthusiasm pleased him. *Look at how his eyes sparkle!* "I have five people who've volunteered to help already, including a trainer and now a vet."

"Do you have anyone who can do a website for you?"

He nodded. "Melissa said she'd do it."

"Melissa who used to work here?"

"Yeah, she said she'd foster cats and little dogs for us too. Her house is too little to do big dogs."

"I'm impressed," Aria admitted. "This is a wonderful thing for you to do." As a vet, she saw animal suffering that would appall most people. Now Caleb, who had little in the way of worldly possessions or even the respect of the world, was going out of his way to alleviate that suffering. In light of his newly proposed adventure, his having stolen a car was even more out of character than she'd originally thought.

Caleb cleared his throat. "We're having our organizational meeting tonight if you'd like to come."

Her heart swelled with emotion when she looked into his eyes and saw the pleading expression there. He wanted her to be a part of the rescue. "Of course I'll come. Would you like to have the meeting at my house? It'll be nice and cool on the river, and I have some frozen barbecue I've been saving for a special occasion. I already have chips and paper plates, so we can have barbecue sandwiches and chips for dinner before we talk business."

The look of pleasure on his face made her breath catch. "That sounds good," he agreed. "I'll let everyone know. How about seven o'clock?"

Aria nodded. "That'll be perfect."

His warm smile stirred up some butterflies in her stomach. Honestly!

Caleb went back to work, but before Aria could get started on anything herself she heard her father's voice booming throughout the waiting room. She jumped up and ran to the front of the clinic. "Daddy! What a nice surprise. Come on back so we can talk."

David De Luca hugged his daughter and followed her to her office. He sat in front of her desk. "I stopped by to see how the new security system is working."

Aria giggled. "It must be working fine. We haven't had any more break-ins."

Her father laughed at her joke just as she'd expected. They were so much alike she could generally guess what he'd find amusing. "Good," he said. "So, what's my favorite daughter been up to?"

"Only daughter, you mean," she corrected. "I just agreed to be the vet for a new animal rescue group."

Her father nodded. "That's certainly a worthy cause. Tell me about it. I know some people who'd be glad to donate a little money." His eyes twinkled. "Or a lot, if I twist their arms."

"Oh, it's just wonderful, Daddy." Aria told her father how Caleb and the other employees had agreed to start a rescue group, but why had he started frowning as if he didn't approve of the rescue after all?

"It's not a good idea, honey."

"Why not? I can't imagine why you'd feel that way. This rescue wouldn't need as much money as the traditional model would, and we'd be doing a wonderful thing for the suffering animals in the community."

Her father's lips tightened. "All right, I'll tell you. Remember that you asked. It's a bad idea because of Caleb's background. No one will want to donate money to a rescue run by an ex-convict." He shrugged. "Neither would I. I know you like him, Aria, but what do you really know about him other than the fact that he likes animals? Even bad guys can like animals. Adolph Hitler had a dog."

Aria broke into laughter. "Daddy, Caleb is hardly another Hitler."

He snorted. "No, but you know what I mean."

"I'm sure he doesn't plan on telling people about his past before he rescues a dog."

"Things like that get out," he father rightly observed. "People *will* find out, and when they do, they'll be angry and feel betrayed. You shouldn't have helped this man, Aria. He isn't our kind, and he never will be."

Anger shot through Aria and demanded expression. "Daddy! What's the matter with you? I never thought you'd act this way. Everyone deserves a second chance."

Her father sat up straight. His eyes bored into hers. "I've seen a lot during my time as a lawyer, things I'm proud to say you haven't seen, and I never want you to. People like Caleb ruin everything they touch. Once a criminal, always a criminal in my book. You'd be shocked if you knew how many repeat offenders I've dealt with in my career."

"Maybe they're repeat offenders because no one would give them a chance!" Oops, she had raised her voice without meaning to.

"And maybe they're repeat offenders because they'd bad people," her father coolly returned. "You have a lot at stake here. Your entire practice could be in jeopardy if Caleb did something to bring negative publicity onto St. Francis. Is that what you want? Think about the people who work for you if you won't think about yourself. What would they do without their jobs? In the current economy, jobs aren't easy to come by. You've known your other employees a lot longer than you'd known Caleb, so your loyalty ought to be with them, not him."

Anger surged hot and fast in Aria's veins. "I'm telling Mama what you said, and I don't care if I sound like a two year old or not! I bet she'll be as mad as I am."

Her father laughed. "You're a lot like me, honey, but when you really get mad, you act just like your mama. Go ahead and tell her if you like. We both know which side she'll take."

"Not yours."

He grinned. "No, not mine. Your mama sees the world through rose-colored glasses and always has. That may be one of the reasons I love her so much, but that doesn't change the fact that I'm telling you the truth. Don't be blinded by a plausible scoundrel, Aria. People aren't always what they seem to be."

He stood and smiled. "Now that I've made you mad I have to go back to my office. Forgive me?"

"Oh, you know I do." Her lips parted in a reluctant smile.

"Thanks, baby. Give your old dad a kiss."

Aria did and walked him back to the reception room. Could her father be right about Caleb? She frowned. The private investigator's report was confusing. How could a man who'd always been on the right side of the law, a man that everyone liked, suddenly break the law and steal a car? It just didn't make sense.

She sighed. Her next appointment was in ten minutes, and before then she needed to see if Lila was back with her lunch.

Eight

Caleb's heart swelled with gratitude as Aria's porch filled with people who wanted to help repair the damage evil people did to innocent animals. Melissa had brought her computer so she could show them the website she was working on. Her baby slept peacefully on her shoulder. Besides himself and Lila, two more of Aria's employees had come as well as several people he didn't know. Optimism surged through him. This was going to work.

Aria and Lila came out of the house carrying buns, barbecue, and a big container of barbecue sauce. "I'll get the chips," Marie, one of the vet techs, cried.

Caleb stood back and smiled as everyone clustered around the table, filling their plates with barbecue sandwiches, cole slaw, and chips. "Save room for dessert,"

Aria warned. "Caleb brought chocolate cheesecake for dessert."

"He knows the way to my heart," Marie quipped.

Lila laughed. "I wouldn't stand between Marie and her chocolate if it were me."

Caleb laughed at the friendly banter. What a wonderful evening. This was what he'd craved and dreamed of his entire life. Oh, not barbecue, but friendship and acceptance. Did Aria have any idea how much this meant to him? No, she couldn't understand. She'd been brought up as the pampered daughter of a well-to-do family. Her background was nothing like his.

"Hey, grab a plate," Aria called to him. "Do you want Peaches to eat your share?"

Caleb laughed. Peaches had been banished to the bedroom when she became too insistent on having some of the barbecue. He picked up a plate and joined the hungry crowd. Aria, who had taken a seat on the porch swing, slid over and called, "You can sit here."

Warmth flooded Caleb clean down to his toes. He'd never dreamed about sitting on a porch swing with a beautiful woman, but he'd dream about it now. The moment he sat, the faint, floral odor of perfume enveloped him. Aria smelled like a temptress even after she'd spent the day at work and came home to get this dinner together.

He set his jaw against the sudden urge to touch her. Her skin would feel like velvet under his hand as he looked into her eyes and slowly lowered his mouth to her moist, red lips. She would taste as sweet as sugar as she allowed him access to her mouth. Then she'd touch him. Her arms would surround him and pull him close. The kissing would intensify as masculine skin met feminine.

Caleb drew a deep breath. This line of thinking had to stop right now. Aria was his boss, not his lover.

She touched his arm. "Caleb? Are you okay? I just asked if you wanted a refill on your drink, and you didn't answer me."

"Er, sorry, I was thinking about the rescue."

"We should go ahead and elect officers first," Melissa said. "Caleb, it's your idea. By rights, you should be the president."

Caleb held up a hand in protest. "Hey, I thought one of you would do it."

"I'm too busy with the baby," Melissa answered. She looked around. "All in favor of Caleb being the president raise your hand."

The vote was unanimous.

Aria smiled at him, her brown eyes sparkling. "Well, Mr. President, go ahead and take charge of your meeting."

They elected Marie as the vice-president and Lila as the treasurer. Melissa set up a PayPal account for them and showed them the website. "We can go live whenever you want," she said. "Unless you want to make changes, the website is finished."

"Hold on a minute. You've forgotten one thing," Aria said.

All eyes swung her way.

She laughed. "A name. What's the name of the rescue?"

Laughter broke out around the porch as possible names were bandied about. "How about Second Chance Rescue?" Lila asked.

Everybody thought about it. "You nailed it, Lila," Caleb said with a smile. "I like that."

Around the porch everyone muttered their agreement.

"So is everybody ready?" Caleb asked.

"Go for it," Aria cried as heads nodded around the room. Melissa added the name to the website and tapped some keys on her computer. "We're live!"

Everyone clapped and cheered.

"We should see about some local press coverage," Lila said, "and maybe we can find a registry on the Internet where we can list our organization."

"We can all work on the internet part," Melissa promised. "I'll check out the press coverage tomorrow. I know a guy who works for *The Daily*. We can also send announcements to all the shelters and rescues in the state."

Caleb reached for his drink. "Word of mouth is good too. Tell everyone you know."

"We can give out flyers at St. Francis," Aria said. "When the clients check out, we'll give them a flyer."

Gradually, everyone packed up and headed for home, leaving Caleb and Aria alone. "I'll help you with clean up, Doc. You have to work tomorrow too."

A look of what he'd swear was pleasure filled her face, but no, it probably wasn't. She just needed some help cleaning up. "That would be great," she said. "It won't take long."

She was right. They finished the cleanup in a just a few minutes. He tied the garbage bag and took it to the bin at the back of the house. "Let's walk down to the river for a minute," he suggested. "It's a pretty night, and the river sounds so peaceful."

Aria linked her arm through his. "Let's do."

The moment her arm touched his side, he broke into a sweat. His breath quickened, and no matter what he did, he couldn't control it. Her feminine scent surrounded him and filled his head not only with her warm fragrance but also with desire like he'd never felt before. He steeled himself against the need to sweep her into his arms and kiss her until they were both breathless and totally devoid of reason, caught up in an act as old as time itself.

They had reached the river. He bent over and plunged his hand into the water, which was cold even in the summer. Splashing the water over his face and head might cool him off a little, but he couldn't do that with Aria beside him. Picking up a rock, he hurled it into the river.

"Isn't it beautiful out here?" she asked, her voice sounding dreamy and relaxed in contrast to her usual brisk tones.

"Yeah, real nice." The less said the better. He didn't have control over his voice at the moment.

"Sometimes on hot days Lila and I tube down the river. It cools you off like nothing you've ever seen."

"I bet."

She turned to him. "Let's do that soon."

Caleb cleared his throat. "Me and you?"

She laughed and seemed amused by his question. "Of course me and you. You aren't afraid of water, are you?"

No, he wasn't, but he *was* afraid of what it would do to him to see her in a bathing suit. Flesh and blood could only take so much, and it had been a long time since he had any female companionship. "Er, no, I'm not afraid."

"Then let's do it on Saturday afternoon. It's supposed to be ninety on Saturday, so that would be a good time to go tubing. After we leave the clinic, we could drive to my house and hop in the river. I have everything we'd need."

What a predicament. He wanted to go, but she was his boss, and he was an ex-con. People might talk about her if they spent time together socially. Besides that, he wanted her so much he was terrified of spending time alone with her. None of that seemed to matter, though. Nothing would keep him from her. Swallowing hard, he said, "Sure, sounds like fun."

Her laughter sounded like that of a happy child, cheerful, carefree, and innocent. "Thank goodness. You didn't sound enthusiastic at all."

"Oh, I am," he assured her. "You have no idea how much."

She stuck one flip-flop shod foot into the edge of the river. "It's cold tonight," she said with a shiver.

"Maybe we'd better go back."

As they strolled from the river to her truck, he had to bite his lip against the temptation to reach for her hand. It would be so easy.

Aria broke the silence between them. "Congratulations on the rescue, Caleb. I think it's a wonderful idea."

Her praise sent warmth racing through his veins. "Well, I saw a need, and it seemed like the least I could do."

Aria smiled at him and pulled her truck key from her pocket. "Shall we go? I don't want my best employee to oversleep tomorrow."

He laughed. She had no idea how good her teasing made him feel. What he wouldn't give to invite her to his house and... No, forget it. Think about the rescue, not Aria De Luca. Her daddy would probably shoot him before he let him anywhere near her.

For the millionth time, he questioned the choices he'd made in the past, but it was too late to change things now. Things were what they were, and all the regret in the world wouldn't make the slightest bit of difference.

~ * ~

Lila dropped into the chair in front of Aria's desk. "The mail just came. Here's the lab report for Mrs. Lane's cat.

Aria reached for the envelope. "Good. I've been waiting for it." She scowled as she read the report. "It's cancer. The aggressive kind." She sighed. "I guess I'll call Mrs. Lane before I leave."

"That's a good idea. She can spend the weekend with the cat before she brings it in. I hate this part of our job."

Aria nodded. "Me too. Mrs. Lane loves Fatima, so she'll want us to put the cat down before it starts to suffer."

"It's for the best. Some owners put their pets through torment before they get up the courage to do what's right, and it isn't fair to the animal to make it suffer."

Aria stroked Peaches' head. "I know, but I do understand. It's hard to lose a friend."

Lila reached over and patted her hand. "You're right. Let's change the subject. What are you doing after you leave work?"

"Oh, I'm tubing down the river with Caleb. We planned it before I took him home the other night."

Lila pursed her lips. "Why won't you listen to me? Leave Caleb alone."

"Don't start with me, Lila."

Lila shut the door with her foot. "I know you like him, Aria, but this time I think you should reconsider how involved you want to be with him. I know he seems like a nice guy. It's easy to like him, but he's been in prison. Do you know how many guys are repeat offenders? They call it recidivism when people go back to prison time and time again."

Aria frowned. "Do you think Caleb is going back to prison?"

Her question brought a thoughtful look to Lila's face. "At this minute, no, but I did the research. We have a huge recidivism rate in this country."

Aria considered Lila's point of view. Her provoking friend was right. Lots of people who went to prison eventually returned, and why was that? Did their early background mark them in some way? Or maybe it was a faulty gene. She bit her lip. As a doctor she had faith in science. Heredity *did* matter. Was Caleb doomed to a life of crime by both heredity and background? Her father and Lila would certainly say so.

She scowled at Lila, who'd made her doubt Caleb. People made mistakes all the time, but it didn't mean they'd all turn out to be criminals. Caleb had made a new start. That's all that should matter to anyone, including Lila or her father.

She stood up, hoping Lila wouldn't say anything else. "I'm going to be late. See you on Monday. Don't forget to lock up before you leave."

Lila sighed dramatically. "When have I ever forgotten?"

Aria made no comment. Why take the chance on getting Lila started again?

She removed her lab jacket, grabbed her purse from a drawer in her desk, and went in search of Caleb who should be ready to go by then. He was putting Rascal back in his kennel when she found him. "Hey, are you about finished here?" she called with a smile that went well with the warmth suffusing her heart.

He smiled back and made her stomach flutter. "Yep, I am. Let me wash my hands and I'll be ready to go."

Minutes later they were walking toward Aria's car. "Did you bring your swimsuit?" she asked. "You don't have anything with you."

He winked at her. "Wore it under my clothes."

"Quaint," a voice behind her broke in.

Aria stopped and turned around. "Hey, Jason, where did you come from?"

He laughed and brushed his hair back from his face. "I came from home," he teased. "I wanted to ask if you'd drive to Pine City with me to look at a piece of property. Then we could have dinner."

"It sounds like fun, but I already have plans with Caleb." She made a face at him. "Next time call earlier."

Some emotion flashed across his face, but he controlled it almost immediately. The wattage in his ready smile increased. "Point taken. What are you doing this afternoon?"

"We're going tubing on the river."

Jason's high wattage smile vanished. "Is that a good idea? By yourself, I mean."

"She won't be by herself," Caleb said. "She told you she'll be with me."

Oh, why did he have to say anything? She didn't want tension between them.

Jason's lips tightened. "And you have knowledge of this river and have gone tubing before?"

"We'll be fine."

Jason ignored Caleb. "If you're determined to do this thing, Aria, maybe I should go with you."

Should she laugh or get mad, and what on earth could she say to Jason? If she and Caleb were only friends, it wouldn't matter if Jason came with them or not, but if, as she suspected, they were on the verge of becoming something more, she didn't want him horning in.

Her eyes cut to Caleb, whose face might have been carved of granite for all the expression he showed. All except for his eyes. They burned with dislike and resentment. If she let Jason come, Caleb wouldn't forget it anytime soon.

"It's okay, Jason. We're only going from my house down to the Porter's Creek bridge."

Jason's face blazed. "Fine." He turned on his heel and stalked away.

Okay, that certainly didn't go well. She drew a deep breath. If she lived to be an old, old lady she'd never understand the male ego. "Ready, Caleb?"

"Yeah, I'm ready. Aria?"

"What?"

"Thanks."

"For what?"

"For picking me over him."

"Oh, I..." Nope. No way would she tell him she hadn't picked anyone, not with that beautiful, warm light shining from his eyes. Hurting his feelings wasn't an option. "I just wanted to say that Jason was rude to invite himself along," she improvised.

They drove to Aria's house where she changed into her bathing suit. Then they pulled their equipment from her storage shed. "We'll have to inflate the tubes," she said, gesturing toward a black one toward the back of the shed. "That one's big enough to hold you without any trouble." She chuckled. "At least I think so. You're a big man."

"Yep, I sure am." His voice turned gruff. "I'm well able to protect you from any danger on the river."

Aria laughed. "Forget about Jason. We won't be in any danger. It'll only take about two hours to get to the place where we're getting out, and there's nothing dangerous between here and there, not even any white water. We're in for a nice, relaxing time."

Caleb detached the air compressor's hose from the tube valve stem. "I hate to break it to you, but that's a nice long walk back to your place if we're carrying these tubes."

"Not to worry. I called Mama, and she said she'd pick us up."

Caleb flashed a smile that made her heart race. "I like your mama."

Aria nodded. "Everyone does. She likes you too."

The smile left his face. "Really? My background isn't anything to brag about, and I know your father doesn't approve of me."

"Oh, that's just because Daddy doesn't know you. He'll warm up. Just give him time."

He looked as if he disagreed with her, but he kept silent anyway. "I'm ready," he said.

Aria slid her tube into the water, then tossed a small, soft cooler to Caleb who caught it with one hand. "We might get thirsty, so I put a couple of bottles of water in there. Do you want to tie the tubes together?"

"Sure."

They put the tubes in the water, roped them together and waded into the river and an incredible afternoon. The sun was hot, but on the water with their hands or feet dangling in the cold river, the sun felt good. Occasionally, they passed a cabin or house, but for the most part they floated along with only trees and the sound of burbling water to keep them company. As they rounded a curve, Aria spotted a small, sandy beach along the side of the river. "Want to stop for a minute? I see some big blackberry bushes over there." She pointed toward the bushes in case Caleb had missed them.

He started paddling toward the shore. "Okay, but you better not let me get into poison ivy. I'm allergic to that stuff."

"Don't worry. I'm allergic too."

Caleb got to the berries first. He leaned over and picked several fat ones, popping a couple into his mouth before passing some to Aria. "Have one. They're good."

They spent the next few minutes eating blackberries. "Your teeth are blue," Caleb teased. He licked his own teeth.

"So?" She threw a berry at him. "You look worse."

He flung one back at her. "No, you look worse."

The berry landed on the white tee shirt Aria wore over her bathing suit, leaving a huge, wet, blue stain. "I'll get you for that," she yelled. Grabbing some berries, she charged toward Caleb and aimed for his face, intending to smash them into his mouth. Caleb sidestepped and Aria's momentum carried her into the water where she fell face first.

"Aria! Are you okay?"

Caleb grabbed her around the waist and pulled her from the water as easily as if she'd been a small child.

She laughed as she swiped at her face. "No, I'm not fine. My pride is shattered."

"As long as that's all that got shattered."

She pulled her wet hair from her face and rolled her eyes. "I'm not that fragile. I promise I won't break."

"Aria."

The soft tone in his voice when he said her name took her breath away. She tried to speak, to ask him what he wanted, but words wouldn't come.

His big hand cupped her face and sent white heat racing through her veins. "You are without doubt the most beautiful woman I've ever seen." He pushed a few remaining strands of wet hair from her cheek. She stepped closer, and he swept her into his arms and laid her head against his shoulder.

The doctor in Aria wondered if her blood pressure was dangerously high. It must be. Her heart was going like a jackhammer, and her knees felt spongy. She held on tight to Caleb as the scent of sun-warmed masculine skin surrounded her.

Her tee shirt was wet, but where he was touching her back, his hand felt red hot against her. She groaned, and he lifted her head from his shoulder. His eyes, filled with heat, locked with hers before fluttering shut. Firm, kissable lips met hers in a sweet, tender kiss that soon morphed into something else entirely.

His hand tangled into her hair, and he kissed her the way she admitted she'd longed for. As his tongue found hers, she shivered and pressed herself against him. His knees must not have been any stronger than hers because both of them sank down onto the damp sand.

A low, sobbing howl filled the afternoon. The sound was filled with so much misery and seemed so close that it jerked both of them apart and to their feet. "What *is* that?" Aria cried.

Before Caleb could answer, the afternoon filled with snarls and sobs. He grabbed her arm, and they ran for the tubes. "Stop," Aria protested. "We have to check that out. It sounded like dogs, and I know there's no house back here. One of them may be hurt."

"No." His crisp, decisive voice was filled with finality. "One, we aren't dressed for tromping through the woods. Do you want to get snake bit? Two, there are a lot of dogs somewhere nearby. I don't think it's in our best interests to take on a pack of feral dogs that just may be eating one of their own. Let's get out of here now while we still can."

Another howl rent the afternoon and sent both of them scrambling to get away. Caleb was right. There was nothing they could do. Both of them watched the shore as they moved back onto the river. They had gone maybe fifty yards when Caleb pointed toward the sky. "Look. Isn't that a chimney sticking up through the trees?"

Aria studied the tree line. "Yes, it is. I didn't know anyone lived on this stretch of the river. I don't like this, Caleb. Something's wrong back there. We need to get the sheriff and let him take us to check it out."

"Check out what? A pack of howling dogs?" Caleb snorted. "The sheriff won't help you."

Aria gritted her teeth. He was right. There was no law against howling dogs, and she had no evidence the dogs were in trouble. "I don't like this," she repeated.

Caleb shrugged. "Neither do I, but there's nothing we can do about it."

Aria searched the riverbank for a driveway or path into the woods. "Jason has a fish camp somewhere around here, but I haven't been to it since I was a kid. I'm not sure where it is."

"So you think the howling was coming from his fish camp?"

"I doubt it. Jason doesn't have any dogs. He doesn't really like them. His dad got him a dog when he was six, but he didn't care anything about it. He could never understand why I loved animals so much." She grimaced. "I didn't and still don't understand his point of view."

The mood of the afternoon hadn't totally been spoiled. Aria shivered, remembering the feel of Caleb's lips on hers. Desire kicked her in her middle. Her knees got weak just remembering how rock hard and masculine his body felt against her.

Maybe it was a good thing they'd heard the dogs. She was attracted to Caleb with every fiber of her being, but her father and her best friend didn't like him. Besides that, something didn't add up in the report the private investigator had made to her.

She sneaked a glance at him. Uh oh. He was staring back at her with fire in his eyes. Unconsciously, her hand sought his.

"Aria! Over here!"

Aria jumped and jerked her hand away. Her mother was standing on the bridge waving to them. "It's Mama," she told Caleb. Duh! Like he couldn't see that for himself.

Clariee ran down the bank to the riverside. "Can I help you with anything?"

"No, we're fine," Caleb answered. "Thanks for picking us up."

"No problem," she assured him with a smile.

They put their tubes on top of Clairee's SUV and started the drive back to Aria's house. "Mama, did you know that there's a house back in the woods about forty-five minutes after you pass the last cottage on the river?" Aria asked.

Clariee shook her head. "No, I didn't. The Lees used to have an old cabin somewhere in that area, but I think the roof fell in a few years ago. I don't know if they repaired it or not, but I doubt it. They've mentioned that they don't have time anymore to use it. How do you know about this mystery house?"

Aria told her.

Clairee's face paled, and her hand went to her heart. "Oh, my darling! Caleb, thank goodness you were there with her."

"Mama! I'm not a child." She scowled at Clariee. "I don't need anyone to rescue me."

Her mother looked downright exasperated. "Everybody needs rescuing at one time or the other. Even you and your father, Aria De Luca."

Aria made no answer to this truthful observation. "I think I'll report to the sheriff and tell him about the dogs anyway. He probably won't do anything, but it'll make me feel better about leaving before we checked things out."

By then, they had reached Aria's house. "Would you like to come in, Mama? I'll rustle up something to eat."

Clariee laughed. "No. Your father and I are going out with the Wilsons." She kissed Aria, waved to Caleb, and disappeared down the driveway.

"I like your mama," Caleb said, repeating what he'd said earlier in the day.

Did he know he had a wistful look in his eyes? He never had a chance to even meet his mother. Aria's heart quivered. Sometimes she took so many things for granted.

They put the tubes back in the storage building and went inside the house. "I'm starving," Aria proclaimed, slipping out of her flip-flops. "Would you like a snack?"

"I could eat. What do you have?"

He moved closer to her, smelling of river water and sun. Where *did* the man get those shoulders? Caleb moved closer still. The air between them sizzled with electricity.

"Aria..." He broke off, and with a look of near desperation on his face, he pulled her against him. Aria gasped when his chest met hers.

With a groan low in his throat, he buried one big hand in her hair and kissed her. Aria shivered and pressed herself against him. When his other hand came to rest on her backside, waves of dark, red heat broke over her. Her breathing sounded like a freight train. She still couldn't get close enough to him.

Caleb relaxed his grip on her and buried his face against her neck, his hot breath scorching her skin. He raised his head and looked into her eyes. "How far do you want this to go?"

For answer, Aria tugged at his tee shirt. She moaned when her hands touched his bare back.

Caleb had the shirt off in seconds flat, which allowed Aria to caress his chest. Her ears roared as she noted the sprinkling of dark hair trailing down the center of his stomach before entering his swimsuit. Her tee shirt joined his on the floor.

"You are so beautiful," he whispered. "So smart. So good. And you feel like heaven in my arms."

His hands moved against her back, and her bathing suit top fell between them. Caleb grabbed it and tossed it away. One hand moved to her newly freed breast. Aria cried out and arched against him.

"Aria! Are you in there? Why aren't you opening this door? Answer me."

Lost in a sensory haze, it took a moment to realize that someone was pounding on her door and calling her name. Jason. The voice belonged to Jason Lee. She grabbed her clothes and ran for the bathroom. Of all the times to have company! What was Jason thinking? Why was he deliberately ruining her day? He knew she and Caleb had plans. When she came back properly dressed, Caleb was sitting on her sofa without his shirt, and Jason sat at the dining room table shooting him murderous looks.

"I didn't expect to see you, Jason," she said, glad that she had some control over her voice.

"I see that." His eyes glittered with what she thought was anger. "I came over to make sure you got back alright, but it looks like you did."

She nodded. "That's right."

He jerked his head toward Caleb. "Do you ordinarily entertain half-dressed men, or doesn't he know that most people wear clothes when they go visiting?"

"Oh, give it a rest, Jason. You know we spent the afternoon on the water." True, but that wasn't why Caleb's shirt was on the floor, not that that was any of Jason Lee's business. He had no claim on her, and she'd not explain herself to him or let him make her uncomfortable. Chancing a look at Caleb, she quickly averted her eyes. Just looking at the man made her weak-kneed.

Caleb lazily got to his feet. Oh, crap, he had a cocky expression on his face. Surely, he wouldn't start anything at her house. His eyes were boring into Jason's. "Do you ordinarily butt in when you're not wanted? She's being polite, but can't you tell she wants you to go and give us some privacy?"

Jason's fists clenched. His face turned red. "Watch your mouth, Hawkins."

Caleb's head tilted. "Or what?"

"That's enough!" Aria's voice rang throughout the living room. "I think the testosterone is a little thick in here. Both of you settle down and stop acting like juvenile delinquents."

Jason sneered at Caleb. "One of us is a delinquent anyway."

"Jason!"

Eyes flashing, Jason strode toward the door. "Mark my words, Aria. You'll regret this."

The door slammed with such force that it seemed as if the entire house quivered. What was Jason thinking? They'd never been involved in a romantic relationship. They were friends. Nothing more than friends. It didn't make sense for him to be jealous of Caleb.

Caleb moved to her side. The cold challenge in his eyes had been replaced by a warm, caressing expression. "Why'd you do that?"

"Er, do what?"

"Pick me again."

Aria sighed. "It's not a contest, Caleb. There's no picking going on here."

"That kiss we shared tells me otherwise." His warm hand caressed her face. "Would you like to pick up where we left off?"

He took her hand and pulled her against him, but this time Aria pushed him away. "No. Things are ...moving too fast. I wasn't ...er ...don't ... things are moving too fast."

Caleb's eyes twinkled as a smile spread across his face. "I don't see you at a loss for words too often."

"What do you mean by that?"

He wound a lock of her hair around his finger. "You're a take-charge kind of gal. You're decisive, confident, and very capable, but right now you can't put two words together without stuttering. I think that's a good sign."

Aria felt hot blood rush to her face. "I think you should go, Caleb. It's been a long day."

His eyes, filled with heat and desire, met hers. "Are you sure you want me to go?"

She was sure she *didn't* want him to go, but she had told him the truth. Things were moving too fast for her. "Not tonight, Caleb. Tonight you have to go."

He let go of her hair and picked up his tee shirt. "Okay. I'll go." He grinned at her. "Do I have to walk back home?"

She sighed and rolled her eyes. "Of course not."

Grabbing her purse, she drove him back to his rental house. For a moment neither of them spoke, then Caleb reached for her hand. "You can come in if you like."

Aria bit her lip against the desire to take him up on his offer. Her body still burned in the places where his hands had rested, and if they could be alone together for five minutes, she'd burn all over. Had she ever wanted a man so badly? No. No, she hadn't. The urge to give in was almost overwhelming.

All she had to do was get out of the car. He'd unlock the house and let her go in before him. The minute the door closed, he'd take her in his arms. She broke out in goosebumps when she imagined his lips against her neck.

She'd throw her arms around him, and he'd lead her to his bedroom. They'd kiss and touch a minute before he pulled her tee shirt off. She'd melt against him from head to toe and feel his arousal hot and hard against her. He'd unzip her shorts and she'd step out of them.

He'd push her onto the bed where their naked bodies would tangle together. His knee would nudge hers apart, and his manhood would fill her. He'd totally fill her; impale her, possess her. She'd be at the mercy of his thrusting body, arching against him and begging for more.

STOP RIGHT NOW! Aria held on to the steering wheel for dear life. She couldn't do this, not now, not yet. She had to clear her throat before she could speak. "I'll see you on Monday."

He stroked her check with one finger. "Call me if you change your mind." He jumped out of the car and waved to her after he unlocked his door. Waving back, she fought against the still potent desire that made her heart thunder and her insides turn to mush. She couldn't stay tonight, but one night in the not too distant future she would. He had thanked her for picking him, and she had assured him that no picking was going on, but he was right. She had picked him.

Nine

Aria heard her phone ringing as she unlocked the door of her house and ran to answer it. "Hello?"

"Hi, honey, it's me. Is Caleb still with you?" Clariee asked.

"No, I just got back from taking him home." Aria slipped out of her shoes and curled up on the sofa. "Jason Lee ruined our evening."

"Jason?" She heard surprise in her mother's voice. "How did he do that?"

Aria scowled, yet at the same time she felt almost grateful to Jason. It wasn't time to be intimate with Caleb, and Jason had stopped her before she couldn't stop. "He came over to see if I made it home alright. He knew Caleb was with me, so he also knew he wouldn't be welcome. I don't understand that, Mama. Jason and I have never been a couple. We played together as children, and we've had dinner occasionally, but that's as far as it went."

Clariee sighed. "I love Jason's mama, and I like his father, but I'm not sure about Jason. There's something hard and self-serving about him. I don't think he ever gave you a second thought until he believed you were getting interested in Caleb. Jason is the kind of person who can't stand it when someone else has something good that he doesn't have."

"I think he's a narcissist."

Clariee laughed. "That's a very good description, considering how full of himself he is."

Aria laughed too. "Talking to you always makes me feel better. Jason was downright nasty to Caleb."

"Tell me about it."

Aria told her mother about the altercation between Caleb and Jason. "I thought they were going to fight. I believe they would have if I hadn't been there to get between them."

"Given Jason's personality, I'm sure you're right, even though I imagine Caleb would have loved to wipe the floor with him." Clariee cleared her throat. "It sounds like you and Caleb are becoming a little more than employer and employee. In fact, it sounds as if you might even be moving past simple friendship."

Aria exhaled noisily. "I guess it's time to face facts. I think maybe we are."

A short silence fell. "Are you sure, honey? I'm not trying to be judgmental, and I think everyone deserves a second chance, but Caleb doesn't exactly come from the same background that you do. If I were you, I'd go slowly. Get to know him better before you enter a relationship you might regret later on."

What excellent advice! Her mother was right as usual, but in this case it was too late to slow anything down. No matter what anyone thought or said, she and Caleb had bonded.

~ * ~

Lila tapped on the door to Aria's office the next morning and came in without waiting for an invitation. "Mrs. Greene called. Her dog just got hit by a car."

Aria groaned. "She can't afford a fence, so she needs to keep the dog inside. I've warned her about it over and over. Let's get ready."

They had set out things Aria thought she might need when Caleb hurried into the room. "Emergency in the waiting room. A dog hit by a car."

They all rushed to the front to fetch the patient. After a quick exploration and X-rays, Aria knew the dog had been lucky. The car had bruised his shoulder but missed all of his vital organs. "He's a very lucky dog," she said to the frantic owner. She told Mrs. Greene how to care for the patient and turned to Caleb. "Could you carry him to the car for her?"

Caleb smiled at Mrs. Greene, who was wringing her hands and fluttering helplessly over the dog. "Sure thing."

He picked up the dog and bore him gently away with Mrs. Greene trailing in his wake, but before Aria could leave the exam room, Lila shot a stern look her way. "Okay, let's have it."

Aria tossed a disposable syringe into a receptacle. "Have what?"

"Oh, please. Don't you think I've noticed those little glances you and Caleb have been giving each other all morning? What happened between the two of you?"

Aria hesitated, then gave in. "Come into my office where we can talk privately."

She shut the office door and sat in her desk chair. "We connected, Lila. It's that simple and that complicated. I know you and Daddy don't like him. I know he has a prison record and his past is probably pretty rough, but none of that matters. I can't stay away from him. He's ...he's wonderful."

Lila's jaw dropped. She shut her mouth with a pop. "I ... I really didn't expect that. I mean, I thought you'd ... Er, I couldn't imagine ... Darn it all, Aria! Why'd you have to fall in love with a criminal?"

Aria sighed and stared out the window toward the parking lot. Nothing much to see there. "I don't know why. I just did."

"But you've always been so smart, so levelheaded," Lila wailed.

"That's true."

Lila bit her lip, a sure sign of agitation. "So did you sleep with him?"

"No, but I would have if Jason Lee hadn't showed up at my house."

Lila smacked her forehead. "You've lost your mind. You can't sleep with an ex-convict!"

It struck Aria as funny. "I haven't lost anything." She giggled. "I found Caleb."

Lila's eyes narrowed. "Don't take this the wrong way, but did it occur to you that maybe Caleb is attracted to your obviously successful practice and to your obviously successful family? He has nothing. Why wouldn't he believe he fell into a nice situation?"

Okay, that was a valid argument. She thought about it, but it didn't feel right. It didn't fit the Caleb she knew. The man she knew was no user, and she didn't think he ever would be. "No, I never thought that, and I still don't."

"Maybe you should."

"Am I so awful no one would want me?"

"Of course not," Lila snapped. She fell silent for a moment. "Okay, if you think this guy is so great, why not hire a private investigator and let them do an investigation for you. Find out once and for all if he's on the up and up."

"I already did."

Lila's eyes widened. "You did? That's awesome! Maybe you haven't totally lost touch with reality."

"Uh huh. Want to see the report?"

"Yes, indeed. Hand it over."

Aria watched while Lila read the private investigator's report. "Aria, something seems ...off someway. Caleb was doing so well, and then all at once he begins a life of crime. I have to wonder if the investigator is missing something, something you need to know."

Aria nodded. "That's exactly what I thought."

"Are you going to do another investigation?" Lila slid the report back across the desk to her.

"I doubt it. Like I told you, we connected, so I know what he's all about. It's like I can see into his heart. I don't need an investigation to tell me he's a good person. What matters now are the present and the future, not the past. Together we'll make a new life."

Lila gasped. "He mentioned marriage?"

"No, he didn't, and neither did I. I just guess maybe we're heading that way. Eventually."

Lila stood when the buzzer over the front door sounded. "Think this over before you make a mistake that could mess up your entire life. Maybe you should give Jason Lee another chance. Jason isn't perfect, but at least we know everything there is to know about him."

~ * ~

Aria took a sip of her soft drink and gently patted Peaches' head. Peaches sighed and closed her eyes after wrapping herself around Aria's feet. It was downright nice to have a dog. Why in the world hadn't she found a pet for herself a long time ago?

From her porch, she watched as fireflies flitted around the yard. What a truly beautiful sight they were. She sighed. The only thing missing from this idyllic setting was Caleb Hawkins. Wouldn't it be wonderful to reach over and take his strong, warm hand in hers? They wouldn't have to say anything, not unless they wanted to. Silence never felt awkward when Caleb was around.

It was funny how things happened. When she read about Peaches in the paper, she'd never dreamed that one day she'd be involved with Caleb. She smiled in the dark. It was too bad Peaches had been abused, but she wasn't sorry she'd met Caleb.

If he were here now, the two of them could walk down to the river and enjoy the way the full moon shone over the busy water. "We'll try to do that very soon, Peaches," she whispered. "And maybe Caleb can even stay the night with us. You'd like that, wouldn't you?" She laughed softly. "So would I."

~ * ~

Caleb had gone to bed an hour earlier, but the bedside clock said midnight, and he was still awake. He flipped over onto his back and stared at the ceiling. The euphoria that had filled him the entire day was wearing off. Aria De Luca was falling for him. She was beautiful, successful, came from a nice family, and could have any man she wanted, and she had picked him. But why? Ah, that was the right question. Aria knew he'd been in prison. She also knew he had no education to speak of, so why was she doing this? Was she just slumming? Maybe she was attracted to him *because* of his background, not in spite of it. A buddy of his had fallen into that trap, and it hadn't ended well.

What did he have to offer a woman like her? Nothing, that's what. A big fat nothing. She'd never be Mrs. Hawkins in the community. He'd be Mr. De Luca, Aria's pet convict.

He punched his pillow, which relieved his feelings somewhat. But what if he were wrong? What if she truly loved him? With all the class differences between them, she shouldn't love him, but just maybe she did. Was he willing to let her go for his own pride and lack of ego?

His attention wandered when he heard the sound of a car door. He slipped out of bed and pulled on his pants just as someone knocked on his front door. Could it be Aria? Had she come to be with him tonight?

Rushing to the door, he flung it open. Three men in jeans and dark tee shirts stormed into the living room. He got in one lucky punch, but two of them grabbed his arms while the third one went to work on his stomach. After several hard blows, they released him. He doubled over and sank to the floor, trying to catch his breath.

"Leave Dr. De Luca alone," the man who'd hit him ordered. "She isn't for scum like you. If you don't do what you're told, you'll be real sorry. You won't like it much if we have to come back."

They strode past him and left without kicking him, which was what he'd expected. Groaning, he held onto the sofa and pulled himself up. It didn't take a rocket scientist to figure out who those guys worked for. Jason Lee obviously didn't like losing, but he was afraid to do his own dirty work. Those thugs probably worked for him on one of his construction projects. One thing was true; Lee had hired a rough bunch. They'd enjoyed working him over.

He sank down onto the sofa. If he had any sense he'd get out of there while he could do it in one piece. It wouldn't work out with Aria, something he'd always known. She was too good for him. Upper middle class women and working class guys had very little, if anything, in common. That job at the Pine City Animal Shelter was his for the asking, so it wasn't like he'd be begging on the streets, and his grandmother would probably put him up until he found a cheap apartment.

He took a deep breath that hurt all the way from his nose down to his stomach. Jason Lee could go to hell. In fact, anybody who disapproved of him and Aria could do the same. This was his business, his and Aria's, and if he left town it would be because he'd decided it was best for her, or she had asked him to go.

Decision made, he locked the front door, took two aspirin, and eased himself back into bed.

~ * ~

Beep, beep, beep. Caleb rolled over and turned off the alarm. Ouch. He felt like somebody had punched him in the gut, which of course they had. Grunting, he got up and took his shower. His stomach felt sore, but he was starving to death, so he chanced a bowl of cereal. It stayed down.

By the time he was ready to go, it was raining outside, a heavy downpour that would leave him drenched before he reached the clinic in spite of the huge umbrella he'd bought. If only it didn't take his entire salary just to live. By eating a lot of noodles, peanut butter, and boxed macaroni and cheese, he'd saved a few dollars, but nothing like what he'd need to buy a car. *Be patient. You have so much more than you ever expected.*

Aria was hand-feeding Rascal when he arrived. "You should have waited for me to do that," he exclaimed as he tossed his dripping umbrella outside the door.

She dumped Rascal's food into his bowl and stood. "If I had stayed in my office, I couldn't do this." She stood on tiptoe and kissed him.

He savored that kiss for several long, wonderful, scorching minutes. "You can feed Rascal every morning," he whispered as his arms tightened around her.

"Maybe I will," she teased, a warm expression in her eyes. "How's he coming along?"

"Did he bite your hand off?"

"No."

"Then he's doing great." He laughed and brought her hand to his lips. "Seriously, he doesn't seem like the same dog anymore."

"You got that right." She stood back and looked him over. "You got wet."

"How observant of you, Dr. De Luca. Didn't you feel the damp when you hugged me?"

She gently touched his face. "No, I was thinking about more entertaining stuff. You need something to drive, you know."

"Can't afford it yet. Don't worry about a little rain. I'm not sweet enough to melt."

Aria laughed and after glancing over her shoulder, she kissed him again. "I think you're very sweet." She licked her lips. "Sweet as sugar."

Caleb pretended to scowl at her. "I don't want to be sweet. Sweet is what women say to the men they reject."

"In that case, you are a beast of a man. A brute. There's nothing sweet about you."

Caleb smacked her bottom. "Don't you forget it, woman."

"Woman!"

Caleb laughed until his sore stomach hurt. "I'm sorry, but the look on your face was priceless."

"Priceless," she repeated, a twinkle coming into her eyes. "Okay, I guess I'll forgive you for that crack if you make it up to me later. Seriously, Caleb, it's raining cats and dogs today. You do need something to drive. How about if I finance a car for you? You can make payments to me."

"I don't think so, Doc, but I appreciate it."

"Why not?" she demanded as a little line appeared between her eyebrows.

He had noticed that little line before when something didn't please her.

"Because I don't want people thinking I see you as a meal ticket, a way to get something for nothing."

Aria's eyes flashed. "What do you care what people say? I don't."

Caleb pulled her against him. "You would if they actually said it."

She fell silent for a moment, but the calculating look on her face told him this particular discussion wasn't over. "I know," she exclaimed. "I'll let you drive the practice truck. It's as old as the hills and looks dreadful, but it runs fine."

He opened his mouth to protest but never did because a huge flash of lightning struck the ground right outside the window. Dogs howled, cats hissed, and both he and Aria flinched. The boom of thunder that rolled around the clinic brought screams from almost everyone in the building.

"Maybe I'll borrow the truck," Caleb agreed with a short laugh. "At least until I can buy something for myself."

"Now you're being sensible," Aria approved.

The rain was falling in streams then and struck the roof with such force it seemed to isolate them from the rest of the world. Caleb gently pulled her against him. "I should be sensible, shouldn't I? I have a very sensible girlfriend."

Aria snuggled her head against his shoulder. "Am I your girlfriend?"

Caleb nuzzled his face against her hair. Even her hair smelled sexy. "I hope so because there's nothing in the world I'd like better."

The sound of briskly tapping heels broke them apart. Lila entered the room and pursed her lips when she saw the two of them together. "If you're finished here, Aria, your mama just called. She wants you to call her back."

Aria nodded. "Okay, thanks." To Caleb she said, "Mama is afraid of storms, so when we have a bad one, she calls me to make sure I'm okay. I guess I'd better call her back, or she'll come down here to find out what's wrong. I'll see you later."

Would she kiss him in front of Lila? Nah, it was probably better that she didn't. Unless he was mistaken, Lila wanted him to leave Aria alone, so there was no use to make her mad. He had enough enemies what with Jason Lee and David De Luca disapproving of him.

~ * ~

Caleb refilled the last water bowl and gave the dog a pat on the head. The animal scarcely responded. It was still raining, which had made most of the animals sleep all day. Well, he wouldn't mind a nap himself. He stared outside the window. Having the practice truck would make everything a lot easier. Maybe he should take Aria out to thank her for her generosity. The people in the Pine City shelter had been nice, but not as nice as Aria. His lips curved into a smile. He hadn't been dating anyone there either. If he lived to be a hundred he'd never forget how it felt to have a woman like her turn to him.

He turned off the overhead lights and walked down the short hallway to Aria's office. She was staring at her computer screen as if she were mesmerized. "Hey, Doc. Can you spare a minute?"

Ten

She looked up, blinked, and minimized whatever was on the screen. "Do you even have to ask?" Standing up, she closed the door behind him and melted into his arms. "I've been thinking about this all day."

"Me too." He tipped her chin up and kissed her, quivering with eagerness.

"What's all that shivering about?" she teased as they broke apart.

He chuckled. "Like you don't know what you're doing to me."

She giggled. "I hope I know." Pulling him against her, she ran her fingers through his hair. "What did you need?"

"I wanted to invite you to dinner tonight. How about going for chicken at Ned's? They have the best fried chicken I ever tasted."

"It's a date." Her eyes sparkled and almost took his breath away. "What time will I pick you up?"

"Oh, you aren't picking me up. I'm picking you up. How about in an hour?"

She nodded. "That's fine. I'll be ready." She opened her desk drawer and took out a key on a big silver ring. "This is the truck key."

It still felt odd to take such a favor, but he wasn't taking advantage of her, so it would be okay for him to use the truck. Anyway, the vehicle was nothing more than a rust bucket, not the thing a gigolo would coax out of an enthralled woman. "See you soon," he said, already thinking about how she'd feel in his arms.

~ * ~

Aria smiled and munched on an appetizer of fried green tomatoes over grits with Ned's secret sauce on top. "Name one place in the whole town with better food, not counting Mama's house."

"My place."

Her eyebrows shot up. "You can cook?"

"Naturally," he said with such a grin that she just had to grin back.

She glanced at a tray of chicken as the waitress passed them. "I don't care how well you can cook. This chicken is divine."

"I know, but I can cook."

"Who taught you?"

He thought for a moment. "I guess I taught myself. I spent a lot of time with my grandmother when I was young. After watching her cook, I knew what to do."

Aria rolled a paper napkin between her fingers, an old habit left over from her childhood, and swiped the napkins crumbs into the floor. "I've wondered why you haven't been to Pine City to see your grandmother."

Caleb lowered the bite of tomato and grits he'd been about to eat. "How'd you know she lives in Pine City?"

She knew it because of the private investigator's report. Praying that he'd swallow her lie, Aria said, "I believe you mentioned it once."

"Oh. I guess we'll need to talk about my relatives and my past if …" his voice trailed off, and his eyes slid away from hers. He wasn't smiling now.

"If you're going to be my boyfriend?" she asked. That was so funny. Boyfriend sounded like the two of them were in high school.

"Yeah."

He looked so uncomfortable! Aria squeezed his arm. "I know you've been in prison. I'm assuming you probably have some things in your past you might not like talking about, but it doesn't make any difference to me. The only thing that matters is now and the kind of man you've become."

"So you say, but you don't know everything."

He clasped his hands together and put them in his lap. His eyes had filled with trepidation.

"Then tell me the things you want me to know." If only he would! As long as he remained silent, there was a chasm between them that could only be bridged by the truth. Uneasily, she shifted in her seat. She'd probably have to tell him about the private investigator she'd hired, but then again, maybe not. He was the one with a colorful past, not her. Did that make a difference? She'd have to think about it.

Caleb was staring at a mark on the tablecloth as if it were a lifeline thrown in a storm. "Okay, we'll talk. I guess it's better to go on and get it over with." His lips turned downward in a slight grimace. "If you change your mind about me, don't be afraid to say so. I'd understand."

Aria reached for his hand since he wouldn't reach for hers. "Just tell me. I don't think it can be that bad."

His fingers clenched hers. He shrugged. "I guess you can judge for yourself after I'm done. My father was no account. I guess that sounds harsh, but it's the truth. He spent a lot of time either in jail or drunk. My mother's family was blue collar, but they all had steady jobs."

"There's nothing wrong with honest work," Aria interrupted.

"No, there isn't. I'm just explaining that my family was as common and poor as dirt."

"Why are you trying to paint your family in such a bad light?" She smiled at a client who had just passed their table. "I don't care that your family was poor, Caleb. There are good people and bad people in all social classes."

He grunted. "As far as I can tell, most of mine were bad. Anyway, my mother died when I was born. I never knew her. Her mother—my grandmother—mostly raised me."

"Then why haven't you been to see her?"

Caleb briefly smiled. "She didn't approve of the activities that landed me in prison. I called her when I got out of jail, but she didn't invite me to come over."

Aria boiled with indignation on his behalf. How could his own flesh and blood treat him like an unwanted piece of garbage? "That is so mean!"

"Oh, my prison sentence made her decide I was like Dad. She never had any use for him, not that I blame her. He was abusive to my mother, which of course burned Grandma up."

"It still wasn't fair to hold your father's faults against you. If I were you, I'd be fighting mad about it."

He shrugged. "You don't come from the same kind of place I do."

"What kind of car did you steal?"

Caleb flinched. He hadn't expected that question. In fact, she had the impression he had to think about it. Considering that he spent over three years in a jail cell for taking that car, how could he ever forget what kind it was?

"Uh, it was a Toyota Camry. They're good cars."

"What color?"

He frowned. "Why does that matter?"

"It doesn't. What color was it?"

"Red."

"What color of red was it?" she insisted.

He stared at her as if she'd lost her mind. "Red like a fire truck."

Aria thought for a minute. She'd seen a burgundy-red Camry, but she didn't think they came in fire engine red. That was weird.

She dipped a French fry in ketchup, but laid it down without taking a bite. "Did you have a girlfriend?" The private investigator's report had said that he did, but she wanted to hear about Molly Daniels from his point of view.

Caleb nodded. Yeah, I had a girlfriend for a little while. I met her when I worked at a big home improvement store, but the better I got to know her, the more I realized she wasn't the one I wanted to spend my life with. We had a messy breakup, and shortly after that I went to jail."

"What happened to her?"

Caleb shrugged. "I have no idea. We didn't have contact with each other after we broke up."

"Was she pretty?"

He grinned, and this time it reached his eyes. "She couldn't hold a candle to you, Doc, and that's nothing but the truth."

Aria laughed. "I wasn't asking for a compliment, but I'll take it anyway. Did you steal the car because the breakup upset you?" Gah! She was beginning to sound like a prosecutor with this inquisition.

He shrugged. "I wasn't upset about the breakup. Remember, I didn't like her."

Aria leaned forward. "So, why'd you take the car? I know it wasn't because it was a good one."

He stumbled around with this question too. "I wanted ...uh ...that is ...well, I can't really ... I just needed a car."

Aria didn't believe him. Nobody would steal a car and think they could drive around in it, not without a lot of phony paperwork and a cheap paint job. Maybe he was afraid to tell her. He thought his story would break them up, that much was obvious, so it made sense that he'd be afraid to confide in her. "If you think ..."

He wasn't looking at her. His eyes were trained on the door, his expression cold and forbidding. Jason Lee was

"Don't even say her name," Caleb warned. "Don't come back here again either. Don't ever call me, write me, email me, or try to talk to me. We're through, and you know why. I was a fool to let you talk me into covering for you." He made a sound that might have passed for laughter. "You never even bothered to visit me in prison. I rotted in that cell for three and a half years, and I didn't see you one lousy time."

A petulant expression marred his father's face. "I'm your father. You owed me."

Caleb gave a shudder of revulsion. "I owed you nothing. Leave me alone. I don't want anything from you, and I sure have nothing to offer you."

He got up and held the door open. The rain blew in and made a wet puddle on the floor. "Goodbye."

His father's eyes narrowed. "Ungrateful little ..."

"Don't bother to insult me."

As his father passed him, Charles' shoulders tensed. "Go on, try it," Caleb urged. "I'd love the excuse to wipe the floor with your sorry ass."

He held his breath, but his father passed into the rain without violence. What a miserable excuse for a human being. Taking long, slow, deep breaths, he attempted to calm himself. When he turned around, he saw Aria in the receptionist's office staring at him through the open window on the wall that separated the waiting room from the office. "Aria..."

"Let's go back to my office where we can talk."

If only he didn't have to! Caleb trailed behind her and shut the door. He'd be damned if he'd let anyone else overhear this conversation.

Aria's chair squeaked when she sat down. A little oil would probably take care of that just fine. Provided he was still here to do it after this little discussion. Aria might finally understand a little of what his family was all about, and if so, he couldn't imagine her wanting him in her life.

Face neutral, she said, "That man is your father."

It was a statement, not a question. He nodded. "Yes, he is."

"You ...didn't seem happy to see him." She steepled her fingers and looked expectantly at him.

"No, I wasn't happy to see him. My father isn't like yours, Aria. He never has had my best interests at heart."

He had expected some platitude about how all fathers loved their children, but instead it didn't seem to surprise her that his father was no good. She didn't even seem angry that he and ...Charles had almost started something at her clinic.

Her eyes had filled with expectation that he didn't understand. "What did he mean about covering for him?" she asked.

Caleb winced as his stomach clenched. Why'd she have to hear that part? "I'd rather not say. I doubt you'd believe me even if I did tell you, and I don't think I can stand for you to think I'm a liar."

Hurt raced across her face. "Why would you think such a thing? Haven't I always believed you?"

He nodded and resisted the urge to jump up and run away, but even if he did, he couldn't run away from his past. "Yeah, you're always been more than fair to me, but this is something different. It sounds too self-serving to be the truth."

She leaned toward him, eyes intense. "Is it the truth?"

He nodded.

"Then tell me what he meant."

Caleb drew a deep breath. His stomach felt shaky, and his hands had started to sweat. Would she believe him or not? "I spent over three years in prison for grand theft auto, but I wasn't the one who took the car. It was my father."

"Your father!"

He scowled at her. "Lower your voice. This is between me and you. Yes, my father took the car. He arrived at my apartment around eleven that night and told me the police were chasing him. He said he was older then and couldn't stand the hardships of prison life." The urge to spit almost overcame him, but he suppressed it and went on.

"He had tears in his eyes when he begged me to say that I was the one driving the car. We look so much alike he knew the cops would believe the story."

What was up with the expression on Aria's face? She seemed lit from within, like maybe she'd finally solved a mystery that had been bugging her. She drew a deep breath. "Why did you cover for him if he was so terrible to you?"

He shrugged. "Maybe I thought he'd love me if I did." It felt as if someone had punched him in the gut again. Yes, that was exactly why he'd done it. A lifetime of neglect demanded resolution that of course he didn't find, not with a father like Charles Hawkins.

Aria's face glowed with color and intensity. "It isn't too late to come clean with the police. If they could take the conviction off your record, it would open a lot of doors to you."

He couldn't sit still any longer. He sprang from his chair and strolled to the window where he stared out into the rain. "He'd only deny it, and since I've already admitted to stealing the car, they wouldn't believe me." He turned and smiled at her. "It doesn't work that way when you're in trouble with the law, not that you'd know."

"But that isn't fair!"

A long roll of thunder sounded as mournful, angry, and disgusted as he felt as it washed across the clinic. "Your parents misled you, Aria. Life isn't fair, not for people like me. Maybe it is for you because you're in a different social class. I wouldn't know." He grimaced. "I guess you should think about things like this before you call me your boyfriend."

He could see her turning it over in her mind. Sweet Aria! So logical and steady. He held his breath as he waited for her to decide.

"I'm sorry, Caleb, but it's too late. You're already my boyfriend." She smiled, and her eyes were so soft it made his knees go weak.

Jumping to her feet, she moved into his arms. "You're making a habit out of picking me," Caleb muttered, "and that's really not in your best interests."

Her breath was warm against his neck, her hands caressed his back. "I've been making my own decisions for a long time, Caleb. I think this is very much in my best interests."

The sound of howling in the kennels broke them apart. "I'll see you later," Caleb said. "That sounds like Rascal." He hesitated, kissed her, and dashed away, buoyed by hope and happiness like he hadn't felt in years, in fact ever.

~ * ~

Aria bit her lip and stared at her cell phone that lay on the coffee table in her living room. Ever since she got home, she'd tried to get up the courage to call her father. If anything could be done for Caleb, he'd know what it was, but he didn't like Caleb. Nevertheless, her dad had spent his entire working life in the courtroom, dealing daily with the realities of the law. It could be that he'd want to see justice done for Caleb.

Maybe she should go over there instead of just calling. She walked outside to her screened-in porch and listened to the rain pound on the metal roof. Everybody was sick of the constant rain, but the weatherman said the low front was stuck in place for at least the next week.

With a sigh, she put on her rain jacket and darted through the deluge to her car. It would be better to talk to her father in person. As she crossed Pigeon Creek, she noticed that the water was pretty high. It wasn't about to flood the road or anything, but it was high. So was the river in front of her house. No more tubing for her and Caleb until the rain stopped and the water receded.

She turned in to her parents' driveway and ran through the rain to the house. After taking off her wet shoes and coat, she padded into the kitchen where her mother and father were having an after dinner coffee. "Hey," she called and hugged both of them.

"What are you doing out in the rain?" Clariee asked. She jumped up and poured a cup of coffee for Aria, making sure to put in lots of both cream and sugar.

Aria sat at her old place at the table and wrapped her hands around her cup. "I found out something today, and I want to help, but I don't know how."

Her father took a sip of his coffee. He took his black, the way his father and mother had done. He sometimes teased her and her mother about the cream and sugar they both liked. "What did you find out?"

Aria childishly crossed her fingers for luck. "I found out Caleb didn't steal the car. His father took it and came to Caleb with tears in his eyes, begging Caleb to take the blame. He told Caleb he was too old to go to prison and that it would kill him, so Caleb agreed to confess to the crime."

Silence greeted her explanation. Her father pressed two fingers between his eyes, a sure sign of stress. "How do you know this?"

"Caleb told me after his father showed up at the clinic looking for him."

"Darling..." Clariee's face looked unhappy as she chewed on her lip. "I know you want to believe in Caleb, but have you considered that maybe he's telling you a little white lie because he doesn't want you to think badly of him?"

"That's right, honey," her father said. "Very few people really go to prison for another person, not even their fathers. I know it happens in movies, but not in real life. I understand why he lied. No man wants to lose face in front of his employer, especially if his employer is a beautiful lady vet. "

"I'm sure you're right, Daddy, but in this case there's a lot more going on. Caleb just wanted to earn his father's love."

Aria told them about Caleb's childhood and how his father had treated him.

David De Luca ran a hand through his hair. His lips had thinned to a straight line so she knew he was struggling to keep his temper. "How do you know about Caleb's childhood? Did he tell you? Honey, can't you see he's just trying to manipulate you? He wants you to feel sorry for him."

"This is just between us, right?"

Her mother squeezed her hand. "Of course."

"Well, I hired a private investigator to look into Caleb's background. Don't tell him, though. He has no idea I did it."

Her father started to laugh. "That's my girl. I was wondering where my cool, rational, daughter had gotten to. Tell me what the investigator found."

Aria explained what was in the file.

David got up and poured himself another cup of coffee. "I admit it does sound a little odd. Caleb was always on the straight and narrow, and out of the blue he steals a car. Curious, but unless his father confesses to the crime, Caleb has no way to prove his innocence."

Aria's heart fell. "So there's no way to get Caleb's record wiped clean? His life would be much easier without a prison record."

Her father shook his head. "No, I can't think of anything, not unless his father confesses that is. Even then, it wouldn't be easy. There'd be a lot of paperwork and time involved."

Aria exhaled noisily. "Having a criminal record closes a lot of doors. I was hoping to make things easier for him."

Her father shrugged. "Some doors close, but not all do. Didn't you give him a job at St. Francis?"

"He doesn't make a lot of money there," Aria said. "If I didn't help him, he'd be living in poverty."

Clariee set her coffee cup down. "What do you mean by that?"

"I let him drive the practice truck, and I'm secretly paying part of his rent."

Her father's face darkened. His cup thumped down on the table. "He's taking advantage of you. Don't you see that? What kind of man mooches off a woman?"

Clariee laid a hand on David's arm. "Honey, if it's a secret, he can hardly be taking advantage of her."

David scowled and shrugged away. "How can you women be so blind where this man is concerned? Liking a dog doesn't make him anything but what he appears to be on the surface."

Aria bit back hot words of defense for Caleb and condemnation for her father. "Then there's nothing we can do for him?"

"Nothing."

That was annoying, but it didn't surprise her. Courts required hard evidence that, unfortunately, Caleb didn't have.

"Thanks anyway, Daddy. I know you'd help if you could."

Her father sighed and shifted in his chair as if the soft seat had suddenly become rock hard. "Be careful with Caleb, baby. I can see you believe in him, but some of the worst criminals I've ever encountered were personable, convincing, and dangerous. Don't let down your guard."

Aria crossed her fingers under the table. "I won't, Daddy."

Oh, what a lie she'd just told, and to her father who trusted her. Where Caleb was concerned, all of her defenses were down.

She said goodbye before she could tell any more lies and drove home. The rain had slacked off so she wouldn't get drenched when she got out of her car. Something had to be done for Caleb and soon. Clearing his name would be of enormous benefit to him, and if she did find a way to expunge his record, he'd be much more acceptable to her father. Well, more acceptable anyway.

She sighed. It would be nice if her father liked Caleb, but whether he did or didn't made no difference to her heart.

Eleven

"Hey, Doc, you got a minute?"

Aria looked up from her computer where she'd been researching both Molly Daniels and Delia Jefferson. She minimized the browser and smiled at him. "Do you have to ask? What's up?"

Caleb entered her office in a manner she could only call hesitant. "I wondered if I could have Friday off. I need to pay a visit to my parole officer, and I've decided to see my grandmother while I'm in Pine City."

From his tone, she could tell he wasn't looking forward to either one. "I really think you should see your grandmother. Attitudes can change, right? How are you getting to Pine City?"

"Don't worry about the truck. I'll take the bus."

Aria jumped up and moved into his arms, praying that today wasn't the day Lila would burst in without knocking. She had no interest in a lecture. "I wasn't worried about the truck. I was just thinking that if you don't mind my company, I'd go with you. The only thing I have on Friday is a spay, and I can do that early before we leave."

"Only one thing? That's odd."

Aria laughed. "There's a free vet clinic in town on Friday. Most of my clientele will probably go there, and the vet techs can handle the few appointments we do have. Anyway, it's been a long time since I took a Friday off. It'll be fun."

She felt his lips against her hair. "I don't see how any of the things I have to do will be too much fun."

Of course she couldn't say so, but both the parole office and his grandmother were of vital interest to her. One or both of them probably had valuable information to share, information that would maybe help her figure out what should be done to clear Caleb's record. "Oh, I'll be fine if you don't mind me tagging along." She wagged her eyebrows at him. "We can go to the mall and do some shopping before we come back."

He grimaced before smiling at her. "Oh, yeah, shopping. Can't wait."

"If we get held up at your grandmother's house, we don't have to shop."

Alarm flashed in his eyes, but he rose to the occasion anyway. "It'll be a red letter day in our relationship. Our first shopping trip."

No, he definitely didn't want her tagging along, but there was no way she'd pass up this chance. Even if she learned nothing from either the parole office or his grandmother, she'd go because spending a day with Caleb would be downright nice.

~ * ~

Aria stroked the cat's glossy, black fur and crooned, "You'll feel better soon, sweet girl, and now you won't have to worry about giving birth over and over again."

Still under the effect of the anesthesia, Miss Priss didn't seem thrilled by this revelation. She didn't even open her eyes. Lila put the cat into a cage so it could wake up, and Aria went to wash her hands and get ready to pick up Caleb.

When she came back, Lila made a notation on a clipboard and passed it to her for her signature. "Aria?"

"What?"

"Let Caleb take the bus to Pine City."

Aria rolled her eyes. "We've already talked about this. Give it a rest."

Lila sighed, an exaggerated noise that seemed to say she had an idiot for a boss. "If you insist on going, maybe you can find out something about Caleb from his grandmother. I don't think his parole officer would tell you anything, that's probably illegal, but a relative might."

Aria put some lotion on her hands and rubbed it in. Washing her hands so often dried them out something awful. "Yeah, I thought about that. I may not get a chance to talk to her in private, but if I do, I've got my questions ready."

Lila blinked. "That's a surprise."

"I don't see why it should be. In spite of what you think, I'm not an idiot. Have you forgotten about the logical, rational streak I inherited from my father? " She grabbed her umbrella and shook it to get rid of some rain left over from when she came to work. "If it doesn't stop raining we may have to build another ark."

Lila snickered. "We do have some animals here."

Aria said goodbye and dashed out into the rain, which wasn't too bad at the moment. It did make the entire landscape look dreary and wet, though. Well, maybe dreary wasn't the right word. All the rain had caused an explosion of plant growth everywhere. Uh-oh. Look at that. Several of the concrete dog runs had standing water on them. The dogs were nowhere in sight. Guess they had the sense to come in out of the rain that was really getting ridiculous.

Caleb was waiting for her. The minute her car turned into the driveway of his little house he bounded out to meet her. He wasn't dressed in jeans and a tee shirt like he usually wore to work. Instead, he had on a pair of khakis and a white, long-sleeved shirt. His shoulders looked so wide, his eyes so blue, she could eat him with a spoon.

He smiled at her and made her heart flutter. "Hey, Doc. It sure felt funny not to go to work this morning."

Aria laughed and squeezed his hand. Honestly, she couldn't keep her hands off him! "Unlike certain people, *I* did go to work."

"That's okay. Unlike certain people, *I* slept late."

Somehow the drive to Pine City had never seemed so short. One topic of conversation led to another, and before she knew it they had arrived at their destination. "Where do we go first?" she asked.

"To see the parole officer. He's expecting me in fifteen minutes."

They found the office that was located in a squat, gray, concrete building. Man, it was ugly. She shivered as she and Caleb entered the building. Everything was drab, cold, and gray. It wasn't a place designed to put clients at ease.

Her hackles rose the minute she laid eyes on the parole officer. His gut hung down over his belt and strained the fabric of his shirt so tightly his buttons might pop off any minute. His face was red, his eyes too small. He raised his eyebrows when he saw Aria. "I hope you don't mind that I came with Caleb," she said, extending her hand to him. "I'm his employer, Dr. Aria De Luca."

Something flickered on the man's face, but she didn't have time to interpret it. "Sam Bowman," he said. He smiled at her and revealed nicotine-stained teeth. "It looks as though Caleb landed on his feet. Just out of prison and he already has a job with a beautiful woman. Maybe I should spend some time in the penal system."

She swallowed hard to keep from reaming him out like he deserved. What a jerk! Did he think that was funny? Was he making insinuations about her and Caleb? If so, she knew what that expression on his face had meant. Drawing a deep breath, she willed herself to calm down in the off chance she was wrong about Bowman. "Caleb learned a lot about animal care in prison, Mr. Bowman, and he's putting it to good use at St. Francis, my animal clinic. I'd say that in his case the penal system actually functioned as it was intended to." Enough said. If she made him angry, this odious man might take it out on Caleb.

Bowman's mouth tightened. Evidently, he understood that he had displeased her. He nodded and sat behind his desk, an old, beat-up metal job that looked as if it needed a good cleaning. "So, Caleb, you're working at the animal clinic now."

"Yes, I am."

"After you got such a glowing recommendation from the Pine City shelter, I figured you'd go back there."

"Dr. De Luca offered more chances for advancement."

Aria bit her lip to keep from laughing at the surprised expression on the man's face.

Amusement fled when Bowman's eyebrows wagged in a suggestive manner. "What kind of advancement?"

"I can answer that," she interrupted. "In the fall, Caleb will be starting school at the local community college. I want him to have a vet tech degree so he can have a bigger role in the treatment of the animals.

"I also want him to become a certified dog trainer. He has a natural talent for training, but he can probably pick up a few pointers if he takes a course.

"I haven't discussed this with him, but if he's interested, a few years down the road I'd like to see him actually become a vet himself. Fairfield, that's where my clinic is, has plenty of work for another vet, and I'd just as soon we kept the business at St. Francis."

She smiled at Bowman. "Of course, he may be perfectly happy to be a vet tech and trainer, and if so, St. Francis still benefits."

Oh, she hoped she hadn't scared Caleb. She hadn't discussed this with him, and she should have before she ran her mouth, but Bowman had made her angry with his snide insinuations. When would she learn to think before speaking?

"They were good to me in Pine City," Caleb said to Bowman, "but they didn't make me an offer like Dr. De Luca did. That's why I'm working at St. Francis."

"Yes, I'm sure," Bowman mumbled.

"I have an address change for you," Caleb continued. "I moved from the motel where I was staying into a house within walking distance of the clinic."

Bowman wrote the address down. He seemed reluctant to bring the meeting to a close without finding something he could be negative about, but there wasn't anything to find. Caleb had been a model prisoner, and he was now a model ex-convict. She had hoped that Bowman would help them to clear Caleb's name, but he wouldn't. His peevish expression made her think he was almost disappointed that a former prisoner had turned his life around. What a jerk!

Bowman rose to his feet. "Same time next month, Caleb. Dr. De Luca, it was a pleasure to meet you."

This guy had a lot of power over Caleb so she smiled and said, "It was very nice to meet you as well."

Caleb nodded, and they escaped from the hateful office. "What's wrong, Caleb? You have a serious expression on your face."

"Nothing."

"Bowman is detestable. He actually seemed sorry you were doing well."

Caleb laughed shortly. "Oh he was. Bowman has a reputation. No one is ever glad to have him as a parole officer."

"He didn't like seeing us together, did he?"

One look at his face told her she was right, but he said, "Oh, forget about it. Bowman doesn't bother me. He's jealous. If he tries to cause any trouble, I'll tell him you broke up with me, and that'll be that."

Caleb was probably right, but there was no use to take chances. She'd make sure Bowman didn't cause trouble for him. Her father knew plenty of important people. If necessary she'd talk him into helping Caleb. No burnt-out, jealous parole officer was going to punish Caleb because he had gotten a job with her.

Things of this nature probably happened to him all the time. Everyone he met pre-judged him because they thought he was a thief. She shivered. Imagine having to deal with the Sam Bowmans of the world on a daily basis. Even her father, who was a good man, had no use for Caleb.

Having set her mind on a course of action, Aria pushed the unpleasant topic from her mind. "Let's go see your grandma." And hopefully it would be a better experience than the one they'd just had.

~ * ~

Caleb's grandmother lived in a neighborhood that had probably been new in the 1940s. All of the houses were small with some being made of brick and others of wooden siding. The yards were all on the small side. Some of the homes hadn't been kept up very well, and Delia Jefferson lived in one of those. Weeds were trying to take over the yard, and several limbs off the big oak tree in the front lay in a large puddle of water in the yard. The steps were made of concrete that had cracked in several places and leaned haphazardly to one side. The doorbell didn't work either, so Caleb knocked on the door.

After a moment, a white-haired woman opened the door a crack and peered outside. Her eyes widened. "Caleb?"

"Hi, Grandma. How are you?"

She opened the door and stepped aside. "Come in."

Caleb allowed Aria to precede him inside. The interior of the home was better than the outside. The house had hardwood floors that looked cleanly swept. The furniture was covered in pink and green floral upholstery that was somewhat old-fashioned, but it too was clean and showed no signs of fading. It wouldn't be faded since the windows were swathed in heavy green fabric that cut out most of the light.

Mrs. Jefferson sat in a rocker that creaked under her weight. She wore white knit pants and a pretty blue blouse that matched the color of her eyes. Caleb had those same eyes. Waving her hand at the sofa, she indicated that they should be seated. "I didn't expect to see you at my front door, Caleb."

"I did tell you I was out of jail."

His jaw had tightened as had his shoulders. Was her presence causing him grief here as well as at the parole office? No, surely his own grandmother would be glad to see how well he was doing.

Mrs. Jefferson pursed her lips and looked Aria over. "He didn't waste any time finding a new woman. What's your name?"

Well, that one came out of left field. She hadn't expected that salvo. Aria smiled in her most winning manner in an effort to charm this woman. "My name is Aria De Luca. I own St. Francis Animal Hospital. Caleb is my employee."

"If you say so."

She'd like to tell Mrs. Jefferson what she could do with that snotty little comment, but the waves of anguish radiating from Caleb were almost palpable, so she let it go. "Caleb is invaluable to the clinic, Mrs. Jefferson, and as soon as he gets his vet tech degree, he'll have even more responsibilities. We're lucky to have him."

Mrs. Jefferson shrugged, clearly unimpressed. "Not my business. Would you like some coffee?"

Aria nodded. "That would be wonderful. May I help you?"

"No, I'll get it."

Mrs. Jefferson heaved herself up and meandered into the kitchen. "I shouldn't have brought you here," Caleb whispered, "not knowing how she felt about me. I apologize for her rudeness."

Aria gave his hand a squeeze. "Don't worry about it. I'm fine." She grinned. "It could be a lot worse, so we'll hope for the best."

Mrs. Jefferson returned with their coffee—instant coffee—and sat back down. "Where are you living, Caleb?"

"I rented a little house not far from the clinic. It's nice."

Her expression didn't change. "Have you heard from your father?"

"Yeah, he came by."

Mrs. Jefferson shifted in her chair. "Goody for you. Now that you're here, make yourself useful. Go outside and clean those tree limbs out of the front yard."

"Okay."

Caleb got up and went outside, making no protest even though his shoes and the hem of his pants would be soaked. He'd get his white shirt dirty too, and Aria doubted he had too many extra shirts hanging in his closet. His grandmother was almost as bad as Sam Bowman.

The minute the door closed him, Mrs. Jefferson went on the offensive. "Don't get involved with him, girl. I know you're pretending there's nothing between you, but I'm not a fool. How often do employers go visiting with their employees? Caleb's good looking for sure, but he's got a lot of his daddy in him, and that man was no good. After he married my poor Ellen…" She broke off before continuing. "He beat Ellen. They lived in a roach-infested apartment with no air conditioner and not much food, and he beat on her night and day, even when she was pregnant with Caleb. It's no wonder she died when he was born."

Aria's heart broke in the face of Mrs. Jefferson's emotion. How dreadful it would be to know that your well-loved child had landed herself in such a situation. She'd like to say something to comfort the woman, but how could anything wipe away such pain? "I'm so sorry."

Mrs. Jefferson's lip trembled. "I think she died just to get away from him. I told her over and over to get a divorce, but she wouldn't listen. She said he'd just drag her back home, and things would be worse than ever."

"Why didn't you try to get custody of Caleb after his mother died?" Her sympathy had waned when she thought of a helpless baby at the mercy of a man like Caleb's father. Her voice probably sounded pretty judgmental, but why wouldn't the woman want to protect a small child, especially the child of a beloved daughter?

"I didn't need to." She jabbed her finger in the air toward Aria. "Charles didn't pay him any attention. He didn't care if Caleb stayed here with me. I've fed him many a night and given him a place to sleep when otherwise he'd have had nothing."

"Did you love Caleb?" Somehow this seemed like the most important question of all. Food and a place to sleep paled beside love. Had Caleb ever known what it was like to be loved?

To her surprise, Mrs. Jefferson gave the question serious thought. "I'm not sure. He looks a lot like his father." She sniffed. "After he stole that car, I knew the resemblance wasn't just on the surface."

"That's not really fair," Aria said. "Anyone can make a mistake."

Mrs. Jefferson snorted. "Do you know about Molly Daniels? Was she another mistake?"

"You mean Caleb's old girl friend?"

She nodded. "What do you know about her?"

Uh oh. Mrs. Jefferson was too hostile to know she had investigated Caleb. "Nothing really. I just guessed he had a girlfriend because of what we were talking about." Lame, but it was the best she could do.

"Oh, there's plenty you need to know." Aria tried not to recoil from the venom in Mrs. Jefferson's voice. "Caleb met Molly Daniels when he worked at the home store on Pleasant View Street. Molly was a pretty thing. She had long blonde hair and a pair of big blue eyes. Nice shape too. Caleb brought her around and introduced us. I liked her, so we had dinner more than once. I was proud that Caleb had found a good job and a nice woman. I started thinking maybe I'd been wrong about him." Her expression darkened. "Then Molly showed up here one night while he was at work."

Aria's heart pounded in her chest. Something bad was coming. She could feel it.

Mrs. Jefferson's expression turned malevolent. "Caleb had broken up with her after he said he'd marry her."

Was that all it was? Relief made her almost light-headed. Caleb's grandmother was mad because she had liked Molly Daniels. "Mrs. Jefferson, lots of people break engagements. Maybe he found out he didn't love her after all. It's better to break it off before you get married than to go through a divorce later."

Mrs. Jefferson chuckled, but she sounded anything but amused. "Oh, he loved her all right. So much so that she was pregnant. That's why he broke up with her. He said he didn't intend to be tied down to a family so soon."

Aria flinched; her head spun. No. He couldn't have done that, could he?

"Surprised?" Mrs. Jefferson asked, her lips turning down into a petulant frown.

"I ...yes ...I guess so. Where are Molly and her child now?"

"Molly lives in Center City. She had a miscarriage during her seventh month, and the baby died. She was fired from her job at the home and garden center for causing a scene at work, and the only job she could get involved some heavy lifting that she shouldn't have been doing. That's why she lost the baby."

Aria folded her arms around her to drive out the coldness inside. "Didn't Caleb help her with expenses?"

"He couldn't. He was in prison for stealing that car."

The front door opened and brought their private time to a close. "I dragged the branches out to the curb for you and did a little weeding in your flowers," Caleb said. "If you want, I can come back next week and finish the job."

Through the pain that wracked her, Aria noted his unsmiling face and wondered if he really wanted to come back, or if he was just afraid his grandmother would reject his offer and didn't want her to see it. Mrs. Jefferson pursed her lips and stared at him. "I guess that would be okay. If you don't do it, I'll have to pay someone else to do it for me, and I'm not rich."

Having made their plans, Caleb turned to Aria. "Are you ready to go?"

She nodded. "It was nice to meet you Mrs. Jefferson."

"You too. Take care."

She understood perfectly. Caleb's grandmother was warning her about him.

Neither of them spoke as they walked to their car. Most of what she'd heard, she already knew from the private investigator, but the PI hadn't discovered the part about the miscarriage. A wave of dizziness washed over her. How could Caleb or any man run out on a woman he'd gotten pregnant? Rejecting someone you found you didn't love was one thing, but to allow an innocent baby to suffer was monstrous.

But wait! The private investigator would have found something so bad, wouldn't she? Maybe, but maybe not. After all, she had asked Ms. Silver to find out about Caleb, not Molly Daniels. Once Caleb was sent to prison, Ms. Silver probably figured there was nothing more to find.

It was imperative that she talk to Caleb as soon as possible. Clearing her throat, she tried to make the words come but they stuck in her throat and refused to come out. Later. They'd talk later after she analyzed this thing. Yeah, she needed to think first.

~ * ~

"Will you *please* tell me what's wrong?" Caleb pleaded as Aria's truck came to a stop in his driveway. His eyes bored into hers and demanded an answer, but Aria remained silent. "You haven't had two words to say ever since we left my grandmother's house. What happened when I went outside?"

"Why, nothing happened."

Caleb drew a deep breath and let it out slowly, struggling not to lose his composure. "That isn't true, and you know it. Things were fine between us before I dragged those limbs out of Grandma's yard, but now you'll hardly speak to me. You refuse to even look at me, so tell me what she said, damn it."

Aria pushed a lock of dark hair behind her ear. "Let's just say your grandmother isn't your biggest fan."

"Tell me something I don't already know."

"She said you ...she talked about Molly Daniels."

Caleb reached for her hand, but she pulled it back and refused to let him touch her. It hurt so much that for a moment it was hard to breathe. "Why are you so upset that I had a girlfriend before we met? I told you about her, remember?"

Aria's face flushed red. Her eyes looked glassy with unshed tears. "I don't want to talk about it right now. I need time to ..."

"To what?" he growled, his hands fisting in his lap. "Find a dignified way to break up with me?"

"No! I mean ...I need time..."

Caleb grabbed her by the shoulders and jerked her around. "You don't need time. What's needed right now is the truth."

Aria's eyes started to snap. "Do you even know what the truth is, Caleb?"

His control slipped. "What the hell is that supposed to mean?" he demanded. God, he was almost yelling at her.

"It means that your grandmother told me how you treated Molly. How could you do it? What kind of man leaves a woman in Molly's situation?"

The contempt in her eyes almost stopped his breath. His voice lowered. "If you won't tell me what she said, whatever story she's spinning is going to ruin our relationship. You know it, and I know it. If you've ever had feelings for me, tell me the truth. Give me a chance to tell you my side of the story. You've always been more than fair to me, Aria. Don't stop now, not if you care about me."

He paused as a new idea struck him. "Of course, you stepped into my world today. If you can't handle it, just say so. Don't worry about being tactful. Tell me, and I'll clear out."

She dropped her head. *Come on, Aria, speak to me.* He held his breath and waited.

"Okay, if you want to know, your grandmother told me you broke up with Molly when she told you she was pregnant. You said you didn't want to be tied down to a family yet."

Caleb's mouth fell open, and he closed it with a pop. "Every word of it is a lie." He sat back against the truck's leather seats. "I knew she didn't like me because of my father, but I never thought she'd lie to spoil my chance with you." He spread his hands. "I don't get it. My mother was her own daughter! Doesn't that count for anything? How can she hate me so much just because I look like my father?"

Was he imagining it, or was Aria's face thawing a bit?

"She also said that Molly had a miscarriage because the job she had to take was too hard for her."

He shook his head. "Another lie. After Molly got fired she started working at one of the branch libraries in Pine City. There's nothing hard about library work, is there?"

Aria shrugged. "Not that I'm aware of."

This time when he reached for her hand she let him take it. "Do you believe me?" he begged. Yeah, he was begging, but who cared as long as it made things right between them. It would kill him to lose her now. That couldn't happen. It just couldn't. Fate couldn't be so cruel to take away the best thing that ever happened to him.

"I guess I believe you. It's ...I mean you've always been truthful with me before."

The uncertainty in her eyes was better than cold conviction. "If you're up to it, on Sunday let's visit Grandma. Let's confront her about the lies she told you."

Her cell phone rang and made both of them jump. "It's Lila. I better take it." She pressed a button on her phone. "Hey, Lila, what's up?"

She listened for a moment to what Lila was saying. "Caleb is with me. We'll be right there." She disconnected and tossed the phone into the truck's console. "You have your first rescue. A woman not far from where I live found a dog that needs emergency help right away."

Neither of them would let the dog suffer just because of their own personal problems so they'd have to postpone this conversation for later. Gah, his stomach had a knot the size of Texas in it. Would she go with him to see his grandmother on Sunday? Everything could be straightened out if she did. His teeth clenched and he fought the impulse to hit something. After the lies she told Aria, he'd never willingly see her again, not after Sunday.

As the truck crossed Pigeon Creek, he noted how high the water was. On a normal day Pigeon creek was placid, calm, and sometimes scarcely seemed to move. In contrast, today it raged and boiled with white water, small tree limbs, and dirt. No wonder with the amount of rain they'd had in the past few days.

Aria passed her own driveway and turned onto Turtledove Lane. She stopped in front of a gray cabin with a nice screened in porch. A petite blonde woman opened the door of the porch when they got out of the car. "Oh, Dr. De Luca, I'm so glad to see you! Something awful happened to this dog."

"Where is he?"

"On the porch."

Caleb followed Aria onto the porch, gasping when he saw the dog. He guessed the animal was a lab mix, but since it had almost no fur at all, he wasn't sure. Its skin looked gray and scaly, and he could see its bones through its skin. A white bone protruded through the dog's back leg.

The vet in Aria had taken over. She cast a practiced eye over the dog. "Caleb, get my bag from the truck."

Ignoring the rain that had started up again, Caleb ran for her bag and rejoined her on the porch. She tossed him a pair of heavy gloves. "Hold his head please. I'm going to give him something for pain."

He didn't need the gloves after all because the dog made no fuss and lay there with its eyes darting from face to face, terror evident in its horrified brown eyes. The needle had hardly been withdrawn before it started to relax a little. "Now let's stabilize that leg for transport."

As everyone watched, Aria efficiently wrapped and splinted the dog's leg. "Do you know what happened?" she asked the woman as she pushed herself up from the floor.

"I didn't see it myself, but my son said that a white SUV came speeding down the road, and a guy tossed the dog out."

Caleb's blood boiled. If only he had five minutes alone with that guy.

After thanking the woman, they drove to St. Francis where Lila waited for them. She ran ahead and opened the door to the exam room for them. "Will you do surgery?" she asked.

Aria nodded. "Let's get his vitals and blood work and do an x-ray. If everything checks out, we'll operate tonight."

Caleb's hands fisted. He was useless in this emergency. Both Aria and Lila were professionals and were working hard to save a life, but all he'd been able to do was carry the animal for Aria. Determination welled up inside him. No matter what it took he'd get that vet tech degree.

Aria studied the lab results and x-rays for a long time before deciding what to do. "The break is bad, but it's not as bad as it looks. I don't think we'll need an orthopedist to fix it. Lila, let's get ready to operate."

Caleb laid a hand on her arm to detain her. "Is it okay if I watch?"

"Yes, of course. Find some scrubs and put on a mask."

The surgery seemed to go on forever, but watching it didn't bother him. He was too interested in what Aria was doing to think of being sick. Her fingers were nimble and sure as she put the dog's leg back together and stitched him up. "We'll dress the wound and start him on an antibiotic, but I think he'll be fine," she said as she pulled her mask off and tossed her bloody gloves in the trash. "Caleb, let's put him in a kennel and cover him with a warm blanket."

"What's wrong with his skin?" Caleb asked.

"It's called Demodex mange, and it's caused by a tiny, parasitic mite. In most cases, it doesn't cause any trouble, but this dog has a lot of parasites and hasn't been properly taken care of. The mites finally just overran the immune system. The skin is crusty and dark because continued exposure to the mites has made it leathery and hard. Besides that, we have some e-Coli on the skin. This boy is pretty sick, but we're treating him with Ivermectin, which is an anti-parasitic drug. I think he'll eventually be fine."

Lila looked at her watch. "It's getting late, and I have a date in thirty minutes. Aria, I'll check back with you around nine."

"That's good. Have a nice time."

Lila paused at the door. "I called Melissa and she updated the rescue website. We already have fifty dollars in donations for the dog's care."

Caleb yelled, grabbed Aria, spun her around and kissed her. Who cared if Lila was watching them? "Doc, that's freaking wonderful."

Lila tried to frown, but she giggled instead and waved goodbye.

Aria hadn't tried to move out of his arms. She rested quietly against his chest, her breathing soft and even. He pulled away from her. "Are you going to Greenville with me on Sunday?"

She sighed and nodded. "Yeah, I'm going. I want to see what your grandmother has to say for herself."

He kissed the top of her head. "I don't know why she lied, Doc, but I promise you I didn't do the things she accused me of. Maybe Molly fed her some garbage to punish me for breaking up with her. Don't you worry about a thing. We'll get it all straightened out on Sunday."

He pulled her chin up and teased her lips with his, marveling at the way she felt in his arms. "You won't be sorry for trusting me. Just you wait and see."

~ * ~

Aria kicked the covers off and sprang from the bed. It was seven-thirty, and she had to be at work in thirty minutes. She tore into the bathroom and took the quickest shower on record, pulled her hair into a wet ponytail and dived into yesterday's jeans and tee shirt because they were conveniently lying in the chair on the other side of the room. Grabbing a banana as she raced out of the kitchen, she yelled, "Come on, Peaches. You can eat at St. Francis."

Lila looked up from her own breakfast when Aria charged into the clinic. "Look what the cat dragged in," she teased. "Did you oversleep?"

Aria nodded. "Yes, and I'm aggravated about it." She eyed Lila's ham biscuit. "I only had a banana."

Lila reached into a McDonald's bag and handed a wrapped biscuit to Aria. "Go to bed earlier next time." She surveyed Aria through narrowed eyes. "Er, you were alone last night, right?"

"Yes." Aria grabbed a can of food from a cabinet and dished it out for Peaches before starting on her own biscuit.

"Just checking," Lila said. "I wondered if maybe Caleb had stayed with you."

No, but Caleb was the problem. She'd tossed and turned all night trying to figure out what to do about him. Based on his behavior since she hired him, it was hard to believe he was anything but what he seemed on the surface, a nice guy who'd done a silly thing trying to earn the love of his father.

On the other hand, what was that old saying her grandmother used to be so fond of...Yeah, where's there's smoke, there's fire. If that were true, Caleb might be exactly what Jason said he was: a con man who was interested in her because of her family's money.

Ignoring Lila, she called, "Let's go out, Peaches."

Peaches whined and slunk to the floor. She didn't like getting wet, but the vet techs didn't like cleaning up dog waste either. The dog did her business in record time and made a beeline for her warm bed in Aria's office. Spoiled creature.

The phone rang, and Aria answered since she was closest to it. "St. Francis Animal Clinic. How may I help you?"

Caleb's voice, throaty and seductive, almost burned her ear. "I can think of several ways, but none of them have anything to do with medicine."

Her heart picked up speed as her breath quickened, and her worry melted away. "Oh? Do tell."

"I'll tell you later. My list is pretty long. Can you come to dinner at my house? I'll cook spaghetti. I have a great recipe, and since this is my day off, it's a good time to impress you with my know how in the kitchen."

She really should keep her distance from him, at least until after they spoke to his grandmother and sorted this mess out, but she didn't want to spend the evening alone, not when she could be with Caleb. "Yeah, I can come. What time?"

"Come over at six."

"Can I bring anything?"

"Just yourself, but if you get bored this afternoon, you don't have to wait until six to come over. We'll start working on my list."

Aria laughed, thrilled by their banter. "I'll see you at six."

Provided she could wait that long.

~ * ~

Aria shimmied into her black skinny jeans. Hmm. Not bad. Not bad at all, and she had just the thing to wear with the jeans, a black and white striped tee shirt with a boat neck collar and three quarter length sleeves. She needed to look good tonight. Looking nice always gave her confidence in herself, and she wanted to feel confident about her choice to trust Caleb. Of course, she did have one or two tiny reservations, but the minute she had heard his voice today they all melted like snowflakes in July.

She paused before leaving the shelter of her porch. It was still drizzling rain. When was this stuff going away? Everyone was sick of it. Goodness. Listen to the river roar. Had it ever been so high? No, not since she moved in anyway.

A smile creased her face. What did a little rain matter when a short trip would take her to Caleb? Opening her wet umbrella, she ran for her truck, laughing at her silly attempt to dodge the raindrops.

~ * ~

The minute she knocked on the door, Caleb jerked it open and enveloped her in a bear hug. "You're late," he muttered seconds before his lips claimed hers.

A bolt of white-hot fire raced along every nerve in her body. His tongue found hers as his hand slid down her side and cupped her bottom. Aria gasped as he pulled her against him. Her hands tightened around his shoulders.

"You are without doubt the most beautiful, desirable woman I've ever met," he muttered. He gently stroked her cheek. "I guess the angels themselves can't hold a candle to you." He laid her head on his shoulder. "What did I ever do to deserve someone like you?" Happiness and wonder colored his voice. "Nothing. There's nothing I could ever do to be worthy of you. Nobody's ever believed in me the way you do." He drew a deep breath. "I love you, Aria."

Aria raised her head and stared into his eyes. They looked soft and joyous, and tender. How could she ever have doubted him? Caleb was no monster. His grandmother was a mean old woman who'd lied about Caleb just because of who his father was. Her mind had probably snapped when she lost her daughter.

This time, she'd follow her heart, which told her to trust him. "I love you, Caleb. So much."

Caleb laughed loudly. He grabbed her and swung her around. "Aria De Luca loves me!" he shouted. "Hey, world! Did you hear? Aria De Luca loves me."

He bowled her over onto the sofa. "I'm not good enough for you," he muttered, "but I don't give a damn about that, and anybody who doesn't like it can go to …" He broke off. "Sorry. I'll have to work on my language. In prison nobody much cares about polite language."

Aria ran her hand through his thick, dark hair, loving the crisp, clean feel of it in her fingers. "Work on it, but first I need another kiss."

"Yes, ma'am. I think that can be arranged." His eyes fluttered shut as his lips found hers.

The heat radiating from his body seared her and made her breath come in gasps. She had to have him or she'd die! Whimpering, she pulled at his shirt, desperate to feel the weight of him on top of her. Caleb understood what she wanted and tried to accommodate her, but the sofa was too small. He hit the floor with a thump.

Aria blinked. She giggled. Caleb looked offended for a moment, but then he too roared with laughter. "This isn't very romantic," Aria teased. "Here I am, totally on fire for you, and you fall off the sofa."

"There'll be consequences if you mock me, woman."

"Oww, I'm so scared. What kind of consequences?"

Caleb leered at her. "Sofas aren't meant for making love, but if you'd care to go to the bedroom..."

She shook her head and sat up, straightening her tee shirt that had ridden up around her neck and was choking her. "Not right now. I can't get serious when I'm thinking of the thump you made hitting the floor."

He grinned and sprang from the floor. "I guess it was kind of funny, and I do have dinner ready."

Aria rolled her eyes. "Spaghetti seems a little prosaic right now, but okay, let's eat."

Caleb laughed and took her hand to pull her off the sofa. "I have no idea what prosaic means, Doc. I'll have to look it up."

Unable to stop herself, Aria rubbed against him. A wave of heat washed over her. "You do that."

"Hey..."

She pulled away with a sultry smile. "Let's eat."

"Oh. Dinner. Yeah."

Aria laughed. "I love it when a man does that."

"Er..."

She gave him a quick kiss. "Let's eat spaghetti."

She had expected something out of a jar with maybe a little hamburger thrown in for good measure, but Caleb surprised her. His sauce tasted and looked homemade. "Did you really make this? It's great."

"Of course I did. This'll teach you to doubt my cooking." An emphatic nod emphasized his words.

Aria wrinkled her nose. "I don't much like to cook."

"Then I'm perfect for you because I do."

"Oh, right, I picked you just because you can cook. I didn't know you could cook until I tasted your spaghetti sauce."

Caleb's eyes glowed with emotion. "Okay, why did you pick me?" He reached for her hand. "What other things can I help you with?"

Aria's breath caught in her throat. She'd been joking with him, but the eager look in his eyes told her that he was dead serious. He wanted her. "Caleb."

She heard the longing in her own voice, so it was no wonder that his eyes started to smolder. As graceful and swift as any jungle cat, he sprang from his seat and pulled her to her feet. "Kiss me, Aria. I'm dying for you."

His lips, firm and warm, met hers. Wave after wave of sensation crashed and broke over her. Her entire body had never felt so alive. Every single nerve seemed ultrasensitive, and the feel of his hands against her almost took her breath away. The unique scent that was Caleb's alone surrounded her. Rational thought left her as more elemental passions surfaced.

"I don't know why you keep picking me," he muttered. "I'm nothing. I'm a nobody with a criminal record, a guy with no family, no money, and not many prospects, but you keep picking me anyway." His hands tightened on her. "I should let you go, but I can't. I never knew I was so selfish, but even though it's in your best interest to find someone from your own social class to get involved with, I can't let you go."

Aria nestled her head against his shoulder and hung on tight. "I can't let you go either. It's like I'm high on you ever single moment we're together." Her face started to burn. "Kiss me."

Caleb buried his hand in her hair and drew her face to his. "I love you, Doc," he whispered, seconds before his lips claimed hers.

Aria's heart pounded like a jackhammer before he finally released her. "I love you too, Caleb. More than I ever thought possible. I wasn't sure I'd ever find a man I could love with my whole being, but I did."

She had thought they couldn't get any closer together, but Caleb was trying. His body pressed against hers from head to toe and sent a shower of sparks straight to her core. Liquid heat filled her and made her knees go weak. In the back of her mind, she heard his heavy, jagged breathing and the sound of thunder.

The scent of lilac wafted around her as her back met the cool sheets on his bed. How did she get here? Had he carried her? Had she followed him? It didn't matter. Not much mattered but him. She took his shoulders and pulled him against her. Oh, Caleb!

Caleb groaned and pressed his lips against her throat. "You smell good," he growled, his voice deep and rough.

He caressed her and kissed his way down her body, leaving a river of fire every place he touched. It was so hot in the room!

Moaning, she clenched his shoulders as heat built inside her. She couldn't take much more of this. Placing quick, frantic kisses on his shoulder she begged, "Now, Caleb. For goodness sake, now."

Caleb obliged. He positioned himself above her. "Are you sure?" His breath was ragged, harsh.

"Yes!"

Time ceased to exist as wave after wave of sensation crashed and broke over Aria. Her skin burned where her flesh touched his. His masculine scent, the taste of him, and the pounding of her heart in her ears surrounded her and set her adrift in an erotic sea. She clung to Caleb's shoulders to ground herself as red heat consumed her, and with a loud cry she found the release she craved.

~ * ~

Aria sighed and snuggled more closely against Caleb as the rain on the roof sang a soothing lullaby. His arm briefly tightened around her but relaxed almost at once. He was sleepy, but even though she was drowsy, she didn't want to sleep. This was an occasion to savor and enjoy. Why waste it in sleep?

Who'd ever have dreamed that she and a guy like Caleb would get together? When she hired him, she had truly expected Melissa to come back to St. Francis once her maternity leave ended. Caleb's job was only supposed to be temporary. A wave of happiness and warmth filled her heart as her lips curved into a little smile. Maybe she should send Melissa a thank you note for not coming back.

The glow in her heart dimmed a little. Of course, her relationship with Caleb did come with a few complications. Her father, for one. He wasn't going to like this at all, but her mother could probably talk him around. Clariee usually could. Once her father got used to Caleb, he'd see what a truly good and fine man she had found for herself.

Lila had been reserved with Caleb, but he was slowing winning her trust by his work at the clinic and with the rescue. She'd eventually be okay with them as a couple.

A frown crossed her face. Tomorrow they had to go and see Caleb's grandmother. She wanted to know why a man's own flesh and blood had lied just to hurt him, but of course not all parents loved and cared for their children as they should. It killed her to think of Caleb as a neglected, hungry child. He had been through so much! It wasn't fair that her life had been wonderful while his had been filled with hardship.

Should she and Caleb really bother talking to his grandmother? If she'd lie one time, she'd lie again, and it truly didn't matter one way or the other what Mrs. Jefferson had to say for herself. She trusted Caleb. If not, she wouldn't be in his bed snuggled against him.

This attraction thing was interesting. Most people would think Jason Lee was the better catch, but she'd never really felt anything but friendship for Jason. Most people would also say that a convict was a flawed person, and if that were true, she was making a mistake by choosing Caleb. But most people didn't know Caleb. They didn't know he was innocent of any wrongdoing. He only took the blame for stealing the car because he wanted to earn his father's love. Naturally, that wasn't really possible, but with Caleb's background, who could blame him for trying? She'd have felt the same way if her life had gone like his.

Her heart picked up a little speed. Caleb had said he loved her. She prayed he really meant it because she'd meant it when she said it back to him. So, where did they go from here? To pick out a ring and a wedding dress?

She shivered when she imagined walking down the aisle on her father's arm wearing a fairy tale creation of lace, tulle, and pearls. Only last week she'd seen a dress to die for. It would make her look like a fairy princess. Oh, and maybe Lila would be her maid of honor.

A new thought struck her. Caleb didn't seem to have any friends at all. The only people he knew were the ones at the rescue, and they were mostly women. He had no one to be his best man.

Oh, it didn't matter. If they had to, they'd tweak the traditional ceremony into something that would be better for him. She blinked. Maybe she was jumping the gun here. He hadn't asked her to marry him. *But he will! Surely he will. It's what I want.*

If all went well, she'd help him pay for school. He could be a vet tech if he wanted, or she'd help him become a vet himself. St. Francis was swamped with clients. There'd be plenty of work for both of them, just as she'd told Sam Bowman.

She caught her breath as he stirred against her. A stab of pure pleasure shook her from head to toe. This magnificent man belonged to her. Caleb was more than just a nice body, though. He had one of the kindest, sweetest natures she'd ever seen.

A sudden flash of lightning illuminated the room. The resulting thunder reverberated through the house and actually shook it. Aria screamed and Caleb sat up as though a puppet master had pulled his strings.

Aria laughed, but even to herself her laughter sounded shaky to say the least. "We're too old to be scared of a little thunder and lightning."

Caleb flung himself back down. "More than a little, if you ask me." He touched her shoulder. "Lie down," he coaxed.

"It's raining and it's so late you may as well stay the night with me. I want to sleep with you in my arms and wake up to the prettiest face I've ever seen."

"Oh, I don't know, Caleb." She brushed her hair away from her face. "Somebody might see my truck here and tell my dad. I want him to like you, and if he knows about this, I can guarantee you he won't like it. Daddy's real old-fashioned."

"I'll move the truck behind the house."

Aria laughed and kissed him. "Okay, you talked me into it. It's lucky I have a toothbrush in my purse. I keep one with me so I can brush after lunch when I'm working. I can't sleep without brushing my teeth, and I don't share with anybody, even you. You'll have to set the clock early so I can get up and go home to get dressed."

Caleb nuzzled her neck and pressed small kisses on her. "Whatever you say, Doc. Could I get another kiss now?"

"I think it can be arranged now that you know about my tooth brushing requirements."

He laughed and kissed her. "I wonder where my pants are?"

Aria gestured over his shoulder. "Behind you on the floor."

"Oh."

"While you're moving the truck, I'll brush my teeth and wash my face."

He leaned over and kissed her again. "It's torture to leave you for even a second, but okay, where are your keys?"

Aria got up and sauntered across the room. Oh my, he was watching her every move.

Eyes burning, Caleb licked his lips. "Do I have to move that truck right now?"

"Oh, yes. There's no time like the present."

He crossed the small room in one big stride. "I'll move it later."

He shooed her back toward the bed, and Aria put her arms around his neck and pulled him on top of her.

~ * ~

"Caleb?"

"Hmm?"

"You have to move my truck."

He groaned. "Okay. I'm getting up, even though you've worn me out."

"Go." She paused for a big yawn. "I'll brush my teeth while you do."

Caleb staggered out of bed and pulled his pants on while Aria found her toothbrush and toothpaste in her purse and went to brush her teeth. She liked Caleb's bathroom. It was basic, of course, but he had hung an interesting red shower curtain with abstract patterns that intrigued her. The man did have a nice sense of style.

Taking the cap off the toothpaste, she squeezed hard, but nothing came out. Empty. No problem. Guess she'd borrow something from Caleb.

The medicine cabinet had three small shelves that were mostly free of clutter. There was the toothpaste on the bottom shelf. Good. They used the same brand. As she reached for the tube, she noticed the bottle on the second shelf, the one partly hidden behind a big can of shaving cream. Her veins filled with ice when she identified one of the missing bottles of painkiller from the clinic.

A wave of dizziness overcame her. She dropped down onto the toilet and hung her head between her knees. There was only one way that Caleb could have gotten that bottle. He had been the one who broke into the clinic. Moaning, she barely kept from throwing up. Freezing. It was freezing in there, but her skin felt hot.

She couldn't breathe! There was a lump in her throat that kept her from drawing air into her lungs. No, she was hyperventilating. No paper bag was handy so she pulled the bottom of her tee shirt over her face. It helped a little.

She heard the front door slam, and Caleb appeared in the doorway. "Doc! What's wrong with you? Do you feel bad? You look sick."

Her lips were numb, but she was still able to talk. "I feel sick."

Caleb knelt beside her, a look of concern on his face. "What's wrong?"

Aria unclenched her hand, no small task since her fingers had frozen around the medication, and held out the vial.

Caleb took it from her and studied it. "This is some of the painkiller we use at the hospital. Why are you carrying that around?"

Aria swallowed hard. Why did she always think she knew best? Everyone had warned her against trusting Caleb, and she had ignored everything they said. She reached for the vial. "I made excuses for you and believed everything you ever told me, but this time you can't lie your way out of trouble. As you well know, I found the vial in your medicine cabinet." A spasm of despair rocked her. It felt as though her heart had just split in two. "The only way it could get in your medicine cabinet is if you put it there, and to put it there you have to be the one who broke into the clinic."

A single sob burst from her throat. "Did you do it because you needed money and wanted to sell it? I would gladly have helped you. Or did you want it for yourself?" She hugged herself and rocked back and forth. "You're fired."

Springing from the toilet, she darted back into the bedroom where she dressed in record time. As she strode past him, Caleb grabbed her arm.

"Let me go!"

His face was calm. It revealed nothing of what he might be feeling. "I'm disappointed in you, Aria. I thought you believed in me so I gave you my heart, and now you're going to break it for me." His façade slipped, and she saw naked pain on his face. "I didn't break into the clinic, but I have an idea who did."

"Oh, right! Blame it on someone else. Some mysterious, shadowy figure that no one ever sees or knows. I've seen movies with that plot! " Her lip curled. "I'm not buying your story this time. Just once, Caleb, be a man and own up to what you've done."

His lips compressed. "I won't ever lie again, not even to you."

Aria jerked her arm away. "Take your hands off me. I'm going home."

The pain on his face was like a living thing. She could almost feel it racing through her own veins, devouring and ruining everything it touched. He held out his hand. "Don't. Don't lose faith in me now. Believe me. Believe in me. Don't you know I'd never hurt you?"

Sorrow and anger nipped and raged at Aria. Would she ever be able to forget about him? Blindly, she shook her head and bolted out into the rain. Within seconds she was drenched. Her keys! Caleb had her keys.

She saw him standing on the front porch and ran back to him. "I want my keys."

Without a word, he tossed them to her. They fell short and landed in the mud. Aria scrambled for the keys and wiped the mud and grass on her pants. A tremendous bolt of lightning split the night sky followed almost at once by a deafening rumble of thunder. Aria screamed and ran for her truck that, of course, was locked. Hands trembling, she stabbed at the lock. By the time she finally got the door open, her eyes were blurred with tears, not just rain.

Caleb was still standing on the porch as she wheeled out of the yard. It didn't look as if he'd moved a muscle since he tossed the keys to her. She felt as if a huge hand had wrapped itself around her heart and was squeezing the life out of her. How could she have been so wrong about him?

~ * ~

As Aria's car disappeared from view, Caleb finally went back inside. The remains of the spaghetti dinner he'd cooked still sat on the table, and from the living room he could see the rumpled covers on his bed.

He methodically cleared the table and carried the dishes to the sink. Some of the spaghetti sauce was still in the pot on the stove, but the sight of it caused the flesh at the base of his nostrils to tighten. With a grunt, he scraped the mess into the garbage can.

It would have been far better if he'd never come to Fairfield. He had thought life had turned around for him, but that just went to show what a fool he had been. Guys like him didn't get breaks in life. That was reserved for people like Jason Lee, who came from a good family and had never been to jail. What made him think it would be different this time?

Aria, of course. Her friendliness and kindness had lulled him into a false sense of security, but deep down he'd always known it couldn't last. Maybe if not for his father and grandmother she'd have stayed with him, but probably not, not with her father and Lila against him. Why had she shown him another world if she didn't trust him enough to let him be a part of it?

A sharp pain in his hand caught his attention. He looked down and saw that he had squeezed a knife blade so tightly that he'd cut himself. Blood dripped all over the dishes in the sink and made him shudder.

Now what would he do? Without her, life really wasn't worth living.

Twelve

Rain sluiced down the windows of Aria's cabin the next morning under menacing, gray clouds. Even through the closed window she heard the sound of the river roaring not too far from the house. If the water continued to rise, it wouldn't be safe to stay there. Her eyes filled with tears. She wouldn't be staying with Caleb, that's for sure.

Don't think about him! But how could she help it? She had believed in him with her whole heart. She had given herself to him. She had done everything in her power to help him improve his life. Why, even her Mama liked him!

In light of all these new developments, she saw his grandmother in a different way too. The old lady seemed less vindictive and spiteful and more concerned that her no good grandson was fooling another naïve woman whose eyes were too filled with stardust to see the truth.

Even Jason's actions seemed—if not nice—at least justifiable. He too had seen the bad blood in Caleb and tried to warn her, but no, she wouldn't listen, and for her trouble she had a broken heart to mend.

Her lip quivered. She was through with men. All they did was cause trouble and hurt the people who loved them. Well, almost all of them. Her father wasn't that way, and she didn't think Lila's boyfriend was either. It was just her. She picked Caleb because he had been nice to a dog! How stupid was that? Some serial killers probably liked dogs too.

She swiped her eyes with the back of her hand. Wonder what he'd think when his rent came due and was much more than he expected? He still had the old truck too. Somehow, she'd have to get that back as well. Ah, never mind. Let him have it. Driving that old piece of junk would just remind her of him and make her feel bad.

Stop thinking about it. To distract herself, she turned on the TV just in time to hear the local forecast. "I wish I had something better to tell you," the weatherman said, "but if you've looked out the window, you know it's still raining. This is our tenth day of rain. In this one month alone, we've received as much rain as we usually do in six months, and with a low front stalled right on top of us, the rain will continue at least through the weekend. Several communities upriver are already coping with flood waters." The TV shifted to a picture of people stacking sandbags along the river's edge. "Officials are hopeful that the sandbags will be enough to hold back the water, but they're making contingency plans just the same."

"Nothing but bad news," Aria exclaimed to the empty room. She turned off the TV and dragged herself to the bathroom for a shower. Even though she'd rather stay in bed all day, she still had to go to work.

~ * ~

Plink. Plink. Plink. Caleb watched as the drops of water falling from the ceiling bounced on the laminate tabletop. Plink. Plink. Plink. The water had reached the edge of the table. Plink. Plink. Plink. It cascaded off the table into the floor.

He'd come so close to having it all, to having everything he had wanted since he was old enough to know what he was missing. It didn't seem like much to ask, just someone to love him and hold him when life hurt too much. To belong somewhere, to have a feeling of homecoming and welcome at the end of the day. Why was that too much to ask for?

Maybe he'd failed some unknown, cosmic test and this was his punishment. "I tried so hard," he muttered. "I even went to jail trying to earn my father's approval. That didn't work, but I didn't care because I found Aria."

His mouth turned down in a grimace. Aria had been slumming when she hung out with him. Why had he ever thought she cared about him? He'd seen where she came from, and it was nothing like his background.

A chill penetrated his bones. So be it. She'd made her feelings real clear to him so he was outta here, and the next time he 'fell in love,' he'd run as fast as he could in the opposite direction. He had tried to do the right thing his entire life, and look what it got him. It was time to look out for number one for a change. For sure, no one else was going to.

~ * ~

Aria patted the dog's back and crooned, "You're a good boy, yes you are."

Margaret White who lived on the river not far from Aria laughed. "I swear that dog loves to come to the vet more than any animal I've ever seen. Sometimes I think he's faking so he can come to see you."

"This puppy is welcome anytime, sick or well." She scratched Duke's ears for him. "In this case, all he needs is a little ointment for that sore. It isn't serious."

"I'm relieved to hear it." Mrs. White took Duke's leash from Aria. "You're listening to the weather reports, I hope."

Aria nodded. "All day. It's getting pretty bad."

"In Chamberlain they're calling for a mandatory evacuation of people living in the flood plain."

Aria bit her lip. "That's only fifty miles from here."

"I know. You really ought to go home and get your important papers and valuables out of your house. As soon as I get back home, my husband and I are leaving until the river settles down."

Aria helped Duke off the table, grunting when the big dog stepped on her foot. "But the river's never flooded where our houses are."

Mrs. White shrugged. "It's up to you, but there's no way I'd spend another night out there."

Aria stood and stared out into the rain as Mrs. White and Duke ran for their car. St. Francis sat on a flat piece of property and already had standing water everywhere. "Lila," she called. "What do we have left this afternoon?"

Lila joined her at the window. "Nothing much. Just a couple of routine well checks left." She frowned at the rain.

"It's getting bad, which is why people are staying home. Maybe we should cancel the two well checks and go home ourselves."

"I think that's a good idea."

The phone rang, and since Aria was closest to it, she answered. "St. Francis Animal Clinic."

"Darling, thank goodness I caught you!"

Aria froze. "Mama, what's wrong? You sound frightened."

"I am. I just heard they're calling for a mandatory evacuation for people living along the river."

Aria ran a hand through her hair. "I'm not surprised. I just talked to Margaret White. She and her husband are leaving until the rain stops."

"Close the clinic and come to our house. The evacuation order doesn't cover us."

"I just told Lila to call and cancel everyone. I'm going to run home to pick up a few things, and then I'll be right over."

Her mother's voice sounded panicked now. "You can't go alone. Wait for me. I'll come to the clinic and go with you."

"All right. See you in a few."

It wasn't necessary for her mother to get wet, but on the other hand, it might be nice to have someone to help her carry things. It would also be nice to have someone to talk to. When she was talking to other people or busy with the animals, she could almost forget about Caleb. Almost. Should she tell her mother and father that Caleb was responsible for the break-in? No. A thousand times no. She couldn't bear her mother's sympathy or her father's relief, not until she'd had a little time to grieve over the loss of so many hopes and dreams.

As she removed her lab coat, a car careened into the parking lot, spraying water everywhere. Quicker than she would have thought possible the doorbell dinged and someone yelled, "Help us! Help us!"

Aria almost slipped and fell in her hurry to see what was wrong. She collided with Lila who had come running from the kennels. A gangly teenager was carrying a big, limber pit bull with a huge chain around his neck. The animal was covered with bites and scars and looked dead. The boy's mama—she guessed that's who it was—tried to help the boy support the big animal.

"In the back," Aria cried, running to show the way.

The boy dropped the dog on the table. "He's drowned. It just happened. We can't revive him."

Aria checked for a heartbeat, but she heard nothing. The dog wasn't breathing either. She cleared the animal's airway of blood and mucus and started CPR. If she could get him breathing, she'd give him Lasix and some steroids and maybe he'd live.

Ten minutes later she gave up. Gently, she stroked the dog's head. "It's no use. He's gone."

The boy started sniffling, and the woman cried.

"Is this your dog?" Aria asked as Lila moved to her side in a show of support. If these people owned the animal, she was getting their names to send to the sheriff. He didn't like dog fighting any more than she did, and he certainly wouldn't want dogs chained up to drown.

The woman shook her head. "No, we've never seen him before. We live on the river and had just gotten word that we had to evacuate when we saw the dog. The river swept him almost to our deck, and he was close enough for us to grab. The poor thing. It looks like something attacked him, but I guess he probably got all those cuts in the water."

Aria believed her story so she didn't tell them that those 'cuts' were bite marks. She'd bet dollars to doughnuts that this dog too had been held in the dog-fighting ring, but there was no use in making these nice people feel any worse. They had done more than most people would have when they brought the poor dog to her. "I thank you for bringing him in," she said. "I wish we could have done more, but I suspect it was too late even before you got him out of the water."

The woman took a tissue from her pocket and blew her nose. "What do we owe you, Doctor?"

Aria shook her head. "Nothing. This one's on me, but if you get a pet of your own, I'd love to be his or her vet. I like dealing with caring people like you."

The boy smiled. "We have two mutts that we got at the animal shelter, but they're great dogs. We love them just as much as if they had fancy pedigrees. Right now they're with my dad at my grandma's house."

The mother nodded. "We don't believe in buying dogs when there are so many animals in shelters that need homes." She tossed her tissue into a wastebasket. "Are you sure we can't pay you? It doesn't seem fair for you to do this for nothing."

"No, you don't owe me a thing. I only wish I could have saved him."

"Then we'll see you when shot time rolls around."

The mother and son were almost at the door when the boy came running back. "I just thought of something. I think someone has a lot of dogs near our house. We can hear them sometimes at night." His eyes begged for a good answer to his question. "Do you think they're safe from the flood?"

"Where do you live?"

The boy told her. Good grief! He was talking about the same stretch of water where she and Caleb had heard dogs howling the day they rafted down the river. The hair on her arms stood up. Had they accidentally stumbled onto the location of the dog-fighting ring?

The boy was waiting for an answer.

"I'm sure all the dogs are fine. Their owner will take care of them. I wouldn't worry any more about it."

He nodded, looking pleased with her reply, and joined his mother in their car.

By the time Clariee arrived ten minutes later, Lila had gone home, the clinic was locked, and she was ready to go.

She gave her mother a big hug. No matter how bad she felt, seeing her mama always made her feel better. Her dad felt the same way, too. He'd come home after a hard day with a scowl on his face and exhaustion in his eyes, but after a few minutes with Clariee, he looked like a new man. "Let's drive my truck, Mama. Your little red sports car is better off staying here."

Clariee laughed. "Don't insult my car, missy. It has class, but in this case, I think you're right."

"Put it in the garage to keep it out of the rain."

Aria was smiling as they piled into her big truck. The truck was a gift from her mother and father, and Clariee had tried her best to talk her and her father into a sports car, but she and her father agreed that for a vet, a truck was more practical.

Aria drove slowly, careful to avoid the deepest looking puddles, but she came to a halt right after she turned off the main road. Pigeon Creek had topped its banks and was cascading over the road.

Clariee grabbed her arm. "Stop! I don't want to go through that."

"We're not," she soothed, remembering her mother's fear of deep water.

Aria jumped out of the truck and ran over to look at the water flowing across the road. It wasn't very deep or swift at the moment. "I can make it with no trouble," she called, her voice sounding thin and small to her. "Wait here. I won't be a minute."

Clariee got out of the truck and hurried over to her. "Are you insane? You can't cross that."

It had started to rain harder. "Mama, you can see the road through the water. It barely covers my shoes. I have some jewelry and pictures that I don't want ruined. It'll be okay. This'll only take a minute."

Clariee scowled at her. "If you cross that creek, I'm going with you."

No use to argue. When Clariee got stubborn, even her father gave in without a fight. "Let's go, then. Hurry so we can get out of here."

They made it across the water just fine, but by the time they reached Aria's house, it was raining heavily and the clouds were so black it looked almost dark. "The river's up, but it still has a ways to go before it reaches the house," Aria yelled above the roaring of the water and the pounding of the rain.

"Just hurry," Clariee begged. She grabbed the hood of her lightweight jacket as the wind tore it from her head. "This place feels dangerous now."

She wouldn't say it because she didn't want to scare her mother, but she thought it felt dangerous too.

Once they went inside, the feeling of danger receded. The power was still working, and when the lights came on, everything looked familiar, safe, and cozy. Aria found two thick, bath towels and handed one to her mother. "We might as well dry off even though in the long run it won't matter much. We'll get wet again when we go back to the truck."

"Lots better," Clariee approved as she dried her soaking hair.

Aria went to the refrigerator and poured both of them a glass of orange juice. "Something happened at the clinic right before you got there, Mama."

"Oh?"

Aria told her about the drowned dog and what the boy had said about the dogs. "I think that could be where they hold the fights, and if so, I bet at least one of them keeps his dogs there."

Horror darkened her mother's eyes. Clariee loved animals. "You said the dead dog was on a chain?"

Aria nodded.

"How do you think he got away?"

"I don't know."

Clairee's eyes looked sick. "If one dog was left chained to die, the others probably are too. People low down enough to torture dogs are too sorry and worthless to care about saving them in weather like this."

Aria's stomach churned. "That's what I was thinking."

Clariee set her orange juice down with a thump and tossed her towel into the kitchen sink. "We have to find them. We have to make sure they're safe."

Aria peeked out the window. It was still raining. "We'll have to go by land if we go at all. We can't take a boat on the river. The current is so swift it would be suicide."

Clariee shivered. "Then we'll go by land."

Aria scrambled to find two big flashlights, a coil of rope, and a scalpel. At the last minute she picked up a grappling iron that the river had washed up a couple of days earlier. Maybe it would prove useful to them although at the moment she couldn't think how. "What else do we need, Mama?"

"Something to cut a big chain."

Aria shook her head. "I don't have anything like that. I'm taking a scalpel so I can cut through their collars if I have to. They're probably made of leather. The dog my neighbor brought in had on a leather collar."

The lights flickered and went out. "Hurry," Clariee cried, a quiver in her voice. "No, wait. We didn't get your things."

Aria ran for her bedroom and grabbed her jewelry box from the dresser. Then she jerked the picture above her bed off the wall. The picture was a painting of her as a little girl holding her first pet, a pretty calico cat named Hannah. Her mother and father had commissioned the painting from a famous artist, and she loved it.

"Put it in a garbage bag," Clariee ordered.

The minute Aria opened the door she saw that things had gotten a lot worse. The rain was falling almost horizontally as the wind screamed and blew. "The river's almost to the steps," she cried as she ducked her head against the fury of the storm.

"Oh, this is terrible!" Clariee shouted. "How could the water rise so much in such a short time?"

"I don't know. Let's get out of here while we can."

Struggling against the stinging rain, almost deafened by the whine of the wind, they laboriously picked their way across Aria's yard. By the time they reached Pigeon Creek where they'd left their car, rain streamed in rivulets from their hair and clothes. The water from Pigeon Creek was running a lot faster.

"Can we cross?" her mother hollered. Aria saw her shiver. Was she scared or just cold? She was cold herself. It was summer time, but the rain was cold.

"We have to get across, Mama. I don't think it's safe to stay here. I'll go first."

Clariee grabbed her arm. "Wait! Tie the rope to the grappling hook and see if you can snag your truck. We can use that to pull ourselves across the creek if we need to."

It took three tries before Aria got the hook set. She winced thinking of the damage she was doing to the vehicle. "We don't have anything to tie it to on this side. We'll have to cross together."

Clariee spit a lock of wet hair from her mouth. "Go."

They both wrapped the rope around their arms, and with Aria in front, they stepped into the water across the road. It was much deeper—it came mid-way up her shin, and Aria felt a suction that threatened to pull her feet out from under her, but she thought they could have crossed it safely even without the rope. "It isn't as swift or deep as I thought," she yelled as she removed the grappling hook from her truck bed.

"That's good, but let's not get overconfident. It's probably worse in some places than others."

A tremendous flash of lightning split the sky. Screaming, Aria and Clariee dove for the truck that, in spite of Aria's unspoken fears, cranked right up. "I remember where Caleb and I heard the dogs howling, but coming from land instead of the water..."

"We'll do the best we can. Nobody can do better than that."

Her mother was right, but time was running out. They didn't have time to wander through the woods looking for the dogs. They'd either get lucky right away, or the dogs would die because as much as she loved them, she wouldn't sacrifice her life and her mother's to find animals that might or might not be alive.

~ * ~

"Mr. De Luca?"

David De Luca looked up and smiled at his secretary who stood in the doorway. "Yes, Patricia?"

"Have you been listening to the weather reports?"

He shook his head. "No, I'm too busy. The Hunt case isn't going well, and... why do you ask?"

"They're calling for mandatory evacuations along the river where Aria lives. I thought you might want to call her."

The skin on his arms broke out in goose bumps. "I do want to. Thanks, Patricia, and you go on home yourself."

"Thanks, I believe I will." She paused. "You should go home too. Nobody knows how high the flood waters are going."

David slammed the Hunt folder shut and stuffed it in his desk. "I think you're right."

Before he left, he called Aria's house, but the odd sound on his phone told him her landline wasn't working. Probably the rain and flood water. He'd call her cell phone. He tried several times, but nobody answered.

She was probably at the clinic. He tried that number, but he got the same weird noise. A slight fission of anxiety shook him. Okay, he'd go on over to the clinic. Everyone needed to get home before dark.

He gasped when he went outside. The entire world looked flooded and wet, and the wind was blowing so hard it was tough to walk against it. In many places he saw standing water that could easily cause an accident.

By the time he reached the clinic, he'd worked up a major case of anxiety. He'd lived in Fairfield his entire life, and he'd never seen anything like this. His stomach rolled over when he saw the empty parking lot at the clinic. No one was there.

Maybe Clariee would know where she was. He called his house where the phone rang normally, but no one answered. Where was Clariee? Had she and Aria gone somewhere in this weather?

No, of course they hadn't. Clariee was slightly phobic about deep water. She wouldn't deliberately go anywhere near a flood. But wait! What if his house had flooded?

He left the parking lot going a touch too fast for conditions and turned toward home. Except for him, the road was empty. Nobody was headed toward the river.

To his relief, his house wasn't flooded, but... No! Oh, please no. Clariee's little car was missing, and there was no sign of Aria's truck. He sprang from his car and ran inside, but the house was empty. He looked for a note, but he didn't see one anywhere.

Taking a deep breath, he attempted to calm down. Lila would probably know. She kept a pretty close watch on Aria. He'd go over to her house and see if he could find them. And this very day he'd get Lila's cell phone number so he could call her if necessary. Lila lived not far from the Fairfield city park that was, unfortunately, on the river. Guess he'd find out just how bad the flood really was.

He never made it to Lila's house, though. As he turned back toward the clinic, he passed her car and sat down on his horn. She looked into her rear view mirror and brought her car to a stop.

He jumped out and ran over to her, ignoring the cold rain running down his neck and soaking his feet. "Hi, Lila, I'm looking for Aria and Clariee. Do you know where they are?" His teeth clenched as he waited for her answer.

"No, I have no idea. We closed the clinic early, and when I left, Aria was waiting for her mother. They were going to get a few things from Aria's house. There's a mandatory evacuation order for anyone living on the river."

His hands fisted. "I'm going to her house. You need to find shelter yourself."

"Not while Aria is unaccounted for. You can check her house, and I'll see if they're with Caleb."

"Good idea. Thanks, Lila. You're a good friend to Aria."

They exchanged cell numbers, and he dashed away and jumped into his car with his blood roaring in his ears and his teeth clenched.

~ * ~

Caleb jumped. Someone was pounding on his front door, and he almost hadn't heard it because of the roaring of the rain and all the thunder and lightning. *Aria!* No, it wouldn't be Aria. She had very clearly explained how she felt about him, so it was no use to think she'd changed her mind. Passing the time of day with a former employee and lover probably wasn't on her agenda.

His jaw dropped the minute he opened the door and saw Lila standing on his doorstep. Except for maybe his grandmother, Lila was the last person he'd expected to see.

"Have you seen Aria?" she demanded, tossing her wet umbrella onto the porch and brushing past him into the house without even asking permission to enter.

Caleb's lips thinned as he slammed the door behind her. Guess he wasn't worthy of common courtesy. "No, she isn't here. Why do you ask?"

"Because no one can find her or Clariee. We closed the clinic early because the National Guard issued an evacuation order for anyone living on the river. Clariee and Aria were going to Aria's house to pick up a few things, and then Aria was going to stay with her mother until things calm down."

Caleb shrugged. "Sounds sensible to me."

"Yeah, it does, but they never made it home, and they aren't answering their cell phones. Mr. De Luca is beside himself."

He knew then exactly what people meant when they said their blood ran cold. A chill had seized him and caused his heart to race as adrenaline pumped through his veins. He drew a deep, steadying breath. "Has Mr. De Luca been to Aria's house to hunt for them?"

Tears filled Lila's eyes. She visibly gulped. "He tried to, but the area around Aria's house is flooded. There's no way to get to it. Mr. De Luca called the National Guard, and they've promised to check into it as soon as they can, but..."

Her voice trailed off, but she didn't have to finish. If Aria and her mother were trapped in the house, there was no place for them to go except up on the roof, and the way it was pouring outside it would be hard to cling to a slippery, steep roof. Even if they did manage to hang on, the water might still rise too high... But what if they weren't in the house? What if their car had been swept away by the floodwater? No! This couldn't happen. Forcing the dreadful picture from his mind, he sprang to his feet. "I'm going out there anyway. If it's humanly possible, I'll get to her house. "

Lila sat down and started to cry, a gut-wrenching sound that perfectly matched his own mood. "Are you coming with me, Lila?"

She wiped away her tears and squared her shoulders. "Yes, I'm going with you, although if Mr. De Luca couldn't get to the house, I doubt we can either."

It took longer than he had expected to get anywhere near Aria's house. Pigeon Creek had flooded and they couldn't find anywhere to cross it. With the land covered by water, they weren't even sure where Aria's driveway really was. In places, if road signs hadn't been visible it would have been hard to even find where the highway lay. Besides that, in several places on the main road they saw downed power lines and feared to go too near them. Caleb hit the steering wheel with his hand. They were so close yet so far away. "Isn't there any other way to her house, one that bypasses Pigeon Creek?"

Lila shook her head. "Not that I know of."

Come on, Hawkins. Think rationally. Figure this out. The truck couldn't make it. If they tried to cross the creek, they ran the risk of being swept off the road and into the river or deep floodwater where they'd surely drown. It didn't matter about him, but he'd hate to get Lila killed too. She had a pretty nice life in front of her. "A boat," he said. "We can cross Pigeon Creek in a boat. Where can I get one?"

Her eyes opened wide. "Why, it's too rough for a boat."

"On the river yes, but a boat might make it over Pigeon Creek."

Sudden calm seemed to descend on Lila. "You'd really try to get to across Pigeon Creek in this weather? Chances are they won't be in the house."

"Of course." Why did she even have to ask?

Lila drew a deep breath. "Then I apologize."

"For what?"

"For thinking that you might be trying to take advantage of Aria.

As if it made any difference now. He'd have laughed at the irony of it all if the situation wasn't so urgent. "Where can I get a boat?"

Her face brightened. "The guy who owns the boat dealership downtown. He's Aria's client. Maybe he'd help us."

"Let's go."

They turned around and headed back toward town as fast as they safely could.

Jimmy Revis, the owner of Jimmy's Boats and Floats, wasn't underwater, but he was locking up so he could go home when Caleb and Lila arrived. Lila hurriedly told him why they wanted to borrow one of his boats.

"You need a connector boat," he said, "but ordinary people don't usually buy them so I don't have one in stock. Have you contacted anyone about this? The National Guard is pretty much running the show now."

"They'll get to us when they can," Caleb growled. "Aria needs help now."

Jimmy scratched his head. "A regular motorboat won't be any good because in some places you'll probably be traveling in some real shallow water. A canvas inflatable isn't great either because it might get punctured by debris under the water." His lips twisted to the side as he chewed at the inside of his cheek. "You aren't going onto the river? You just want to get across Pigeon Creek?"

Caleb nodded.

"Then I guess the inflatable might be best. Come and let me show you how to use it."

~ * ~

Lila stepped on her brakes and put her car in park. "This is as far as we can go."

Caleb watched the water swirling a few feet from her car. "I appreciate all you've done to help me, Lila, but as soon as we get the boat unloaded, you've got to get out of here. The water's higher now than it was when we left, and we only have about forty-five minutes more daylight. You don't need to get caught in the dark out here."

She scowled. "Oh no, I'm not going anywhere! I'm coming with you to find Aria."

Caleb gave her a brief hug. "Thank you for caring so much, but you can't risk your life this way. You really could die out here."

"You might need me. You don't know what you'll find in that house, and even if they're there and okay, you'll need someone to help you cross the creek again."

"Just say a prayer for us. That'll be more than enough."

Lila looked ready to argue, but she knew he was right. Risking her life wasn't an option. He put on the life jacket Jimmy had given him, readied the boat, and jumped in with her protests still ringing in his ears.

"I'll wait here as long as I can," she yelled.

Waving his hand in reply, he turned the canvas boat toward Pigeon Creek. He felt the current the moment he crossed the creek, but it was nothing compared to what he felt when he finally got within sight of Aria's house. He had told Jimmy Revis he wouldn't be on the river, but he'd been wrong. It wasn't Pigeon Creek that was tossing torrents of water and all that debris against the house. It was the Wendell River, and he was rapidly being carried away from Aria's house.

Changing direction, he tried to get out of the river's grip by traveling at an angle instead of straight into the rushing water. For a moment, the inflatable obeyed, but a huge wave splashed over the side and knocked him to the bottom of the boat. By the time he got up, he was racing past the place where Lila was parked. The way her mouth was moving he thought she might be screaming.

Thirteen

"That's it." Aria gestured toward the top of a chimney sticking through the trees as she brought the truck to a stop. "We might have missed it if the rain hadn't stopped."

"Why that's the old Lee place." Clariee stared at the flooded world around them. "I had forgotten how isolated this house is." She shivered. "If it weren't for the dogs... I don't like deep water, and I never did."

"We can go back."

Clariee laughed and opened the truck door. "I don't think so."

Aria followed her lead and stepped out of the truck into ankle-deep water. In the fading light, the Lees' dirt driveway led through the woods and looked dark and dangerous. She shook her head to clear her mind of such fantasies. Both she and her mother were getting spooked by the isolation and the flooded world.

She thought of the night Jason told her not to visit the fish camp because homeless people might be using it. At the time she had no reason to doubt him, but now she had to wonder if maybe he'd had another, more compelling reason to keep her away from the place. Huh! No surprise that this new idea felt right. "Jason's involved in the dog fighting ring, Mama. I know he is. That's why he warned me not to come out here."

Clariee shrugged. "We'll find out if we can get to the cabin. Let's take a look."

"The water isn't deep here, but the cabin is closer to the river. We'll need to be careful."

Clariee stared at the dark water in front of them. "Find some big sticks. We'll use them to feel our way if necessary."

Easier said than done. After five minutes of searching, they found nothing they could use. Aria splashed her way back toward her mother who was searching on the other side of the driveway. "The water's higher now. If we're going, it has to be now."

"Let me get my flashlight out of the truck. Do you have the scalpel?"

"Yes."

Clariee grabbed her flashlight, and Aria led her mother down the old driveway. "It's pretty easy to follow the road, Mama. I think it's well maintained."

Clariee nodded. "It is and that's a surprise considering the Lees say they never use it."

It took about ten minutes to get to the cabin that had a wrought iron gate blocking the road. A wire fence surrounded the property. Clariee kicked at the gate and splashed water everywhere. "Is it locked?"

Aria nodded. "Yes, but we can get through. Part of the fence is down." She pointed to a large gap to the left of the gate.

She went first and Clariee followed. They paused to stare at the house. At one time, the cabin had looked like something out of a fairy tale. Painted white and trimmed in gingerbread woodwork, a narrow porch ran the entire length of the home. Aria imagined red petunias in the empty window boxes, the kind Mrs. Lee had planted when she and Jason were kids. And hadn't Mrs. Lee had red checked curtains at the windows?

She blinked and saw the place as it really was. The peeling strips of paint gave evidence that it hadn't seen a painter in a long time. The windows all seemed intact as did the roof, but a brooding stillness hung over the whole place even though the rushing of the river was anything but still. Her heart pounded. "Let's check inside first."

The front door was locked. Aria turned to go to the back side of the house, but Clariee grabbed her arm before she stepped off the porch. "This is easier, Aria." She picked up an old clay flowerpot and smashed it through the window.

Aria laughed, a touch of hysteria in the sound. "Way to go. I can add breaking and entering to my resume." Briefly, her thoughts turned to Caleb, but no, she had to think of the dogs now.

Clariee used the flowerpot to clear the remaining glass from the window frame and gestured toward the opening. "After you. No. Wait. If the dogs are in here, are they likely to attack us?"

Aria hesitated. "I don't think so. Most fighting dogs aren't dangerous to humans, but there are exceptions."

"Then you'd better take out that scalpel. You may have to kill a dog to get us out of this place alive."

Aria roared with inappropriate laughter as she withdrew the scalpel from her pocket. Her nerves were about to get the better of her. She drew a deep breath and entered the house through the window with Clariee following right on her heels.

They were in the living room, and it was still dry. "I bet my house has water in it now, Mama, but this place is dry."

"It's on higher ground. If not, we wouldn't have been able to get here."

The cabin muted the sounds of the storm, which somehow made the dim place even spookier, but even though they searched every room, they didn't see any dogs. They ended up in the kitchen. "I don't see any bowls, collars, or leashes either, Mama."

Clariee gestured toward the drain board beside the sink. "Look at that. Those cups aren't dusty or dirty. They've been used recently. And look. There's a coffee maker with coffee still in it. This house is anything but abandoned."

"Or filled with squatters," Aria agreed. "Squatters would have made a mess in here." She sank down into one of the old hard-rock maple chairs around the kitchen table. "Maybe I was wrong. I don't see any evidence of dogs here."

Clariee turned her flashlight toward a door in the far corner of the room. "Let's try the basement before we leave."

"Basement?"

"Not a true basement, maybe, but yes, they have a cellar even though it always stayed pretty wet."

As the door opened, the sound of running water, howls, and barks filled the kitchen. "We've found them! Mama, are they underwater yet?"

Clariee shone her flashlight down into the cellar. Four dogs were chained to the wall. The smallest dog was obviously dead. Even from where they stood she could see the rips and bites on his body. He was thin too, almost a skeleton really. The river water in the cellar hadn't killed this dog, but she knew who did. Jason Lee whom she'd trusted and called a friend was responsible for this horror. If only she had him in front of her right now!

Clariee peered into the cellar. "Let's go on down, but be careful. They don't have real steps, just a ladder."

The dogs went wild when the women entered the cellar, barking and lunging as they begged for help. The water was up to their shoulders.

Aria gasped when she turned her light on the big dog in the far corner. The poor thing was holding one puppy in her mouth, trying to keep it out of the water. She'd bet the farm there were dead puppies under the water surrounding the mama.

She splashed through the water to the mama dog, wincing when she stubbed her toe on something she couldn't see. "Please, mama, let me take the baby. I'll help you both."

Slowly, she reached for the puppy, surprised when the mama dog let it go without complaint. The puppy was still alive, so she stuffed it into her blouse to keep it safely out of the way. She had expected she'd have to use the scalpel to cut the collar off the dog, but she didn't. The chain unhooked easily from the dog's collar.

"I've got the chain off this one," Clariee yelled, "but the water's rising. Hurry, Aria, we still have one more to free."

The last dog was chained near some metal shelving that looked heavy. As Aria reached for the dog's collar, Clariee studied the bottles sitting on the shelves. "I bet this is from the break-in at the clinic."

One of the dogs rushed by Aria and made her loose her balance. With a little cry, she toppled over into the murky water. Clariee held out her hand, and helped Aria scramble to her feet.

Aria's heart almost broke when she saw the items on the shelf. Painkillers, syringes, sutures, and several bottles filled with pills were laid out in a neat row. Other medicine boxes were floating in the water. *Oh, Jason, how could you!* "I bet it's from the clinic too. All of those items were among the things that were stolen." She took a deep breath. "How could he have done this? Why would anyone do this?"

Clariee's eyes flashed fire. "I have no idea, but we'll see that Jason pays for it. How are we going to get the dogs out of here?"

"They'll have to follow us. We can't carry them."

"Hurry." Clariee shoved her wet hair behind her ear. "The water's up to their necks now. You go to the top of the ladder to pull them up while I push from behind."

With lots of pushing, pulling, and grunting, they got the dogs out of the cellar and into the kitchen. "Come on up," Aria yelled. "We have to go *now*."

"Comin...."

A shriek that seemed to go on forever drowned out her mother's voice. Frozen with fear, Aria saw the metal shelves wrench away from the wall and knock her mother to the floor. "Mama!"

Aria slid down the ladder and pulled at the shelving unit, but it wouldn't budge. "Mama, Mama, where are you?" she sobbed.

"Over here. In the corner." By nothing short of a miracle, Clairee's face was still above the rising water. "I'll push, you pull," she panted.

Aria pulled until she felt like every blood vessel in her face was popping, but the shelves wouldn't budge. Clariee groped for her hand. "It's no use, Aria. They're too heavy, and I think something is wrong with my leg. It hurts pretty bad." She attempted a smile. "Save the dogs. If you leave now, you can still do that, and there's absolutely no use in both of us dying here."

~ * ~

The current wasn't as swift there so the canvas boat had slowed considerably. In fact, Caleb was pretty sure that with the hard paddling he'd done he was over land now and not Pigeon Creek or the Wendell River. He should feel grateful for this miracle, but he didn't. He just felt sort of numb. If Aria and Clariee had been caught in Aria's house, the odds that they'd be saved weren't all that good. She had rejected him and believed the worst of him, but the idea of a world without Aria De Luca in it was too monstrous to be believed.

The boat got caught in a small eddy that jerked him out of his reverie. The eddy spun him in a different direction, and when the boat rounded a curve, he saw Aria's truck sitting on the side of the road. Water covered about a third of the tires, but it looked as if the motor was still dry. His hands clenched around his paddle. Where was she? Why was her truck parked there? What could have motivated an intelligent woman to purposely drive into a raging flood zone?

He stared into the trees on his right and saw a chimney sticking up. This looked like the place where he and Aria had heard the dogs! She'd come here to see if they needed rescuing. Cursing the river, the dogs, and even Aria herself, he paddled the boat between the trees down what he assumed was a driveway and shortly saw a faded white house.

Uh oh. There was a fence around the property, but no, it didn't matter. Look at that big gap in the fence. Holding his breath for fear of damaging the boat, he floated across and tied the canvas boat to a rail on the small front porch. Someone, probably Aria, had broken out the window. Stepping inside, he was greeted by three big dogs, all of whom milled about and seemed desperately glad to see him. The light was dim, and their coats were wet, but he could still see scars and some fresh bites on them. "Aria," he yelled. "Are you in here?"

For a minute no one answered, but then Aria bolted out of the kitchen. She was soaking wet, and a puppy's head poked out of the front of her blouse. "Help me! Mama's trapped in the cellar, and the water's rising fast."

She plucked the puppy from her blouse and laid it on the floor, and one of the dogs promptly picked it up in its mouth. "Hurry, Caleb, hurry!"

Caleb took two steps down the ladder and jumped the rest of the way. Dear Lord! Could it be any worse? Except for

Clariee's face, there wasn't much of her that wasn't underwater.

At his side, Aria pulled and tugged on some shelves. "She's trapped by the shelves. They're so heavy!"

Caleb heaved and strained, but he couldn't move them either. They might as well be bolted to bedrock. Probably were. Clariee sputtered and tried to tilt her head backward to get more of her face from under the water. Her eyes met his and conveyed a message he immediately understood.

He took a deep breath and prayed Aria would listen to him. "I can move the shelves, but it's going to take a minute. You get the dogs to your truck and take them to safety. I'll free your mother."

Her eyes opened wide. "Are you crazy? I'm not leaving..."

"You have to. The little boat I brought won't hold the dogs and all of us. If you wait much longer, your truck's going to be flooded. Go. I'll take care of Clariee."

"But..."

"Aria, I said go!" He tried to make his voice sound both stern and comforting at the same time. "Go now, or you and the dogs are dead. I'll follow with Clariee."

"But...Are you sure?"

"Yes, I almost have her free. Go."

Doubt filled her face, but Clariee waved her hand toward the ladder, and Aria gave in. "Shall I wait for you in the truck?"

"No. I have a boat. Go."

Aria scrambled toward the ladder and paused at the bottom. "Caleb..."

"Go! I have her."

Aria vanished, taking her flashlight with her and dimming the faint light in the cellar even more. Caleb sighed and turned to Clariee. "I can't move the shelves, Clariee. I lied to get her out of here, but I'm not giving up. I'll try to find something to use as a lever."

With most of her face under the water, Clariee nodded, and Caleb began the search for anything he could use to save her.

~ * ~

Aria tried to pick up her pace. "Hurry! Hurry! Move dogs, move!" The water came up to her knees, and on lower ground it came almost to her waist. The dogs had had to swim more than once, but they stayed with her as closely as if she had them on leashes. The mama dog kept her eyes fixed on the puppy whose head again stuck out of Aria's blouse. From time to time he howled for his mother, but the big dog didn't try to get to him.

"I see the truck! Look, dogs, I see the truck."

Her stomach clenched. Would it crank or not? The water was so deep! She dropped the tailgate, jumped into the back of the truck, and whistled. All three dogs scrambled in and immediately started shaking water off their coats. What should she do with the puppy? Leave it with its mother? Take it with her? Take it with her. It had started raining again, and she couldn't leave the little one exposed to the elements.

She swept her flashlight in all directions. The flood had surrounded them. Her knees literally shook. The weatherman had said just yesterday that twelve inches of water could sweep a car away. He'd also said that floods might erode the earth under a road and collapse it. 'Go to high ground,' he had said. 'Don't try to drive unless you have no other choice.'

Did she have another choice? Not that she could see. The rising water had taken the choice away from her. If only she knew how high it would go! She jumped from the back of the truck, but she landed on the edge of the pavement and lost her balance. It hurt her foot so much she screamed and swallowed some of the filthy water as she rolled off the road into a shallow ditch. Gah! She'd probably get ten different diseases from this nasty stuff. What had she done to her foot? It felt like she had a toothache in every bone.

"Please crank," she muttered as she dragged herself out of the ditch and into the cab, trying the whole time not to put any weight on her left foot. She held her breath as she turned the key. The truck roared to life, but then she had to get out of there. If only she could see the highway better. If only it wasn't pitch black dark. If only Jason Lee was a decent human being. She bit her lip. Had the river crested yet? How much higher would it rise?

She got the truck turned around, expecting each moment to fall off the pavement into mud that would suck them down and never let go, but she made the turn safely. Her hands gripped the steering wheel so tightly her knuckles turned white. The darkness made it likely that she wouldn't be able to see Caleb's boat even if he and Clariee were right behind her. Oh, but they had a flashlight!

She set her jaw. Might as well face reality. The truth was that she might or might not be able to see the flashlight, and if she lingered any longer with the water rising, she might be signing her own death warrant. Swiping tears away and praying for safety for them all, she put the truck in drive and started creeping down the road.

She ran off the highway almost immediately. Gasping, she jerked the steering wheel to pull the vehicle off the road's shoulder. Why was she trying to drive in the correct lane? Driving in the middle of the road gave her a better chance to get safely home.

Fifty yards down the highway, the truck's right front wheel left the road again. She'd expected this and stopped the vehicle immediately even though she'd rather not stop in water this high. Her heart pounded so hard she could hear the blood roaring in her ears. Unless she'd gotten turned around in the dark, they were near the railroad crossing. If she misjudged the turn again, the truck would plunge into the deep ditch that lay on either side of the rails, and it would stay there until the water receded and a wrecker pulled it out. She and the dogs would probably stay there too.

"I'll get out and look for it," she cried. The puppy howled back, appearing to understand the danger, or maybe he just wanted his mama. She wanted her mama too.

The moment her foot touched the ground, she fell. Shooting pains streaked up her leg, and her foot felt like she'd stuck it into a blazing inferno instead of a watery hell. "Broken," she mumbled. "Or badly sprained."

She took a tentative step forward and fell again, inhaling some of the filthy floodwater at the same time. If she had a walking stick or cane, she could make it, but not this way. Hopping on one foot, she managed to get back into her truck where she blew her nose and tried to get rid of as much water as possible.

She hadn't wanted to think about it, but the floodwater had been a little higher. Not much, but she couldn't take the chance of staying where she was until daylight. One of the dogs howled, the sound so mournful yet full of hope it gave her courage. Easing the truck back onto the road, she steadily inched down the highway.

Five minutes later she saw the railroad crossing. "I forgot about the sign," she yelled. "There's a sign. Oh, thank you, God, there's a sign. I can see the crossing under the water."

With the sign to guide them, they safely crossed the railroad tracks. "How far are we from home, puppy?" The puppy couldn't answer, but it seemed to Aria as if driving had gotten a little easier. Staying on the road didn't present nearly as much of a problem as it had when she left the Lee's driveway.

Oh my goodness! In some places she could actually see the road in the headlights. "The water isn't as deep here, puppy! We may actually make it!"

Resisting the temptation to speed, Aria steadily crawled her way forward. "Puppy, look! I see the town limits sign." Oh, and there was Master's Ice Cream Parlor up ahead. She'd been there so many times!

Euphoria quickly faded in the face of reality. What did she do now? She had to tell the authorities about Caleb and her mother.

Flashing blue lights took the decision out of her hands. "Aria De Luca, pull over," an amplified voice ordered. Stan! It was her friend Stan from the police force. Aria parked in front of the ice cream parlor and hopped out of her truck, making sure not to step on her hurt foot.

"Aria!" Her father jumped from the police car along with Stan, ran to her, and smothered her in a big bear hug. "Where have you been? I've been worried sick about you and your mother. Where is she? Why are you out in weather like this? Don't you realize we have a serious situation here?"

"Daddy, wait, let me explain."

By the time she finished her story, her father's eyes looked sick, and his hands trembled. She had known her father would be upset, but oh, look at Stan's face. Her heart flip-flopped in her chest. "What is it, Stan? The look on your face is scaring me."

Stan's eyes dropped. It was bad. It must be very bad. "I don't want to scare either of you, but..."

"But what?" David snapped. Aria groped for his hand.

"That's the hardest hit area within fifty miles, and the water is still rising. Not as quickly as it was, though. We think it should crest within the next eight hours or so."

Aria's insides quivered; her knees trembled. She got the picture all too well. Stan hadn't said it, but he thought Caleb and her mother might not get out. "What can we do?" she begged. "There has to be something."

"You were out there, Aria. Until morning there's nothing anyone can do."

Her shoulders slumped. "He's right, Daddy. They'd be risking their lives looking for a needle in a haystack."

"Nonsense!" David snapped. "You made it through, didn't you?"

Aria's eyes widened. "It was just dumb luck. You don't know what it's like along that river."

Her father's face looked as dark as the sky above them. "Your mother is still out there. Do you honestly think I'll stay here in town when I could be looking for her?" He shot Stan a malevolent glare. "If I hadn't listened to you, Clariee would be safe now instead of..." His voice trailed off, and Aria knew he couldn't bring himself to say the words.

Stan cleared his throat. "Mr. De Luca, you can take Aria's truck and try to drive to the Lees' house, but until the river crests, the water's going to get deeper and deeper. You can't make it. I know you're hurting, but you can't make it. Would Mrs. De Luca want you to lose your life on a fool's errand?"

"Saving my wife is no fool's errand! Man up, mister. If you're too scared to go, I'll go alone."

"Daddy, please listen to him! If it weren't dark I'd go back with you. I wouldn't hesitate, but you can't see out there. We wouldn't be able to find the house. We'd just keep driving until there was no way back, and we still couldn't save them. Trust Caleb. He said he almost had her free when I left. They're probably on their way to town right now. Caleb's strong. He can make it. I know he can. Please, Daddy. I can't stand to have you out there too."

David scowled and rubbed his hand across his face. "First light. We go at first light."

"First light," Stan agreed. "Tom Bradley down at the station has a boat we can use. I'll pick it up tonight and meet you at the station at five. If we get lucky, EMS or the National Guard will be free to take us, but either way we go. I haven't forgotten all Mrs. De Luca did for my mother and father when Daddy lost his job last year."

Aria's heart warmed. Her mother offered help to anyone in need, but Clariee never blew her own horn. Forgetting about her foot, Aria touched it to the ground and stepped on it. "Ow, that hurt! Daddy, I need to go to the emergency room. My foot's either broken or sprained, but before we do, I need to take the dogs to the clinic."

David stared at the three big dogs who all stared back at him. "They're all trained fighters?"

"I guess so."

"Take them to the animal shelter. They're too dangerous for you to deal with."

"No way! They're going to the rescue for rehabilitation. That's why Mama and I went out there. She wanted to save them, not destroy them."

David nodded. He knew her mother as well as she did, so he knew she was right on this one.

"I'll follow you to the clinic to make sure you get there all right," Stan offered.

Aria nodded. "Thanks, Stan. I owe you one. Next time you bring in your cat, the visit's on me."

"Just doing my job." He grinned. "But I'll take you up on that offer."

"I'll drive," her father said. He helped Aria into the truck and turned toward her clinic. "I talked to Lila. She said there's some standing water outside, but the inside of the building is dry."

He was making conversation so he wouldn't think about her mother. The distracted look on his face gave him away. "Daddy, she'll be okay. Caleb almost had her free when I left them."

His eyes turned fierce. "Caleb could have been lying to you just so you'd leave. Have you thought of that?"

Aria gasped. "No! He said he'd be right behind me."

"He wasn't though, was he?"

"I...I don't know. It was dark, and the water was so high..."

Her father gave her shoulder a squeeze. "He tried to save both you and your mother, Aria. No matter how this turns out he'll always be welcome in my home. I want you to know that."

Aria bit her lip until it hurt. She'd never have a better time to tell her father about Caleb, but she couldn't do it, not with his words of approval ringing in her ears. "I don't understand how Caleb knew where to look for us. I didn't tell him where we were going."

"I guess he must have found you by chance, or maybe he remembered the day when the two of you heard the dogs. He could have guessed that's where you went." Her father explained how Lila had gone looking for her and Caleb had joined in the search. Her stomach rolled when she heard how the river had swept him away.

She hadn't had time to think of Caleb since before she and her mother set out to rescue the dogs, but her father's words brought it all back in a sickening rush. She had blamed Caleb for the break-in at the clinic, but after what she'd seen in that cellar, it was obvious he wasn't to blame. Jason or one of his men had broken into the clinic. Could they have put a bottle of painkillers in Caleb's medicine cabinet to frame him?

A frisson of doubt assailed her. Jason obviously wasn't the man she'd thought he was, but somehow she couldn't imagine him planting evidence in Caleb's house. Of course, she hadn't thought he'd torture dogs or hire men to beat Caleb up either.

So, did she believe Caleb or not? Could he have taken the first bottle that went missing, and then Jason broke into the clinic and took the rest of the stuff? Yes, it was definitely possible. Unfortunately for her, the disappearance of the first bottle of painkiller happened before the break-in, and right now the two events seemed unrelated. Nothing that had happened cleared Caleb.

She bit her lip to hold back tears. Had she ever felt so wretched in her entire life? No, she hadn't. Caleb had made her fall in love with him, yet she couldn't trust him. No matter how she felt about him, they didn't have a future together. She couldn't lie beside him at night if she wasn't totally convinced of his honesty and truthfulness.

He had risked his life to save her and her mother. Didn't that count for anything? She wanted it to. She wanted it so bad her heart was pounding like a drum. Maybe Caleb didn't know any better. His father certainly didn't teach him any morals. If he felt confident in her love, he might let her teach him what he should or shouldn't do. Her heart sank. Guess she was her father's daughter after all because she couldn't take Caleb under those circumstances.

Her father gestured out the front window. "Lila's still at the clinic."

The truck had barely stopped before Lila charged out the clinic door. "Aria," she yelled. "Aria."

Aria hopped out of the truck, and Lila ran to her and almost bowled her over with a huge hug. "Oh, thank God you're okay. I've been so worried."

Aria almost smiled. "Yeah, me too."

The big mama dog laid her puppy down and barked.

"Where did they come from?" Lila demanded.

"It's a long story. Could you help me get them inside?"

Lila ran for some leashes, and after she and Mr. De Luca got the dogs inside, Aria told her about the rescue. It was a terrible story. Why didn't Lila look upset?

Lila gave her another hug. "Don't worry about your mother. Caleb is with her. If he said he'd save her, he will."

Caleb's conduct had certainly changed Lila's opinion of him. If only... No use to go there. Things were what they were. "Daddy, I still need to see a doctor. My foot's swelling bad."

He nodded. "Okay. Lila, is your house flooded?"

"Yeah, it is. I thought I'd stay here tonight. I set up a cot in the back room."

Aria's stomach flipped again as a new thought struck her. "Daddy, is your house under water?"

"Just the first floor, but we'll be back to join Lila later. I think I've got us two connecting rooms at the motel just down the road, but we can't check in until tomorrow."

"I'll hold the fort until you get back," Lila promised.

Aria had expected a long wait at the emergency room, but they got her back within fifteen minutes. After doing an x-ray, the doctor came to speak with her. "You have a metatarsal fracture. The side of the bone is sheared right off." He passed the x-ray film to her. "You can clearly see it right here." Aria held the film to the light, and the doctor pointed out the break.

"We have a sports medicine specialist in the hospital who happens to be on duty tonight," the doctor continued. "I think he can maneuver the chip back in place without any surgery being necessary. If all goes well, afterward we'll put you in a cast, and you can go home."

Aria nodded. "Sounds good."

An hour and a half later, she and her father were on their way to the clinic. "I wish we could check into our motel," he said, "but they've been renovating the rooms, and they won't take us before tomorrow, no matter what." He scowled. "I might sue them."

"That's okay, Daddy. I only want to lie down somewhere for a few hours."

In their absence, Lila had scrounged up an air mattress. "We can share it, Aria, and your dad can have the cot."

Aria nodded and hobbled over to the cabinet where she kept the painkillers. "They didn't give me anything for pain, so I'm going to medicate myself."

Her father frowned. "Is that legal?"

"I don't know, but who's going to tell?"

By the time they turned out the lights, her foot had eased off enough for her to sleep. Her last conscious thought was a prayer for her mother and Caleb.

Fourteen

Caleb plunged his hands into the murky water, frantically feeling the bottom of the heavy shelving unit. No, oh no. Two thin bands of steel anchored the shelves to the floor in spite of the fact that they'd fallen over. They held Clairee's leg in a vise grip. Needed something heavy to pry them loose. Where to look? Corner? Work table? Nothing.

Upstairs, maybe. No. Crow bar? No. Try something. Anything. Out of time. Out of time. Out of time.

"Clariee!" he roared as water totally covered her face. Grabbing her under the arms he jerked and tugged even though he knew he wouldn't be able to move her.

At that moment something big and heavy struck the house from the river side. The cabin shivered, and he felt it shift on its foundation. The shelves! The shelves were moving! The bands must have twisted loose.

He pulled Clariee from the water. "Clariee?"

No answer.

"Clariee?" He was yelling now.

No answer.

The water in the cellar came to his chest. He threw her over his shoulder and bolted up the ladder into the kitchen. He laid her on the floor and commenced CPR. "Breathe! Breathe, damn it, breathe!"

She gasped and coughed up a torrent of water just as the flood entered the kitchen through the cellar door. He sprang to his feet, tossed her over his shoulder again, and ran for the boat. Darkness almost swallowed the thin beam from his flashlight, but he saw the boat bobbing wildly on the choppy current. Could they really reach safety in the dark on what amounted to a canvas raft?

Something cold and wet covered his ankles. No choice now. They'd have to take their chances. They couldn't stay here.

He wrestled Clariee into the boat and climbed in after her, the raw power of the current sending a spike of adrenalin racing through his veins. If he untied the rope that secured them to the porch, the current would sweep them away, and in the dark he wouldn't be able to see where they were going or what might come out of nowhere to crush them.

He grabbed for Clariee as a particularly big wave sent her tumbling toward him. Oh, sweet goodness! A bone was sticking out of her leg just below her knee. What to do? What to do?

~ * ~

Aria awoke the next morning when she heard her father stirring around. Wiping sleep from her eyes, she sat up on the air mattress. Her father saw her and smiled. "Go back to sleep, honey. I'm going to meet Stan."

"But I'm going with you."

"Not this time. You can't walk on that ankle, but even if you could I'm not taking you anywhere near the flood."

He was right. With a broken foot she'd be a handicap to him, not a help. "Okay, but I'm at least going to meet Stan with you. He'll have news of the flood. I'll try to find some food for Lila and me while I'm out."

"Get dressed."

Since she'd worn her clothes to bed, all she had to do was put on one shoe and find the crutches the hospital had given her. After swiping her hands through her hair, she was ready to go.

The sun came up as they turned into the police station. "It isn't raining!" Aria cried. "The sun's shining. I've never been so happy to see the sun."

Stan was waiting for them inside. "The river crested an hour ago. If we take care we should get to the Lee's place safely."

Her father's grim expression told Aria that he dreaded what they might find there. Her stomach clenched. Surely nothing bad had happened to either Caleb or her mother.

"Are we going alone?" her father asked.

Stan smiled for the first time. "No. EMS is taking us in their boat." He looked at his watch. "Let's get going. We have to meet them on Canal Street."

At that moment, David's cell phone rang. "David DeLuca. Yes. Are you sure? I'm on the way."

Her father looked as if the weight of the world had fallen from his shoulders. "That was the hospital. Your mother is safe, but they've had to admit her. She has a broken leg and has to have surgery."

Stan smiled and pumped her father's hand. "That's great. Tell her I'll be by to see her as soon as I can."

"I will."

Aria kissed Stan's cheek. "Thanks for everything."

She climbed into her father's SUV and stuck her crutches between the two of them. "Did the hospital say anything about Caleb?"

"No, not a word, but I assume that's where we'll find him."

Did she really want to find Caleb? She'd like to thank him for saving her mother, but nothing had really changed between them so seeing him would make her feel even worse than she already did. If she had known that giving her heart away would end like this, she never would have done it.

~ * ~

The hospital nurse twisted her hands helplessly. "You can't just leave."

Caleb sighed. "I'm not just leaving. You've called Mrs. De Luca's family, right? They'll be here shortly."

"Do you know them personally?"

He nodded.

"Then they'll want to thank you for helping her. You saved her life, Mr. Hawkins. They'll want to talk to you."

Caleb almost smiled at the nurse. Nobody in the De Luca family wanted to talk to him. He shook his head and walked away, leaving the nurse sputtering and protesting. He'd done what he needed to do in order to save Clariee and Aria, but he refused to hang around and have Aria kick him in the teeth yet again.

Sunshine stirred his soul like a benediction as he walked out of the hospital, but reality still bit and stung. Some people had probably lost their lives in the flood while others had lost their homes and everything they owned.

He forced himself to think of something else. Did his house flood last night? Probably not. From the conversations he'd heard around the hospital, the water didn't make it that far. Should he bother to go home to get his things before he left town? Yeah, guess so. No use to throw away his clothes. They cost money, and he didn't have a job.

He knew where he could get one, though. The people at the Pine City shelter would have him in a jiffy. His heart sank. They had been so kind to him he'd have to tell them why he was leaving St. Francis. Would they believe him? Yeah, he thought they would.

Abruptly, the temptation to see Aria overcame him, but he resolutely turned his face away from the hospital and started walking. Five miles was a way to go after the night he'd had, but the sooner he started, the sooner he'd get there.

~ * ~

Clariee was in surgery when Aria and her father got to the hospital. "We tried to wait for you," the nurse explained, "but the injury to her leg was too bad. She said to tell you she loved you both."

Aria shamed herself by bursting into tears. "What was wrong with her?"

"She has a compound fracture. They have to do surgery to fix it."

As a vet, Aria knew what a compound fracture was. Her mother's broken bone had poked through her skin. She shivered, remembering Clariee trapped under those awful shelves as the floodwaters rose

An hour later Dr. Matthews, Clairee's surgeon, came to see them. "She did fine, and her leg'll be as good as new as soon as it heals." His huge smile dimmed. "The way I heard it, she's lucky to be alive." His eyes scanned the waiting room. "Where's the guy who brought her in?"

"We don't know," her father replied.

"Well, no doubt about it; he saved her life."

Aria wondered how two such different natures could reside in one person. Caleb was a thief, yet he truly risked his life to save her mother. She'd been there; she knew what he'd faced. It would be wonderful to thank him, but seeing him would hurt too much. Best to let it alone, no matter how badly she wanted to see him. It would take a while, but she'd forget him. Of course she would. Mind over matter. That's all it took.

~ * ~

"David?"

Clairee's weak voice brought both Aria and her father out of their seats. She stroked Aria's face and reached for David's hand. "Aria, I was so worried about you. Are the dogs okay?"

Her father's smile lit up the room and made both Aria and Clariee smile in return. "Yes, the dogs are fine and so is Aria. Do you feel like telling us what happened after Aria left?"

"Why, didn't Caleb tell you?"

Fearful of upsetting her mother, Aria skirted the truth for the time being. "He left right after he got you to the hospital. I guess he's helping out somewhere." And he might be, for all she knew."

David squeezed her hand. "Can you tell us what happened after Aria left the Lees' house?"

Clairee's face scrunched up. Tears rimmed her eyes. "It was awful. I was sure I was going to die." She told them how the shelves had finally torn loose and freed her leg. "When the water covered my face, Caleb grabbed me under the arms and started pulling, but my leg was caught between what felt like two steel bars. He'd never have been able to free me without help from the river."

Aria wiped her own eyes. "Where did you spend the night? Were you lost in the dark?"

Clariee shook her head. "The water was too high, and the current was too strong for us to leave the house. We stayed tied to the porch all night." She swallowed hard. "A couple of times we thought we'd have to untie the rope. If the water had kept climbing we probably would, and if that had happened, I don't think we'd have made it."

Neither did Aria, not after all she'd seen. She shivered and tried to banish the dreadful images of the rising water. "Daddy, what are we going to do about Jason? Everything that happened is his fault."

The professional look Aria had known since childhood slipped over her father's face. "We'll prosecute aggressively."

"Ask him about the clinic break-in. I'm sure those medications and syringes belonged to me."

"Oh, don't worry. We will."

Clariee yawned again and made David smile. "Go to sleep, sweetheart. We'll talk when you wake up."

Aria kissed her mother's forehead. "I'm going home to... Why, I can't go home. My house is flooded." She bit her lip to hold back tears. "I...I loved that place."

Her father gave her a hug. "Don't worry, baby. The insurance company will write you a check, and we'll get your house back in order in no time. Meanwhile, you'll stay with your mother and me."

"But the first floor..." Oh, why had she said anything? Now her mother would learn that the first floor of her beautiful home had also been filled with river water and nasty, muddy sludge.

"Here's a key," her father smoothly inserted, pointing to an address written on a plastic card attached to the key.

"Okay. See you guys later."

Thank goodness for her father's connections. It couldn't have been easy to get the motel to let them have two rooms, not when a lot of people had had to evacuate their homes, but as soon as her mother got out of the hospital, they'd need the space. She couldn't wait to get some clean clothes... Her clothes were under water at her house. All she had in the world was the dirty stuff she was wearing.

She stopped by a discount store that had opened for business and bought toiletries, underwear, and some clothes. Then she drove to the motel to shower and get ready for work. She'd probably have some clients that afternoon, and sticking to a schedule would help her as much as anything right now.

As she turned in at St. Francis' driveway, Lila came out the front door with Peaches. The dog barked and ran toward Aria's truck. Aria jumped out and buried her face against the animal's soft fur. Peaches and Caleb wouldn't see each other again.

She swiped her tears away before Lila could see.

"How's your mom?" Lila asked.

Her eyes grew wide and scared-looking as Aria told her what had happened to Clariee. "Oh, Aria, I can't imagine being in that flood. I don't see how you and your mother were brave enough to go out there in the first place." She shook her head as if to clear it of pictures she'd rather not see. "Where's Caleb anyway? I thought for sure he'd come in today."

Oh, this was hard! Lila had warned her about Caleb, but she wouldn't listen, and now she'd have to confess that she should have. She cleared her throat, which had almost closed up. "Caleb won't be coming back."

Lila frowned. "Why not?"

Aria told her. She had expected Lila to say 'I told you so.' Instead, she twisted her mouth to the side as she sometimes did when she was thinking. "I think you're making a mistake, Aria."

"A mistake?"

Lila nodded. "Why would Caleb take that first bottle of narcotics? I never saw him when he looked either high or sedated. Besides that, you two were going out. Why would he mess that up?"

"Old habits?"

Lila snorted, an unladylike sound that made Peaches' ears twitch. "Caleb's on the up and up. Go and find him. You'll regret it if you don't."

Was Lila right? Had she made the biggest mistake of her life when she stormed out of Caleb's house?

Before Aria had time to think about it, the bell above the door sounded, and the afternoon's work began. Several emergencies came in, and by the time she left the clinic she was too tired to think about Caleb or much of anything. After checking on her mother, she'd grab some fast food and go to the motel to eat it. Thank goodness it was Friday and she only had to work half a day tomorrow. This flood or something had really done a number on her.

Fifteen

Caleb stood on the sidewalk in front of his grandmother's house and stared at the place where he'd spent a significant amount of his childhood. Had the place always looked so run down and dreary? He didn't think so, but at present, this wasn't a neighborhood people actually wanted to live in. Judging by the number of empty houses on the street, people with the means to do so were abandoning ship in droves.

He took a step and then stopped. Why put himself through another meeting with this woman? She'd just hurt him again like she'd done so many times before. Drawing a deep breath, he marched down the cement path to her front door. He had to know why she'd try to ruin his chances with Aria. Not that it made any difference what she'd said. Aria didn't trust him and had left him high and dry, and she wouldn't be coming back. No, it made no difference, but he still had to know.

He rapped on the door a little harder than he'd meant to and stared into the peephole. His grandmother always looked through it before she opened the door, which in this neighborhood was probably a wise move. He waited a moment before the door swung open. His grandmother's lips pursed as she looked him up and down.

"Well, Caleb, I didn't expect to see you again."

"Really? Why not?"

She shrugged. "No reason. Do you want to come in?"

No, he didn't, but he didn't want her slamming the door in his face until he'd finished with her so he stepped inside.

She sat down in her accustomed place and crossed her ankles. Her slippers looked new, but she'd worn the same style ever since he'd known her. The color of the fake leather ballerina flats varied from year to year, but the style never did.

He felt like standing, but he sat down across from her anyway. "I want you to tell me why you lied to Aria, but first I'd like you to give me my mother's ruby ring."

"Fired you, did she? Good for her."

Caleb's teeth ground together. "You didn't answer me. I want to know why you lied to her, but first get me that ring."

She heaved herself from her chair and vanished into the bedroom. After a moment she returned with the ring that she thrust at him. "Here. Take it. I don't need a ring to remember my poor Ellen."

"I do. I never knew her at all. Now tell me why you lied to Aria."

Two round red spots appeared on his grandmother's cheeks. "I don't lie. Every word I said was the truth."

Caleb shook his head. "You lied about me. You fed Aria some garbage about a miscarriage."

She primly re-crossed her ankles the other way. "Molly herself told me what happened." She stared at him with a genuinely curious expression on her face. "Did you never care for her? Is that why you abandoned the woman who was carrying your child?"

"So that's where you got your information." The sadness he'd carried around ever since he left Fairfield deepened. "Grandma, I know you don't like me because I look like my father, but before I leave here forever, I'll set the record straight. If Molly was pregnant, and that's a very big if, the baby didn't belong to me. We never slept together. She told you all that crap to turn you against me, not that you ever cared about me to start with. Didn't it bother you to persecute a child just because he looked like his father?" He gave her a long, hard look. "What would my mother say if she knew how you've treated me?"

A long and dreadful silence fell on the room. Just when Caleb was about to get up and walk out, his grandmother spoke. "I don't know what to tell you, Caleb. How can I believe a man who spent time in prison for grand theft auto?"

"Oh, I went to prison, all right, but I didn't steal a thing."

Confusion filled her face. "What?"

"I have another story for you, Grandma. You probably won't believe this one either, but I intend to tell you anyway. Now, let's talk about that car."

His grandmother listened to his story, he'd give her that, but as he expected she didn't believe him. "That doesn't make a lot of sense. Your father is scum of the earth. Why would you go to prison for him?"

"Because I wanted someone to care about me. You never did, and my mother never got the chance to. Yeah, I know how needy and stupid I sound, but I don't care. Everybody wants acceptance and love, even guys like me." He spread his hands. "So what if I look like my father? I'm not my father, and I never will be."

His grandmother's lips moved, but no sound came out. They stared at each other for a moment, and when she remained silent, Caleb rose to his feet. "Goodbye."

He strode out of the house and practically ran down the walk. He'd never willingly come to this house again.

She made her way toward him while still wearing her slippers. She *never* wore them outside. What was wrong with her? Was she having an attack of some sort?

She was breathing heavily when she reached him. Obviously, she wasn't used to hurrying. "I...I wondered if you'd like to have dinner with me on Sunday. I could make a chicken pot pie."

Chicken pot pie. One of his favorites when he was a child. He could practically taste the flaky crust and smooth, creamy gravy.

He struggled against the unaccustomed emotion that gripped him. "Yeah, I guess I can come."

Eyes watery, she snapped, "Twelve-thirty. Don't be late."

Caleb nodded. "Twelve-thirty, and I won't be late."

~ * ~

Caleb dipped his mop into the water and swished it around. This was the third time today he'd had to mop up urine. When the animals got scared, they usually wet the floor. The current mess had been made by a big pit bull. His owners had had to drag him inside where he'd howled as if all the demons from hell were after him. Caleb grimaced. The dog was here to be neutered by the shelter vet so it had a right to complain. He wouldn't want to be in its place even though it was better for the animal.

A bell above the door tinkled just as he set the wet floor sign in front of the damp place he'd just cleaned. He and Bonnie Martin, who sat behind the desk, both turned to see who'd come in. *Oh sweet goodness! It's Molly.* Molly, the woman who'd lied to his grandmother and convinced the old lady to believe the twisted story she had concocted.

She saw him at the same time. Her entire body twitched as if an electric current ran through her veins instead of lies and deceit. "Why, Caleb, I didn't know you worked here."

She looked as fresh and pretty as ever with her cornflower blue eyes and silky blonde hair. A wave of sympathy for his grandmother washed over him. No one would expect this sweet, innocent-looking woman to be a liar. They wouldn't expect her to be a vindictive witch who'd gone out of her way to hurt him either, but she was.

Bonnie was staring at both of them so he nodded and said, "Hello, Molly."

She smiled at him. "I'm here to get a kitten. It's lonesome living by yourself."

Was that her way of letting him know she was available if he should want to rekindle their romance? If so, he had news for her. Hell would freeze over before he went back to her.

"Could you show her the way to the kittens, Caleb?"

With Bonnie smiling like a Cheshire cat, there wasn't anything he could do except nod. "Sure. Follow me."

Actually, they had a nice selection of kittens to choose from. Several people had brought in big litters so Molly would probably find one she liked. He supposed it was okay to give a kitten to her. Being a lying witch didn't mean she disliked animals.

He stopped in front of a big cage bursting with lively, playful kittens. "Here you are. If you see one you like, I'll carry it to the bonding room for you."

"That's clever," she enthused. "That way you get the perfect kitten." She pointed toward a black kitten with four white socks. "That one."

Caleb took the kitten from the cage and escorted her to the small bonding room. Shelter rules mandated that he stay with her, so he closed the door and took a seat on the other side of the room.

She picked up a piece of yarn and dangled it in front of the kitten. "How long have you been working here, Caleb?"

"Not long."

"When did you get out of prison?"

"Not long ago."

Molly pulled the yarn from the kitten's mouth, but the little creature promptly captured it again so she picked him up and stroked his head. "You must live in Pine City."

"That's right."

Her eyes narrowed. "You're hard to have a conversation with. Wouldn't you like to know what I've been doing since you dropped me?"

He shrugged. "Not really, but there is something I do want to know."

She pulled the kitten off her shoulder. He saw that its claws had picked her blouse. "What do you want to know?"

"I want to know why you lied to my grandmother. You went to her house and filled her head with a bunch of garbage about me. We never had sex, not one time. If you were pregnant, it wasn't mine."

"Oh, that." She shrugged dismissively. "You hurt me, Caleb. We had a good thing going, and you ruined it. I was angry." She smiled as if it didn't make a single bit of difference. "I'm over it now. Would you like for me to talk to your grandmother for you? She'll be disappointed in me, but I can talk her around. Nothing needs to be spoiled for us."

Caleb took a deep breath. This whole conversation bordered on the ridiculous. "There is no us, Molly, and there never will be. Get that out of your head."

Tears formed in her eyes. "Do you still not understand? They paid us peanuts at that store. What was wrong in taking a few things to bring our salary up to an acceptable level? Everyone does it, and you know the store can afford it."

This was the same argument she'd used back when he broke up with her, and he still didn't buy it. "It was stealing. No matter how hard you try, you can't justify that or make it all right."

Molly stood up. Her face looked as cold as January. "I took a couple of small things that nobody missed. You took a car and spent time in prison. Don't preach to me."

"You don't have to worry about that." Indeed she didn't. He hoped he never laid eyes on her again. Should he tell her the truth about the car? Nah, why bother? Her opinion meant nothing to him. "Do you want the kitten?"

"Yes."

"Let's go."

He walked her to the front so she could pay for her kitten and went to the dog pens without a word of goodbye.

~ * ~

Lila waved goodbye to Mrs. Burton who had just dropped her cat off for its yearly physical. Most of the time people waited with their animals, but today Mrs. Burton couldn't stay. She had a doctor's appointment herself and would pick up Missy when she got finished.

Aria reached for the overweight Persian. "I've tried and tried to get her to cut back on Missy's food, but she just won't do it. This cat is a butterball."

Lila giggled. Aria knew she liked fat animals.

They dealt with Missy and put her into a cage to wait for Mrs. Burton. "Lila, are you busy?"

Lila rolled her eyes. "Of course I am. I work for you, remember?"

"Yeah, yeah. I just wondered if you'd like to go and look at a house with me."

"A house?"

"Yes. I got my insurance check in the mail yesterday so I'm going house hunting."

Lila washed her hands and tossed the paper towel into the trash. "Let's talk before we go."

Aria glanced at her watch. She had time. "Okay. We can do it in my office."

As Aria closed the door, a disturbing thought occurred to her. "I don't like the serious expression on your face. You aren't quitting, right? I can't run this place without you."

Lila sniffed. "Of course not. Somebody has to look out for you."

Gratitude filled Aria's heart as her eyes misted. "You're the best friend anyone could ever have. I love you like a sister."

Lila rapidly blinked her eyes. "Hush now. You'll make me cry."

"Okay, what do you want to talk about?"

"Caleb."

Aria threw herself into her desk chair. "Oh, Lila, we've already talked about this. I told you why Caleb and I can't be together."

"Yes, you did, but I have an idea that Jason really did take the first bottle and put it in Caleb's bathroom."

Aria ran her hands through her hair and sighed. "Yeah, but you don't have any proof."

A look of compassion crossed her friend's face. "Sometimes you're too much like your daddy. Can't you think with your heart instead of your head on this one?"

Aria sighed. "I guess not."

"That's what I thought. Do you want me to go with you when you confront Jason?"

"What!"

Lila shrugged. "You're never going to be at peace with this thing until you find out exactly what happened with that first bottle of medication, and Jason is the only one who can tell you."

Aria scowled. "Like Jason would tell the truth about anything!"

"It's worth a try. I've never seen you so miserable. I know you're thinking about Caleb all the time. I've even wondered if buying this new house is some kind of knee-jerk reaction to what happened with Caleb."

Aria shivered. "That last part isn't true. I have terrible dreams about the river, which is why I'm buying a new house. It has nothing to do with Caleb."

"Okay, if you say so." Lila stood up. "Are you ready to go?"

"To see the house?"

"No, to see Jason."

Nope, no way, but on the other hand... Yeah, I need to see him because the truth is important. Caleb is never far from my mind, and Jason is the only one who could tell me what really happened. "Let's go."

Lila beamed as Aria grabbed her purse. "You won't regret it. I have a good feeling about this."

~ * ~

Jason Lee lived in a luxury condo in a development he'd built himself. "I bet since Jason lives here, the workmanship in this place is top notch," Lila said as Aria parked her new truck in front of number twelve. The flood hadn't damaged her old truck, but it had tainted the vehicle in some way, so Aria had traded it for this shiny new model with glistening red paint.

"Do you want me to go in with you?" Lila asked.

Aria shook her head. "No, I can handle it, but thanks for the offer."

She got out of the truck before her courage failed and rang Jason's bell. Of course, he might still be working, but since his arraignment he'd been keeping a low profile so there was a good chance of his being at home this morning. She'd thought she was prepared for this meeting, but shock ran through her and caused her heart to pound when he opened the door.

His jaw dropped when he saw her. "Aria! What are you doing here?"

"I came to see you."

He stood aside and motioned for her to come inside. Her eyes darted around the room. As Lila had guessed, everything looked expensive and tasteful. "Have any of your buyers in this complex complained about shoddy workmanship?" Yikes, what was wrong with her? Hadn't her mother taught her that you could catch more flies with sugar than with vinegar? If she started off by antagonizing him, she'd get nothing.

His eyes turned wary. "Is that why you came here? To discuss my construction business?"

She shook her head. "Hardly."

"That's what I figured." He flung himself down into an expensive looking club chair and propped his feet on the matching ottoman. "Have a seat."

She did. If he thought a little rudeness could get rid of her, he had another think coming. "Let's start with the easy part, Jason. Why did you torture those dogs?"

Surprise flashed across his face. He had expected something about Caleb, and she wouldn't disappoint him. They'd get to that in a minute.

"They're animals," he said, his voice indifferent.

"Do you think they don't feel pain?"

He shrugged as if it didn't matter one way or the other. "I don't know. I didn't think about it."

The hard, bitter anger she'd held against him faded in the face of this answer. "What happened to you, Jason? When we were kids, you weren't ruled by money. You weren't cruel either. You never liked dogs, but I remember the time we found a baby bird that fell out of the nest. You tried to nurse it back to health and cried when it died. I certainly never caught you in a lie, and I don't think you stole things either. So, what happened?"

He grunted. "I grew up. The world isn't as rosy and good as you think. Ask your daddy if you don't believe me. Better still, go on and tell me why you really came here."

Aria nodded. "All right. The night that Caleb, Lila, and I were treating your dog, the one at death's door because you made him fight, did you take a bottle of painkiller from the clinic and hide it in Caleb's medicine cabinet?"

He laughed, but it wasn't a pretty sound. "I might have known. I heard that the loser finally left town. You're well rid of him."

"You're entitled to your own opinion about Caleb, but I'm not here for your opinion. I want to know if you took that bottle."

"Are you looking for another charge you can bring against me?" His eyes mocked her. "The charges are serious enough without you searching for more."

She sighed. "This is just between you and me. Tell me the truth and it goes no further."

His face took on a melancholy expression. "We'd have been so good together." He paused. "Okay, for old times' sake, yes, I took the first bottle. I met Caleb's worthless father at a bar and hired him to break into his house and plant the bottle in the medicine cabinet. It was a long shot, but I hoped you'd find it and jump to conclusions, which obviously you did."

Did she ever! With his grandmother's words ringing in her ears, she'd been all too willing to blame Caleb for the theft.

Emotion rose in her throat. It was time to get out of there because breaking down in front of Jason Lee wasn't an option. She leaped to her feet and bolted from the room without a word. Lila saw her coming and threw the truck door open. "Are you okay?" she cried.

Aria shook her head in the negative as she slammed the door behind her. "No! Let's get out of here."

Caleb had told the truth, and she hadn't believed him. She had let a pack of lies break her faith in the man she loved. The pain she'd felt ever since Caleb left Fairfield was no more than she deserved. What idiot threw away the best thing that ever happened to her because she didn't trust her heart? She knew Caleb the way no one else did. How could she have been so stupid?

Lila cleared her throat. "Do you want to talk about it?"

No, she didn't, but she probably should. Clearing Caleb's name with the people at St. Francis was important. "Jason admitted that he took the first bottle. Caleb didn't do it."

"I see." Lila stared out the window for a moment. "I guess the ball's in your court now. What are you going to do?"

"I don't know."

~ * ~

"Caleb, you have a visitor."

Caleb gently laid a groggy kitten into a cage and covered it with a blanket. The Pine City Animal Shelter was busy. This kitten was the fourth spay/ neuter they'd done that morning. The shelter's vet Carl Stephens cared about all the animals so he had earned Caleb's respect, just as Aria had... Don't go there.

"Who is it?" The idea of someone stopping by to see him here at work was kind of odd, but it would be odd if anyone came to see him after work either. He'd been back at the Pine City Shelter for three months, but except for the people at the shelter and his grandmother, he hadn't made any friends or been able to feel at home here. Uh-oh. Had Molly come back?

The receptionist smiled. "Come and see."

"Okay." With his luck, it would be somebody he had no desire to see, like his father maybe, although he couldn't imagine the man knew where he was, and even if he did, he'd hardly pay a visit to his son.

As he approached the front lobby, he heard a familiar voice say, "No, I don't recommend that particular antibiotic for cats."

Aria! What is she doing here? Eagerness flooded him, but common sense tamped it down. He'd learned the hard way that his past would always make her suspicious of him, so why should he let her hurt him again? And it *would* hurt him to see her. Turning on his heel, he sprinted down the hall and left the building by the back entrance. He'd hide in one of the shelter's outbuildings until she left. So it sounded cowardly to run from a woman. Who cared? He was too sad and miserable for a confrontation with her right now.

As he strode out the door, a shiny, red truck caught his eye. Someone had laid out big bucks for that thing. He paused to look at it. Wonder if Aria had to buy a new truck? Did the flood damage hers too badly to use? The early autumn afternoon was warm and balmy, but he shivered when he thought of that dreadful night on the river. He'd even had a couple of nightmares about it. In his dreams, Clariee was always under water, and no matter what he did, he couldn't pull her out.

A voice behind him snapped him out of his reverie. "Hello, Caleb."

Caleb froze. He had waited too long to hide. He drew a deep breath and steeled himself to show no expression. Turning around, he answered, "Hi, Aria."

She looked different. Her eyes had lost their sparkle, and she'd lost some weight. An air of sadness clung to her. His heart leaped in his chest. Maybe Clariee didn't make it! "How's your mother?"

"She's mad at you."

Caleb blinked. "Mad at me? What did I do?"

"You left before she could thank you for saving her life."

Caleb shrugged. "I don't want any thanks for that, but tell her I appreciate her thinking of me."

Aria nodded. "I'll tell her." She licked her lips that looked dry to him. "Everything's back to normal at the clinic."

"Good to know."

She pushed her hair behind her ear. "Daddy's house was flooded, but it's fixed now."

"What about your place?" He hadn't meant to get involved in any kind of conversation with her, but he couldn't seem to help himself.

"I sold the property. The new owners tore the house down."

But she had loved her house. "Was it too expensive to rebuild? Is that why you left?"

She shook her head. "No, I left because I'm afraid of the river now. I can't bear to go anywhere near it. I never see it the way it really is. In my mind it's always wild and angry, and it's pouring rain. I've had some nightmares about it."

So he wasn't the only one who had bad dreams about the flood. "Where are you living?"

"With Mama and Daddy. I put in an offer on a house just outside of town. It's in a neighborhood built in the 1950s, and it still has a lot of retro details in it. I like that, so I hope they accept my offer."

"Lila didn't get caught in the flood, did she?"

"No, she got back to town before the water totally covered the highway."

"That's a relief. I worried about her. Is Peaches okay?"

Exasperation filled her face. "Peaches is fine. Lila is fine. Rascal is fine. Everyone's okay except Jason. He's been charged with breaking and entering, dog fighting, and illegal gambling, and some of the people who bought houses he built are suing him because the work isn't holding up." Tears filled her eyes. "Don't you want to know why I'm here?"

Weakness swept through him, and he struggled to maintain his detachment. "I'm not trying to hurt your feelings, but to be honest, I don't want to know. I just want..." Good question. What did he really want? To turn back the clock? Yeah, too bad he couldn't.

She swiped at her eyes with the back of her hand, a child-like gesture that tore at his heart. "I don't blame you for not wanting to talk to me, but I'm going to tell you why I came anyway. I came to apologize." Her eyes fell. "I would have come sooner, but there was so much to do after the flood. After we got that settled, I waited. I wanted to see if you'd come back on your own, but you didn't so I had to come to you." She almost smiled. "I should have known that was the way things would play out."

Caleb clenched his teeth against the desire to grab her and kiss her silly.

"Jason..."

"I do not want to talk about Jason Lee!" he snapped.

"Oh, I think you will."

The sound of a dog barking as it left the shelter distracted Caleb. It was time to end this pointless trip down memory lane. "I have to get back to work. I'll walk you to your car."

Her shoulders slumped. "Please, can I say one thing? Only one."

"Say it." *Say it before my resolve crumbles.*

"Jason was responsible for the break-in at the clinic. He also confessed to taking the first bottle of narcotics, the one that went missing. He said he was hoping we'd suspect you because you'd been in prison."

Just what he'd thought. Just what he'd tried to tell her the night she fired him and stormed out of his house. Even now it made him angry to think of it. "Thanks for telling me."

He took two steps down the path, and Aria burst into tears. *Well, damn!* He stopped and turned to her even though he wanted to sprint down the path with everything that was in him. "What's wrong?"

"Everything!" Tear drops glistened on her dark, lush eyelashes. Her chin trembled. He had never seen her so vulnerable, not even when they made love. "I'm so sorry, Caleb. I'm sorry I doubted you. I'm sorry I fired you. I'm sorry I didn't believe in you. I'm sorry I didn't trust our love enough." She sniffed. "I'm sorry for everything."

She swiped at her eyes again and wrapped her arms around her middle. "I guess I was hoping if you forgave me that maybe ...maybe you'd give me another chance."

"You cut my heart out and served it up warm," he answered, aware that he sounded angry, but he was angry. No, he was fighting mad over it. "You should have believed in me, but no, I was an ex-con whose word was no good. The great Aria De Luca couldn't have a man like me hanging around." He skewered her with a fiery glare. "Even if I had stolen the medicine, why couldn't you give me another chance? Didn't you love me even that much?" He took a deep breath and blew it out to calm himself. "You were just having a summer fling, and I was stupid enough to think it really meant something."

Aria grabbed his arm. "It did mean something! I love you, Caleb. I love you so much life isn't worth living without you." She held out her hands in a gesture of supplication. "Please? If you love me, please give me another chance. I'll never doubt you again if you'll only give me another chance."

He closed his eyes against the hope on her beautiful face. The pressure in his chest was about to kill him. The rising tide came from the region of his heart and almost choked him. Gasping, he pulled her into his arms and held her so tight he was afraid he might crush her, but she was holding him just as tightly.

Maybe he should say something, tell her he loved her too and couldn't stand another minute of torment without her, but his voice was frozen and wouldn't work. He could kiss her, though. His lips found hers, and they kissed until he was breathless.

Aria pulled away from him and cupped his cheek in her hand. "Caleb..." For a moment her voice failed her. "Will you come back to Fairfield with me?"

He pretended to think about it though he felt light and happy enough to float all the way to the moon, much less Fairfield. "I don't know. My rental house was leaking pretty bad."

Her face flushed. "I didn't mean the rental house. I meant my house."

"You want me to move in with you?"

She nodded.

It was a tempting offer, one he'd give anything to take her up on, but... "I can't just move in with you. If I come back, you have to promise to marry me. Will you, Aria? Will you marry me?"

Joy filled her face and warmed his heart. "Yes, I'll marry you. Aria Hawkins has a lovely ring to it."

And that reminded him. "Speaking of rings, are you dead set on a diamond? My mother had a ruby ring that belonged to her grandmother. Grandma—the one you met—had it, but I made her give it to me after I left St. Francis. I'd like you to wear it. The ring and one picture is all I have of my mother."

Aria reached for his hand. "Rubies are my favorite. I'd be proud to wear your mother's ring."

A shadow of doubt pierced him. How could it not after all they'd been through? "What about your parents? Your father doesn't like me very much."

"Are you joking?" Aria laughed, a carefree sound that made him smile. "Daddy's been pushing me for a month now to make up with you. After you saved my mother, you can do no wrong with Daddy."

It must be a miracle. Only supernatural intervention could have brought about this turn of events. He pulled Aria against him. "This is a lot to take in."

She nodded. "I know." The smile left her face as her arms sneaked around his waist. "I thought I'd lost you."

"Yeah, I know what you mean."

She shook all over as if she were shaking off the problems and troubles of the past. "Will the shelter be mad that you're leaving?"

He shook his head. "I'll give them two weeks' notice so it won't put them in a bind. Lots of people want to work here."

The door opened behind them, and the pretty, dark-haired receptionist poked her head out. "Have you made up yet? Can we start celebrating now?"

Caleb and Aria burst into laughter. "Yes," Caleb answered.

She rushed outside and hugged both of them. "I'm so happy for you both. Extra cheese?"

Aria giggled. "What?"

"We're ordering pizza for everyone. Do you want extra cheese?"

"Of course. That's the way Caleb likes it."

The receptionist grinned. "I know. Any other news you'd like to tell me?"

Caleb picked Aria's hand up and kissed it. "She promised to marry me."

"Get out! I've got to go tell everyone. Come on in whenever you're ready."

She vanished into the shelter, and Caleb pulled Aria into his arms. "Are you sure?"

"I'm sure." She dazzled him with her smile.

"What about the things my grandmother told you?"

"She was wrong."

"Don't you want to talk to her?"

"Nope."

Wasn't it funny how things could change so quickly? His life sparkled with promise even though when he got up this morning, it had felt just like another ordinary workday. He took Aria's hand, and side-by-side they went inside to celebrate new beginnings with pizza and extra cheese.

Epilogue

"Daddy, grab Peaches!" Aria yelled as she wrestled a huge garment bag through the door of her bedroom. The silly dog was stomping all over the train of her beautiful wedding dress.

David grabbed Peaches collar and hauled her away from Aria, not an easy task since the big dog had displayed intense curiosity about the garment bag. "Honey, are you sure you want Peaches to be in the wedding? I mean, that's kind of …silly."

Aria giggled. "I know, but she brought Caleb and me together, Daddy. Why wouldn't we want her in the wedding?" She laughed again. "After her bath she smells good, and I love her new collar."

The collar was pale green, the same shade that the bridesmaids were wearing and was studded with big rhinestones. Lila, as the matron of honor, was going to lead Peaches down the aisle and turn her leash over to Clariee who'd be sitting on the front row.

It had taken some doing to persuade the minister to allow a dog in church, but the pastor liked Caleb, and the De Lucas had been going to his church for a long time. He had given in with a chuckle and begged them not to take his picture with Peaches. They'd promised, but Aria planned on getting a shot of the bride and groom, Peaches, and the minister just for her and Caleb.

"You're going to wrinkle your dress!" Clariee exclaimed. "For goodness sake, David, help her."

Aria took Peaches' leash, and her father took the garment bag, and everyone trudged downstairs to the limo that had been hired to take the family to the church. After the ceremony, Caleb and Aria would use the limo to take them to the airport for their flight to France. Caleb hadn't wanted Aria to pay for the honeymoon, but when he'd seen how much she wanted to visit Paris, he gave in with grace. 'We're taking a second honeymoon on our tenth anniversary,' he'd insisted, 'and I'll be paying for that one.' Aria had no problem with that idea.

She smiled as she opened the limo door for Peaches. Caleb was going back to school after the first of the year. After he got his undergraduate degree, he intended to study veterinary medicine at the local university. Only yesterday she had shown him her idea for a new sign for the clinic. 'St. Francis Animal Hospital' was going to be on the first line along with a simple drawing of St. Francis, and on the second and third lines they'd put their names. The corner of her lips curled up. Caleb had truly liked the sign. To prove it, he'd kissed her until she was breathless.

The limo pulled into the church parking lot and parked near the side door that all the brides used to enter the church. It would never do for anyone to see the bride before the ceremony.

Aria, Peaches, and her mother hurried into the bride's room where Lila was waiting for them. "You look beautiful!" Aria cried. "That pale green is so pretty on you."

Lila smiled and preened. "Thanks. That's what I thought, but this is your day. Let's get that gorgeous dress on you."

"I don't mind if we do." She hugged Lila. "This is good practice for your wedding."

"Oh, I've thought of that." Lila studied the diamond on her finger. "You'll be my matron of honor, right?"

"You know it! Are you having a dog in your wedding?"

Lila rolled her eyes, which everyone took as a no.

Clariee reverently unzipped the garment bag. "Oh, darling, your dress is wonderful." Her eyes filled with tears. "I promised myself I wouldn't cry."

Both Aria and Lila hugged her.

Aria's wedding dress took her breath away. She had picked a strapless mermaid gown made of lace with a semi-cathedral train. The bodice had an eyelash fringe that she loved. The dress fit her like a glove and had made her eyes bug when she first tried it on. 'I've got to dress up more often,' she'd cried when she saw herself in the figure-hugging gown.

Taking care not to mess up Aria's elaborate hairstyle or her makeup, Clariee and Lila eased the dress over her head and zipped it up. "I still can't believe it's me," Aria cried. "I look like a princess!"

"Caleb is sure to think so," Lila said with a smile. "I can't wait to see his face when you and your dad enter the sanctuary."

Neither could Aria. Emotion swelled in her heart and overflowed in a tremulous smile. The logical part of her personality had been totally submerged today. Actually, she'd felt emotional for a week. She'd cried buckets when a mama cat died following the birth of her kittens. Thank goodness for Caleb's rescue. They were taking great care of the babies, a yellow - boy and two calico girls.

A knock on the door announced her father. "Five minutes, baby." He moved to her side and took her hands. "You may be getting married, but you're still my girl. Don't forget that."

"As if I could!"

A tear streaked down Clairee's face. "Oh, my darling, I hope your entire life is as happy as your wedding day."

Everyone laughed and cried at the same time. Then her father looked at his watch. "It's time, ladies. Let's get this girl married."

Laughing, they exited the bride's room into the empty vestibule. An usher seated Clariee and Caleb's grandmother. Aria still had a hard time believing that Caleb and Mrs. Jefferson had reconciled, but it had actually happened. Mrs. Jefferson had apologized to her for repeating the lies Molly had spread, and that too had shocked Aria. She was glad for Caleb, though. He needed some people of his own in his life.

The sound of 'Trumpets Voluntary' filled the air. Lila took Peaches' leash and made her walk down the aisle. The music changed, and the wedding director opened the doors of the sanctuary for the bride and her father to make their walk down the aisle. The entire church was full to overflowing, but Aria only had eyes for one person. He was staring back at her with such warmth, love, and happiness in his eyes that it was all she could do not to sprint down the aisle to him.

They reached the altar. As her father placed her hand in Caleb's, tears of gratitude filled her eyes. Only God could have brought about this miracle. She was going to spend her entire life with the man she adored. One lifetime together probably wasn't enough, but they'd give it their best shot. They'd make every day count, and in Heaven they'd be together forever.

Oh, Caleb! I do so love you!

Meet Elaine Cantrell

Elaine Cantrell was born and raised in South Carolina where she obtained a master's degree in personnel services from Clemson University. She is a member of Alpha Delta Kappa, an international honorary society for women educators, and Romance Writers of America. Her first novel, *A New Leaf*, was the 2003 winner of the Timeless Love Contest. When she's not writing or teaching, she enjoys movies, quilting, reading, and collecting vintage Christmas ornaments.

Works From The Pen Of Elaine Cantrell

The Welcome Inn - Julianna can't stand Buck Abercrombie! He's rude, chauvinistic, and exasperating, and he's her new boss. Why wouldn't the bank loan her the money to buy The Welcome Inn? As manager she has proved her worth.
Worse yet, Buck's criminal brother Travis works for him, and her friend Melanie likes him!

The Captain and the Cheerleader - Susan English can't stand Robin Lanford! She's so full of herself she irritates everyone on the faculty of Fairfield High. When Robin bets Susan fifty dollars that she can't get a date with Kurt Deveraux, the head football coach, Susan jumps at the chance to put the little heifer in her place. She had no idea that teaching Robin a lesson would irrevocably change her life, strain treasured friendships, and throw two families into chaos.

Flood - Drawn together by their love of animals, Aria De Luca and Caleb Hawkins burn for each other. They never suspected that malignant forces around them were successfully plotting Caleb's ruin from the moment he entered her life. When the flood of a century strikes Aria's hometown, an alienated Caleb is all that stands between her and catastrophic loss

Turnaround Farm - Dedicated career girl Holly Grant has no time for romance. She doesn't need a man to complete her, thank you very much. Building Grant Realty takes all of her time and attention. If she can close a deal for Turnaround Farm, her business will take off like a rocket. Her first problem is that Jeb Wakefield doesn't want to sell his farm, and her second problem is Jeb's grandson Dan, the finest looking man Holly's ever seen.

A Message to Our Readers

Enjoy this book?

You can make a difference.

As an independent publisher, Wings ePress, Inc. does not have the financial clout of the large New York publishers. We can't afford large magazine spreads or subway posters to tell people about our quality books.

But we do have something much more effective and powerful than ads. We have a large base of loyal readers.

Honest reviews help bring the attention of new readers to our books.

If you enjoyed this book, we would appreciate it if you would spend a few minutes posting a review on the site where you purchased this book or on the Wings ePress, Inc. webpages at:

https://wingsepress.com/

Thank You

VISIT OUR WEBSITE
FOR THE FULL INVENTORY
OF QUALITY BOOKS:

*Quality trade paperbacks and downloads
in multiple formats,
in genres ranging from light romantic
comedy to general fiction and horror.
Wings has something
for every reader's taste.
Visit the website, then bookmark it.
We add new titles each month!*

www.ingramcontent.com/pod-product-compliance
Lightning Source LLC
Chambersburg PA
CBHW061021120726
47910CB00006B/2052